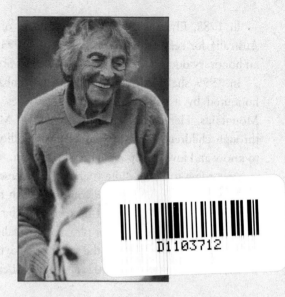

$\mathcal{E}$lyne Mitchell is regarded as one of the most distinguished writers of children's books in Australia. She wrote books for over sixty years and her *Brumby* books have been published in over forty countries, taking Australia — and the Snowy Mountains — to the world.

She was born in Melbourne, in 1913, and her interest in horses began as a child when her father, Harry Chauvel, commanded the ANZAC Mounted Division and Desert Mounted Corps. She had lessons at the army horse-riding school and developed her passion for horses. Following her marriage to Tom Mitchell, she settled on her husband's family farm at Towong Hill in the Snowy Mountains.

Her first children's book, *The Silver Brumby*, was written for Indi, the eldest of her four children, 'to give her the magic joy of reading', and the view from Elyne's home and her rides through the Upper Murray have inspired her writing, becoming vivid parts of her *Brumby* stories.

In 1988, Elyne was awarded the Medal of the Order of Australia for services to literature, and in 1993 was awarded an honorary doctorate of letters from Charles Sturt University.

In 1999 she was both delighted and embarrassed to be honoured by a tribute weekend of festivities in the Snowy Mountains. Her contribution to the Snowy Mountains area through children's literature has brought millions of children to know and love this special part of Australia.

According to Elyne, 'Life is about achievement and service and doing something for your country. I wish that the young people of today were brought up to realise the joy of serving their country. It gives me great pleasure if I realise I have done a service to somebody. That's the secret of enjoying life.'

Elyne Mitchell died in 2002, at the age of eighty-eight.

ELYNE MITCHELL

The Silver Brumby

Including Elyne Mitchell's last
brumby story, *Wild Echoes Ringing*

Angus&Robertson
An imprint of HarperCollins*Publishers*

Angus&Robertson
An imprint of HarperCollins*Publishers*

The Silver Brumby first published in Australia in 1958
This edition published in 2003
by HarperCollins*Publishers* Pty Limited
ABN 36 009 913 517
A member of the HarperCollins*Publishers* (Australia) Pty Limited Group
www.harpercollins.com.au

HarperCollins*Publishers*
Level 13, 201 Elizabeth Street, Sydney NSW 2000, Australia
Unit D, 63 Apollo Drive, Rosedale, Auckland 0632, New Zealand
77–85 Fulham Palace Road, London W6 8JB, United Kingdom
2 Bloor Street East, 20th floor, Toronto, Ontario M4W 1A8, Canada
195 Broadway, New York, NY 10007, USA

National Library of Australia Cataloguing-in-publication data:

Mitchell, Elyne, 1913–2002.
   The Silver Brumby: includes new story Wild echoes ringing.
   For children ages 8–12 years.
   ISBN 0 207 19862 4.
   I. Horses – Juvenile fiction. 2. Wild horses – Juvenile fiction.
   I. Mitchell, Elyne, 1913–3002. Wild echoes ringing.
   II. Title. (Series : Mitchell, Elyne, 1913–2002. Silver Brumby)
A823.3

Cover photograph © Getty Images
Illustrations by Margaret Power
Internal and cover design by Lore Foye, HarperCollins Design Studio
Typeset by HarperCollins in 10.5/14 Sabon
Printed and bound in Australia by Griffin Press.

60gsm Bulky Paperback used by HarperCollins*Publishers* is a natural,
recyclable product made from wood grown in a combination of
sustainable plantation and regrowth forests. The manufacturing processes
conform to the environmental regulations in Tasmania, the place of
manufacture.

Merry Christmas 2014

This book was written for Indi,
who loves horses.

My darling Claudy,
Have a wonderful year
and lots of happy
horse-riding.
Giddy-Up!.
Love, Daddy xxx

CONTENTS

The Silver Brumby

Mt Kosciuzko
7,308'

L. Cootapatamba

Ramshead Range ~ Granitt Tors

North Ramshead

South
Ramshead
Thowra born here

To
Thowra's
Secret
Valley

Paddy
Rush's
Bogong

Crackenback River

Dead
Horse
Hut

The
Brindle Bull

Dead Horse
Creek

The Big Bogay

Dead Horse Ridge

Yarraman's Valley

Swamp

N
W   E
S

Cascade
Creek

Purgatory Hill

Cascade
Hut

Jerusalem
Hill

Steep
Mountain Ash
Forests

The Brolga's
Country

Brumby
Country

Born in the wild wind

Once there was a dark, stormy night in spring, when, deep down in their holes, the wombats knew not to come out, when the possums stayed quiet in their hollow limbs, when the great, black flying phalangers that live in the mountain forests never stirred. On this night, Bel Bel, the cream brumby mare, gave birth to a colt foal, pale like herself, or paler, in that wild, black storm.

Bel Bel had chosen the birthplace of the foal wisely. He was on springy snowgrass under a great overhang of granite that sheltered them from the driving rain. There he lay, a pale bundle in the black dark, while Bel Bel licked him clean and nuzzled him. The wind roared and howled through the granite tors above in the Ramshead Range, where the snow still lay, but there was no single sound of animal or bird except the mournful howl of a dingo. Once, twice, the howl rang out and its echo answered, weird and wild.

Bel Bel lifted her head at the sound, and her nostrils dilated. From the shadowy mass between her forefeet came a faint nickering cry and she nuzzled him again. She was very alone with her newborn foal, and far from her own herd, but that was how she had felt it must be.

Perhaps because of her colour, so much more difficult to hide than bay, or brown, black, grey or chestnut, she had always led a hunted life, and when a foal was going to be born she was very nervous and hid herself far away. Of the three foals she had had, this was the only one who was creamy, like herself.

Bel Bel felt a surge of pride, but the pride was followed by fear. Her son would be hunted as she was and as her own cream-coloured mother had been before her. Hunted by man, since these pale-coloured horses were so strange-looking in the wild herds. And this colt would have another enemy too, as every stallion would be doubly against him because of his colour.

The wind roared and the rain was cold, so cold, it felt as if it could turn to snow. Even with the shelter of the rock, the storm was beating down on them, the moving darkness becoming a thing of terror. The howl of the dingo came again. Bel Bel nosed the tiny colt to get up.

He heaved up his head, stuck his long forelegs out in front of him, and gave a little snort of fear. Bel Bel pushed him up till he stood, his feet far apart and his long legs, trembling. Then she nosed him, wobbling, bending, step-by-step to the sandy mouth of a cave, and there, just out of the rain, she let him tumble down again.

Soon it would be time to make him drink, but for the moment, out of the wild storm, he could rest. Dawn must come soon, and in this storm there would be no men abroad to see a cream brumby mare lead her newborn foal through the snow gums to where there would be grass for her to eat and longed-for water to drink. Bel Bel knew that there would be very few men in the mountains till all the snow had gone and they came driving their herds of red-and-white cattle, but the fear of man was never far from her thoughts.

Dawn came very slowly, showing first the dark outline of the cave mouth against a faintly lighter sky, then, on the hillside below them, reaching long fingers of forest right up to the rocks, the wind-tormented heads of snow gums, driven and lashed as though they must tear themselves up by the roots. The rain had stopped.

Great massing clouds kept racing up over the mountains, but, as the light grew strong, the sky began to look as if it was being torn in shreds by the wind. Flying streamers of rain-washed blue sky appeared and Bel Bel, feeling very hungry herself, decided it was time the foal should drink and that the day would be fair enough for a newborn colt to go with his mother to some better pastures.

'I will call you Thowra,' she said, waking him with her nose, 'because that means wind. In wind you were born, and fleet as the wind must you be if you are to survive.'

On that first day, while the storm blew itself out, Bel Bel did not take Thowra far, only down through the snow gums to a long glade that led to a heather-banked creek where she could drink. That night they went back to the opening of the cave and the foal slept on the dry sand curled up against his mother's flank.

The next day she decided to take him further, to a wide, open field in the snow gum forest, where the grass grew very sweetly, even as early in the spring as this, and where the creek ran shallow over a sand and mica bottom.

The storm had died in the night and there was warm spring sunshine. Bel Bel noticed with pride how the foal trotted more strongly by her side. She did not hurry him, often stopping to graze as they moved under the snow gums or in the long glades. She never left the shelter of the trees without first pausing and looking carefully into the open country ahead. Thus it was through a curtain of the leathery snow gum leaves that she looked out on to the wide, sunny field and saw a bay brumby grazing in the distance by the creek.

Bel Bel became completely still, watching; then she recognised the bay as a mare of her own herd, Mirri, who had been caught by a stockman as a yearling, and managed to get free. Mirri, for this reason, was very nervous of men, and she and Bel Bel had often run together, away from the herd, when they thought the others were too close to the stockmen's huts.

Now Bel Bel made out a dark shape on the ground near Mirri and knew that she, too, had had a foal. Unafraid, she led Thowra out to join them.

When Mirri saw them coming she gave a whinny of greeting, and Bel Bel arched her neck a little and stepped proudly beside her creamy son, thinking how beautiful his silver mane and tail were and how they would someday look like spray from a waterfall as he galloped.

Mirri was pleased to see her.

'Hello, Bel Bel,' she said, 'what a fine foal you have — creamy too! I must stir my sleepyhead to show him off!' And she nosed the bright bay at her feet.

The bay raised his head sleepily, but, seeing strangers, he became wide awake and struggled to his feet.

'A fine intelligent head,' Bel Bel said. 'What do you call him?'

'Storm,' Mirri answered. 'He was born in the worst of the weather, two nights ago. And yours?'

'Thowra, for the wind. He was born then too. They will be great mates for a year or so.' Both mothers nodded wisely, for it was the way of the wild horses that the young colts should run together, after they left their mothers, until they had reached the age and strength to fight for a mare or two of their own and start their own herd.

Storm and Thowra sniffed at each other curiously and then both turned back to their mothers for a drink.

Sunny spring days came, and the grass grew fresh, and green, and sweet. The two mares stayed in Snowgrass Plain, eating, basking in the sun, drinking the cold, clear water, growing strong and sleek after the hard winter, and giving their foals plenty of milk. The foals grew strong, too, and romped and galloped, and rolled in the sun.

Soon they learned to recognise the great wedge-tail eagles floating in the blue arch of sky above them, knew the call of currawongs, and were unafraid of the friendly grey kangaroos or little brown wallabies.

The two foals were equal in strength and size, and when they were able to follow their mothers for a long distance, Bel Bel and Mirri, who had become restless to rejoin their herd, started moving off to the south.

For an hour or so they travelled across the ridge tops, in the fringe of the snow gums, and by mid-morning they came out on an immense open hillside, which was half of a great basin in the hills. Bel Bel and Mirri spoke to their foals at the edge of the tree line.

'Never run out into clear country without first taking a very good look,' they warned.

The foals could see nothing except steep snowgrass and rocks dropping down beyond their sight, and away in the other direction, a rough, timbered hillside.

'That's where we will spend some of the summer,' Bel Bel said. 'It is too rough for the men and their cattle, but we get a good picking there.'

Neither Thowra nor Storm knew what she meant.

'Down there,' said Mirri, 'is the Crackenback River. A nice, cool stream to drink at on hot days, and good sandy beaches, in places, for young ones to roll on.'

They moved out on to the clear hillside, but never went far from the shelter of the trees. Thowra and Storm were too pleasantly tired to want to play and soon went to sleep in the sunshine. Bel Bel and Mirri grazed contentedly, a little distance off. All was quiet. There was the far-off sound of the river, running full and strong with water from the melted snow, and the sound of currawongs, but otherwise a profound silence. Even the mares had grown sleepy, when all of a sudden there was a shrill whinny of fear from Thowra.

Bel Bel whipped round in time to see Thowra and Storm leaping up from their sleep, and there, grabbing at Thowra as he leapt, was a man. She neighed, calling her foal to come quickly, and started galloping towards them, ready to strike at the man. The foals, with long legs flailing, were racing towards her, wild with fear.

She heard Mirri scream with rage behind her. Then the man turned and ran into the trees.

The mares stopped in their headlong chase to snuff their trembling foals all over and make sure they were unhurt.

Bel Bel was all for chasing the man.

'He wasn't a stockman as he had no rope or whip,' she said.

'No,' answered Mirri, 'but even a man alone, walking through the mountains, sometimes has a gun. No, we will just take our foals and go.' She turned to Storm. 'See, my son, that was a man. Never go near man, nor his huts, nor his yards where he fences in cattle and his

8

own tame horse. Man will hurt you and capture you; put straps of leather rope upon your head, tie you up, fence you in, beat you if you bite or kick ...' She was sweating with fear as she spoke, and the two foals' trembling increased.

'And you, Thowra,' said Bel Bel, 'I told you, you would have to be as fleet as the wind. For you will be hunted for your creamy coat and your silver mane and tail, so that the hunters may ride astride your back over your own mountains. Beware of man!'

Still sweating with fear, the two mares led their foals away, slipping like wraiths between the trees, trotting steeply down.

After walking a long way they were nearing the head of the stream. Here the mares went more slowly, stopping to sniff the air.

'The man must have come from this hut, but he is not back yet,' Bel Bel said.

'There may be others.' Mirri's nostrils were quivering.

'I can't smell any fresh smoke.'

'But, still, let us drop much lower down and cross the stream there, rather than follow the track near the hut.'

Bel Bel rubbed one ear on a foreleg.

'The foals are very tired,' she said. 'We had better spend the night near water. A drink for us will help us have more milk for them, too.'

They slept that evening well below the head of the Crackenback, with the singing stream beside them, but occasionally when the north wind blew, the two mares would wrinkle their nostrils and mutter between their teeth, 'Smoke!' So when the moon rose, they nosed the foals up on their tired legs and started the long climb up the Dead Horse Ridge.

Once on top, they could afford to rest again, but it took the foals hours to climb it, and when they found a soak of water to drink, just beyond the top, the mares let the little ones drop down on the soft ground and sleep undisturbed till daybreak.

From there on the travelling was easy, and Bel Bel and Mirri were not so anxious. They were a long way from the hut, and getting very close to the wild horses' winter and spring grazing grounds where, until the snow had all gone, they were never bothered by men.

There had been a time once, years and years ago, when four people had come whizzing down the snow-covered ridges with great wooden boards on their feet, and one of them had a lasso and had roped a bay colt. They had been laughing, almost mad in fact — for all they wanted was to cut off some of his tail to wear plaited and pinned on their coats. This was a legend among the wild horses, a tale every foal heard. But it had happened a long time ago, and man was not expected in the Cascades until the herds of cattle came for summer grazing.

It was evening when the four of them looked down into a narrow valley off the Cascades and saw their own herd grazing. Just then the great, golden chestnut stallion, leader of the herd, raised his head and saw them and let out a shrill, trumpeting cry of greeting.

The two mares neighed in reply and started trotting down the long slope, followed by their nervous foals.

Yarraman's herd

Thowra and Storm were both really frightened by the excitement of the great stallion, their father, and the curiosity of the other mares and foals.

One huge chestnut foal sniffed at Thowra and then gave him a sharp, unpleasant bite on the withers. Thowra dodged behind Bel Bel who promptly laid her ears back and chased the foal away. A small, mean-looking brown mare came prancing up and bared her teeth at Bel Bel.

'That's my foal, Bel Bel,' she snarled.

'Should have thought as much,' Bel Bel said. 'There's nothing in your looks that a foal *could* take after, so it had to be the image of its father.' But when the brown mare had moved off and left them, she said to Thowra, 'Watch that foal, son. It may only be as much as a week older than you, but it's much bigger, and though it's got its father's looks, it has inherited its mother's mean spirit.'

'What's more,' said Mirri, 'Brownie will be trying to queen it over everyone just because she has produced a foal so like Yarraman.' Then she called out loudly to Brownie, 'What have you named your colt?'

'Arrow,' came the answer.

Though the weeks that followed were peaceful for the herd, they were not really peaceful for Thowra and Storm. Arrow seemed to hold it against them that they had been born far off below the Ramshead Range, farther and higher than he had ever been. Whenever Bel Bel and Mirri moved off grazing, or the foals galloped away from their mothers, Arrow would appear slyly beside them, giving a quick bite, or kicking as he galloped past. The other foals were mostly afraid of him, too, but apt to follow his lead — when they could be bothered. Fortunately for Thowra and Storm they could not often be bothered, it was so much more pleasant to gallop and prance on the soft grass, or to splash in the ice-cold creek, watching the golden spray fly up.

Bel Bel and Mirri knew that Arrow was bossing all the foals, and that he was being particularly spiteful towards Thowra and Storm. They kept an eye on any rough games, but realised that the foals must learn to take care of themselves, too.

To the foals, almost every day was the same. They drank their mothers' milk, slept in the sun and played. They learned to stand with forelegs far apart so that they could stretch down and nibble the sweet snowgrass. They learnt other things, too. Bel Bel and Mirri taught them to recognise the track of a dingo, whose cry they heard through the darkness of the night, to tell the wombat paths through the damp bush, and the narrow trail of the Evil One, the snake, over sand. They taught them, too, to recognise the hoofmarks and scent of each member of their herd, and to tell when strange horses came close.

Several other herds of brumbies grazed in the Cascades. They saw a large herd one day when Bel Bel and Mirri felt they must wander and took the foals up Salt Yard Hill at the head of the huge Cascades Valley. Thowra became very excited over their tracks, and proud of himself for recognising them as strangers. He became prouder still when Bel Bel and Mirri showed great interest in one particular set of hoofmarks, one particular scent.

'That's The Brolga,' they muttered, and blew through their nostrils with excitement. 'And he's got a big herd.'

'Who's The Brolga?' the foals both asked.

'He is a young, grey stallion. A fine horse. Very strong. Some day he may be the leading stallion, for he will beat Yarraman when he attains his full strength.'

Thowra and Storm had learnt enough by now to know that this would be a terrific fight, and they wandered up on the grassy hill dreaming of perhaps seeing the great Brolga and his herd.

The restless mares grazed their way on to the southernmost flank of the hill and there, below, on a flat valley floor, were The Brolga and his mares and foals.

Storm started to whinny with excitement, but Mirri gave him a swift nip on the shoulder.

'Be quiet, silly fellow,' she said. 'They might not be pleased to see us.'

Thowra was trembling.

'See,' said Bel Bel, 'three grey filly foals.'

'Come on,' Mirri nudged Storm, 'we'd better go back the other way.'

The sun was warm, and it was good to be up above the valley. They could look down on all the familiar country with its gleaming creeks that ran on down till they joined together and rushed over the rocky rapids. These rapids were the start of the huge waterfall that tumbled down and down, how far, no brumby knew.

That day there was a particularly shining look to all the snow gums, as if the sunlight was dripping off their leaves. The four horses looked around with satisfaction, grazing back across the face of the hill, sleeping for a while in the sun, before wandering back towards their own herd.

Bel Bel looked behind her several times, as was her usual habit, and just as evening was drawing on, she saw something which made her heart jolt inside her. Nose down to their tracks, following a long way behind, was The Brolga with several other horses — young colts and dry mares, she guessed.

'Look behind, Mirri, we'd better run for it as fast as the foals can go,' she said.

Mirri looked back over her shoulder and snorted quietly, but her ears flickered back and forth.

'You two should know your way back to the herd,' she said sharply to Storm. 'Bel Bel and I will just plod along and keep The Brolga thinking.'

'It would be better to keep together,' said Bel Bel, knowing that even in the dusk her foal would show up clearly. 'Come quickly.'

She led off at a hard gallop with the foals following and Mirri bringing up the rear. She knew that The Brolga and his companions would hear them as soon as they started to gallop, but there was a good chance that, despite the slow foals, their lead on The Brolga would allow them to reach their own herd before he caught up with them.

'Hurry!' she called back over her shoulder. And even though she couldn't hear any sound except their own hoof-beats, she caught a glimpse of galloping horses way behind.

They galloped on and on and she could hear the foals beside her blowing. Then she led them splashing through the creek and swung round some rocks and up into the narrow valley where Yarraman's herd had spent each night for some time now. There, she raised her head and let out a high-pitched neigh for help, urging the foals on.

In the gloom near the top of the valley she saw Yarraman, head up, light golden mane and tail foaming, trotting along, looking inquiringly down the valley. She called again and he and some of the herd behind him started to gallop.

From behind her she heard the wild scream of a stallion. She looked back again. The Brolga was standing at the turn into the valley, one foot raised, his head thrown up as he called.

Bel Bel whistled through her teeth. Now what was going to happen? She slowed up. The foals need not gallop so fast, The Brolga would forget all about everyone except Yarraman.

Yarraman began to gallop in earnest. He went thundering past them down the valley, golden mane and tail streaming out on the wind that was made by his own speed. The two mares stopped and turned round to watch. The Brolga was advancing up the valley, rearing and screaming. Bel Bel looked at Thowra, who was giving little whinnies of fear, his eyes and nostrils dilated.

'Oh well, he must learn what fighting is like,' she thought, 'because he, too, will have to fight.'

As he drew close to The Brolga, Yarraman stopped in his headlong gallop and pawed the ground, screaming. Then the two horses advanced, rearing and trumpeting until they were within striking distance of each other and could aim wicked blows with their forefeet.

Even in the half light into which, being grey, The Brolga seemed to fade, the other horses could see how much less heavy and less developed he was than Yarraman. They all knew, too, that in years of fighting Yarraman had learnt every trick. Perhaps, they thought, he will not consider it right or worth his while to kill or maim a much younger horse, and will only punish him for following some of his herd.

The screaming was tremendous. All that could be seen were the two horses, on their hind legs, one a streak of chestnut, pale in the pale light, the other a fainter streak of grey in the gloom, sometimes locked together, biting, striking. Occasionally they broke apart, dropped to the ground and danced around to get in a good position to kick. Yarraman tried not to let The Brolga break away too often because the lighter, younger horse was more nimble on his feet and he had already managed to give one very savage kick.

All the watching horses were trembling and sweating with fear and excitement. Those from The Brolga's herd had drawn a little down the valley. Sometimes their neighs could be heard above the noise of the two stallions.

'Listen! They are calling the foolish one away,' said Bel Bel, and added softly, 'it grows dark.'

Soon they could barely see the two horses.

'See! They are backing off, looking at each other,' Mirri murmured. 'It is too dark, and Yarraman has punished him enough.'

Bel Bel could just distinguish the grey shadow of The Brolga, risen on his hind legs, but backing down the valley. Then it was night.

Yarraman, snorting, whinnying and tossing his fine head, a dark stain of blood on his shoulder and neck, came trotting up the valley.

Leading the foals a dance

Not long after, when the weather was becoming much warmer, Yarraman suddenly led his herd off, away from the Cascades towards the rough range that the mares had pointed out to the foals on the other side of the Crackenback River. When they arrived there was a whole new world to be discovered — not the wide valleys and spacious grassland of the Cascades, with large snow gums and sometimes candlebarks — but rough, rocky ridges and stunted trees, tiny threads of streams, and hidden pockets of snowgrass.

The foals enjoyed it. They played hide-and-seek in among the rocky tors and challenged each other to races down the steep hillsides where the stones broke away from under their hooves and went clattering down, even faster than they could go. Best of all were the bathing parties in the Crackenback, when they would splash and blow bubbles in the water that ran over the cool, brown stones and the shining mica, and then chase each other and roll in the sand.

The foals were now two months old, and Mirri and Bel Bel had lost no opportunity of teaching them their way around the new country. None of the other mares wandered so far off on their own and, when it came to a really good game of hide-and-seek, none of the other foals knew the country as well as Thowra and Storm did.

Brownie was a lazy mare. She stayed around near Yarraman, queening it, as Mirri had guessed she would, and Arrow learnt little else than to be a nuisance — in fact, what else could Brownie teach him, Bel Bel said — but he was still the biggest and strongest foal in the herd. Several times he had given Thowra or Storm vicious bites, and once Thowra was lamed for a week by a kick on the hock.

Then one hot, sultry day, when big thunder clouds sat lazily along the mountain tops, Arrow became especially nasty and he chased Thowra, biting him unmercifully.

Thowra called Storm, 'Come on!' he said. 'He won't catch us!' And away they galloped with Arrow and half the other foals after them.

'We'll lead them a dance,' Thowra said to Storm, as they galloped side-by-side down into a steep ravine. 'If we can lose Arrow, we will!'

They went crashing down, Arrow and his followers not far behind, down, down the rocky slope and then into some very thick scrub. Here, Thowra pulled up sharply on his haunches, and swung on to a tiny narrow track that led towards the head of the ravine.

They heard the other foals go thundering by straight on down, while they went trotting quietly on, making as little sound as possible. The track turned upwards, and they knew they would be quite a height above the other foals when they got out of the scrub.

Thowra led the way on to the rocky hillside again and, sure-footed as a wild goat, cantered across it upwards to the tumbled mass of rock that formed the

18

headwall of the ravine. He and Storm had found a track through, but he was pretty certain Arrow would not know it. He looked down once and saw the other foals far below, but already starting in pursuit.

They had to let their pace drop to a walk when they reached the rocks, and for a moment it was hard to find the start of their track. Then they picked their way carefully through, round and over the great rough rocks with almost a sheer wall of rock up on one side of them and a tremendous drop on the other.

They could hear the other foals crashing and stumbling across the side of the hill, but they didn't stop or look back — they had to watch every step they took on the cliff or they might find themselves hurtling down through space to the floor of the ravine, far below. Thowra felt his coat prickling with fear, and then the sweat running on his neck and flanks. How foolish it would be to fall! But at last they were over, and there, safe on the other side, they neighed and mocked at Arrow who was still looking for a way across the headwall.

At this, Arrow became so angry that he started to climb right round over the top. Thowra and Storm could afford to rest before galloping off. Then they were off again, moving through broken country of granite tors, rough scrub and low snow gums, directly away from where the mares had been grazing. There was no grass here, and Thowra guessed that the other foals had never bothered to explore this way.

Both foals noticed how hot it had become. Thowra's cream coat was all dark with sweat. They stopped for a moment to get their breath and watched black clouds massing over the sky.

'We may be glad we know our way,' Thowra said.

The others were drawing nearer, so they led them on, up a little hill, which was already covered in grey mist.

As soon as they saw the other foals following up the hill, they went through the mist and quickly down the other side, then jumped down into a sharp-sided creek bed that cut straight across the foot of the hill. They turned east up the creek and trotted along, before stopping for a drink.

There was no sound of pursuit, although once Thowra thought he heard a neigh.

'This creek will take us nearly all the way home,' he said.

'Yes,' Storm answered. 'Come on!'

'I'm wondering about the others.'

They both looked around. Clouds had boiled up and poured right over the mountains, and it was impossible to see more than a few yards.

'It's all very well to lose Arrow on a fine day,' Thowra said, 'but the weather is changing. Also,' he added, 'the mothers of the other foals will be wild with us, even if they do think Arrow deserves all he gets.'

'That is quite true,' Storm said. 'Perhaps we had better go and find them.'

They went back along the creek and scrambled up on to the hillside again. Now, they could hear neighing coming from the top of the hill.

Storm threw up his head to listen, 'I expect they are wandering round in circles,' he said. 'Don't let's hurry; give them time to get to know what it's like being lost in a cloud.'

But when they reached the top of the hill they could just make out the group of foals through the cloud, all huddled together in the shelter of some rocks.

Thowra and Storm went up to them, emerging like shadows out of the mist.

'Don't you know your way home?' Storm asked.

Arrow said nothing, but the other foals came crowding round.

'Can you lead us back, even through these clouds?' they asked.

Thowra looked at them without speaking for a moment, then he turned to Arrow.

'Do you want to go home, O swift Arrow?'

Arrow nodded glumly. Just then there was a great roll of thunder, and a whip-like streak of lightning seemed to strike the rocks. Thowra took no notice.

'Are you going to behave yourself and be nicer to everyone?' he asked Arrow.

There was no answer.

'Oh well,' said Thowra, 'Storm and I will go home on our own,' and he moved as if to go back into the cloud and mist. More lightning blazed behind him, and he seemed to be made of silver.

The other foals crowded after them but Arrow stood quite still.

'Arrow will behave, or we will all set on him this minute,' spoke up Star, a brown filly who had always wished she could go wandering with Thowra and Storm and their mothers.

'All right,' Thowra and Storm both agreed. 'Follow us then, closely.' Their last words were almost lost in the rumble of thunder and the sudden sound of pouring rain.

Shivering with cold now as well as fear, the foals followed them as they turned and made their way down into the more sheltered creek bed. Here, the noise of the thunder was almost like something striking at them, and

Thowra noticed with pleasure that Arrow was as frightened as the others.

In places the creek bed widened, and there was grass or sand over which they could canter; sometimes they walked through stones. Then the creek turned in a long northward curve that led them back towards where the herd had been. Even when they were quite close to the mares, the clouds were so heavy and black that only Thowra and Storm knew they had arrived back.

Quietly, they led the foals into the herd. They could tell by the restless moving of the mares that they were worried. Brownie gave a silly-sounding neigh when she saw Arrow and started sniffing him all over.

'What have you been up to?' muttered Bel Bel as Thowra came up beside her for a drink.

'Trying to teach Arrow a lesson. Maybe he won't be such a bully for a while,' Thowra answered.

'Take care — that colt may always be bigger and stronger than you,' Bel Bel said.

Just then Star's mother came up.

'No good will come of you teaching your sons to be so independent,' she said to Bel Bel and Mirri angrily, and then turned to Thowra. 'Where have you led our foals to today?'

But Star, looking miserable, said, 'It was our fault — and Arrow's.'

'That Arrow!' said the mare sourly. 'He will grow into a bad horse.'

'He'll be a bad enemy,' said Mirri, looking with meaning at her own son and at Thowra.

22

Brumby drive

On very clear days the wild horses could see the cattle grazing on the other side of the Crackenback River. Sometimes they might meet a beast or two down drinking, but the horses mostly kept to drinking places where the cattle never came, because where there were cattle there could be men.

One day Bel Bel and Mirri and the two foals were climbing up behind a particularly high granite tor. They were still in the trees, and out of sight themselves, when they saw a man standing upon the top of the tor, gazing over the country.

The wild horses came to a dead stop, nostrils quivering. There the man stood, a wide hat shading his eyes, a red scarf round his neck, wearing faded riding trousers, and with a coiled whip in his hand.

'Stockman,' whispered Bel Bel. 'His tame horse must be somewhere, and maybe a mate or two. Our scent must be blowing straight to him.'

'*He* won't smell it,' said Mirri scornfully.

'His horse may, though.'

Sure enough, there came the sound of neighing and stamping, and even the jingle of a bit.

'He's not very far away. We must go!' Bel Bel turned to Thowra, 'Take a good look at the man, my son. He is your greatest enemy.'

Thowra could not really remember the man who had tried to catch him as he slept on the slopes of the Ramshead Range, but that day had planted the fear of man deeply in him. All he said now was, 'Let's go!'

They moved away quietly, and that evening, as they grazed with the herd by a wide creek bed, Bel Bel and Mirri told Yarraman and the gathered mares and yearlings what they had seen.

'I don't like it,' said Bel Bel. 'He was a mountain man and he will have come here for some purpose, not just curiosity.'

'They are sure to know that many of us always spend the summer here,' Mirri said. 'It wouldn't be good if they came back to hunt us.'

'We know this country too well,' boasted Yarraman, but he did not look happy with the situation.

The two mares kept an even more careful watch on their foals, and would only let them go down to the river very early and very late in the day when men who live in huts or tents are always busy with their pots of water that bubble by their smoking fires.

Once again, the man was seen, this time by Yarraman himself as he and the herd were in their customary grazing ground. The man was standing right above them as though he were cut out of rock.

The news of this was very disquieting to Bel Bel and Mirri, and they kept an even stricter watch.

There were many hot, sleepy days that summer, and though the foals lay stretched out in the grass, their switching tails the only sign of life, the two mothers kept watch in turns, never, during the day, sleeping at the same time. Even so, one day they were both sleepy enough to get badly frightened when they heard an unusual noise far below them.

What was it? Something was moving through dead timber the way no wild animal would move. Perhaps it was a tame horse with a man on its back?

They could not smell anything. Nostrils to the wind, they listened. There was the sound again. They roused the sleeping foals and began to move quietly upwards.

When Thowra made to jump up on a large rocky outcrop, Bel Bel nipped him and pushed him back.

'Don't be so silly,' she said, 'making yourself a clear mark for anyone to see! Stay in the trees and keep quiet.'

Sometimes they stopped to listen, but for a while there was no sound except that of a currawong and the chatter of gang-gangs in the trees. Then, during one such stop, they heard a faint sound of movement, so faint that no one except those who lived in the bush would have heard it, and they knew it was something wild like themselves. Before long, three silver-grey kangaroos went hopping by.

Thowra and Storm were delighted to see them, but both Bel Bel and Mirri looked worried. Not long afterwards, they saw four young colts making up the hill too.

They came to a small, clear stream where the foals wanted to play.

'Have a short drink, and come on,' said Bel Bel. Three black cockatoos flew out of the trees by the water, with their weird, wild crying, and the foals jumped back, startled.

Mirri looked back fearfully.

'Something's happening, I'm sure,' she muttered.

Even a gust of wind rustling the shiny leaves made the mares start nervously, then they saw some of their own herd heading towards their main camping ground, which was in an unexpected hanging valley not far from the top of the range. They caught up to these mares and foals, and Bel Bel said, 'Have you seen anything strange as you travelled homewards at midday?'

Star's mother answered fearfully, 'No, but we heard the sound of horsemen and a faint whip crack. What business have men here?'

Then through the bush, some distance off, they saw several more kangaroos flitting between the trees, moving upwards.

Bel Bel turned to Mirri.

'We're being driven uphill,' she said. 'There must be a great many men.'

'Well, we're going,' said Star's mother. 'We'll be safer with Yarraman and the others.'

Bel Bel looked at Mirri.

'It must be us wild horses they're after, not kangaroos,' she said.

'Good luck!' said Mirri to the others, as they jogged away, then to Bel Bel, 'Shall we try to go across the hill and escape the men?'

'That's the best thing I can think of. We might make the ravine and hide there, but the men will probably have dogs and though *we* might race them, it's not going to be so easy with the foals — but we must go.' And, as usual, the creamy mare led off, the two foals following her, and Mirri close behind them.

All of a sudden, the bush seemed dreadfully still and very hot, and the scent of the turpentine bush was all around. Bel Bel leapt to one side sharply as a big copperhead snake slid across some warm, bare earth almost under her feet, and she felt the sweat break out behind her ears.

Coming up the hill towards her she saw a pair of brown wallabies.

'Yes, we're being driven,' she whispered to herself.

Further on they met more brumbies, panting and sweating. The leader only stopped for a second to say to them, 'You'll meet stockmen if you keep going that way. They're not far behind. Better follow us.'

'There are men everywhere,' said Bel Bel. 'The only thing to do is to try and get back between them.'

But the other horses just went on upwards, their flanks heaving and the smell of their sweat heavy on the air.

Bel Bel led off again, faster, threading through thick snow gums, even breaking into a fast canter when they reached a grassy glade. As much as possible she avoided rocks on which their hooves would make a noise. If only they could reach the ravine ...

Then she saw the first of the men, sitting easily on a neat, grey horse, a Queensland blue heeler padding along beside him.

She doubled back quickly, driving Thowra and Storm in front of her. Perhaps he had not seen her. Perhaps he would not hear them. If they went back a few hundred yards, and then turned downwards, they might just get through the cordon of men and dogs. But when she turned down, there, galloping across in front of her, was the same man and his dog.

The dog saw the wild horses and rushed to head them, snapping not at her or Mirri, who might have kicked, but at Thowra.

Thowra, who had never seen a dog in his life, turned in a frenzy of fear. Bel Bel galloped after him, trying to swing him back to make another effort to beat the man and the dog downhill, but the dog knew his game too well and kept heeling Thowra. Thowra was soon beyond being able to hear anything his mother neighed to him, and all that Bel Bel could do was to go with him in his mad gallop up the hill, trying to strike or kick at the dog. At last she quietened the blue heeler by galloping at him when he snapped at Thowra's heel and giving him a nasty bite on the back.

Bel Bel then galloped shoulder-to-shoulder with Thowra, speaking to him, trying to steady him, and all the time wondering what they should do next. In a few quick, backward glances she could see no sign of Mirri and Storm. The man was a good way behind and had called off his dog, who had done his job of heading them uphill very well.

Bel Bel gave Thowra a gentle nip on the shoulder.

'Slow down!' she said. 'They are not following.'

Thowra was really blowing. He slackened his pace and at last dropped to a walk.

'We will have a little rest in that thick belt of snow gums,' Bel Bel said, 'and, from there, try and cut across to the ravine again.' But the time had gone for escape. The men and their dogs were closing in.

Bel Bel found herself and her foal driven relentlessly uphill. Each time she hoped to cut across she saw a man. Presently, they caught up with several trembling mares and foals, and they could hear others moving on ahead. Bel Bel made one more bid to break away south to the ravine, but just then she heard a whip crack, and another, from the direction of the ravine, and some more brumbies came galloping towards her.

'Don't try to go that way,' they said. 'Lots of men and dogs are there. Quick, quick!' and they galloped on in terror.

Bel Bel realised that they were all being swung round in the direction of their main camping ground.

'The men will have made a yard somewhere,' she thought, because this was not the first time she had been caught up in a big hunt when the stockmen came after the brumbies. She wished Mirri was still with her. Mirri was a good friend, and she understood more about the habits of men. Mirri would know where they would build a yard in which to catch wild horses. As for Bel Bel, she could think of no place more likely than in the narrow mouth of the valley at its farthest end.

She tried to talk to Thowra before he got completely infected with the panic that was gripping all the other horses.

'Son,' she said, 'you must stay beside me. Somewhere these men will have put up fences to stop us escaping. If you stay right next to me, I may be able to just miss going into their yard and we might escape.'

Thowra thought he would never forget all that happened after that. First he heard sticks and branches breaking as though hundreds of men and horses were chasing them. Then he heard the unknown ring of a shod horse's hoof on stone, and *then* whips cracking, many whips, cracking and cracking, right behind them.

The brumbies really started to gallop, and he and his mother galloped with them.

The little foal stretched his legs out beside his mother. He stretched his neck out, too. He could feel his heart thundering unevenly in his chest. He and his mother were right in the centre of the mob. Bel Bel's shoulder touched him on his near side, and he felt her hot breath. Everything was bound up with the tremendous pounding, the thundering of hooves on hard ground, the pounding and thundering of his own heart, the blowing of breath, the gasping of all the horses.

A snow gum branch whipped him across his eyes, and brought stinging tears. He could hear his own breath sob and felt as though his pounding heart would burst. His legs and hooves no longer seemed to belong to him.

Then they were out of the trees and they spread apart a little in the open valley of the camping ground. The men forced them together again into a mob that moved almost as one horse, but, while they were spread out, Thowra had felt Bel Bel pushing him over to the left wing, not quite on the outside of the mob, because their colour would be too noticeable there, but just near the edge. He heard his mother give a gasping sort of whinny and, through the tired haze that was over his eyes, he recognised Mirri and Storm on the wing.

The noise of whips never ceased now, as the men drove them faster and faster. The horses were in a frenzy of fear. Thowra wanted to cry out with the terror that seemed to run like a flame through the mob, but he had no breath for anything except to keep going. Bel Bel spoke to him several times and he hardly heard. Then he knew she was saying something that mattered.

'In a second we will swing to the left,' she said, 'through the gap in the trees.'

With a tremendous effort he focused his eyes on something other than the outstretched noses and heaving flanks beside him, and saw that they were nearly at the end of the valley.

'Now!' said Bel Bel, and edged him out of the mob, neighing to Mirri as they went.

Only a few strides and they would be in the trees. Thowra realised it was Storm beside him and that the two mares were driving them. He felt a searing cut across his face from a whip. A dog fastened on his heel and he heard Bel Bel's scream of rage, but his mother and Mirri forced them on.

There was a jumble of men's voices, one calling, 'Hold the ones we've got!' Another singing out, 'No! I swear I'll have the creamies.'

Then they were in the trees and pounding over rocks, one man and his dog still with them. Bel Bel raced into the lead and Thowra suddenly knew why. There was quite a drop ahead of them, over some rocks. He and Storm had played there often and knew just where to jump. All at once he felt strong enough to go at the faster pace that his mother was setting.

Bel Bel leapt over the edge, jumping on to a little rocky shelf, sliding down from it on her haunches, jumping again, and he was following, legs trembling so much that he could barely stand up when he landed.

Standing at the foot of the little cliff, legs apart and shaking, he looked up. Mirri and Storm were nearly safely down, but the man had reined in on the top and was left behind.

'Come on,' said Bel Bel, and the four brumbies vanished into the trees.

Man, the invader

That night the weather changed suddenly. Stars faded under cloud, a whining wind crept around the rock tors and down the grassy lanes between the snow gums. Far up on the range, the dingoes howled.

There was no other sound except the whining wind and the dingoes where Mirri and Bel Bel and their two foals lay, but nearer the top of the range there were rustlings and stealthy movements. Kangaroos that had been driven from their usual haunts were carefully looking around and starting home again. Birds were disturbed and anxious, unable to settle for the night. Brumbies who had escaped the hunt, or broken out of the yard, footsore and exhausted, moved fearfully into the back country.

A large campfire blazed in the grassy valley and nearly a dozen men slept around it. In the rough yard they had built, there were about fifteen brumbies. There would have been more, but a great heavy colt had smashed one corner of the yard when it tried to escape, and quite a few — including Brownie and Arrow — had escaped. Yarraman and others of the herd had never been in the original round-up.

All night long the brumbies trapped in the yard neighed and called, walked and walked. Rain came in fitful showers, hissing in the fire, steaming on the brumbies' sweating coats. Raindrops woke Bel Bel and Mirri, who were barely sleeping anyway, but no raindrop could have disturbed the two exhausted foals. They slept deeply, occasionally half-neighing at the ugliness of a dream.

During the next day, they lay quietly hidden in thick snow gums and hop scrub by a water soak where the wombats and shy brown wallabies came to drink. They could hear the noise of whips and voices, but knew that it was only the sound of the preparations the men were now making to take the brumbies away with them. It was very unlikely that there would be any more hunting unless the creamies were seen, so it was better to lie low till the men had gone.

Before midday, the sounds of whip cracks had become far distant, and by afternoon the bush had returned to its usual silence — a blend of water music, the sound of wind, of moving branches and moving soft-footed animals, and the song of birds. All that was different was the hanging smell of smoke; and there, in the camping valley was the trampled, spoiled grass, the dead fire and the hidden remains of the trap-yard.

Bel Bel and Mirri did not go to see what was left. Instead, they took their foals and skirted round the valley to the north and east, searching till they found brumby tracks, and the tracks of Yarraman himself.

Yarraman's tracks were over a day old, but there were fresher ones — Thowra discovered the tracks of Brownie and Arrow and gave a squeal of excitement. They followed along the tracks for some miles to a spot where Yarraman had deliberately led the herd over a great, rough cliff of rock and stone, where no track would remain.

'I know where he's gone,' said Bel Bel. 'He will have headed for the Hidden Flat,' and she struck off across the cliff.

It was evening when they reached a narrow, grassy flat, deep down in a gorge. Since the walls of the gorge were so steep, and the trees on its side so tall, no one approaching could see down into the Hidden Flat, and they did not know if the others were still there till they reached the grass. Then they heard a welcoming neigh from Yarraman as he came trotting to meet them.

The herd stayed around the Hidden Flat till the days grew shorter, the nights frosty and bright; till the rivers were stilled with the cold, and so clear that you could see each stone in the bottom, and every reflection, so deeply. Then the wild things in the mountains knew that the snow must be coming soon and the stockmen would be too busy mustering their cattle to have any more brumby hunts. Now it was safe to go back to Paddy Rush's Bogong and watch over the other side of the Crackenback for the going of the cattle herds, when they could return to the Cascades for the winter and spring.

Thowra and Storm had both grown a lot, but Arrow was still the biggest of all the foals. He was arrogant and mean-minded, but, since Thowra and Storm had so easily lost him in the clouds and brought him ignominiously home again, he had left them in peace from petty bites and kicks.

The other foals had learnt to hate him yet admire him at the same time. Although Arrow was bigger, stronger, and faster, he could never be acknowledged leader of the foals. Thowra and Storm knew the country better than he, and knew all the signs and sounds of the bush. Also, it was well known among the mares that Yarraman admired Bel Bel and Mirri and never bossed them around like he did the others — after all, mares that could fend for themselves and who knew the mountains better than he did could hardly be bossed by a stallion.

Autumn was a happy time for Thowra and Storm and their mothers.

The brumbies listened to the sounds of herds of cattle being mustered above the Crackenback. Finally, the last bullock and the last man left the mountains, and there was no more smoke coming from the chimneys of the huts. Thowra and Storm were as eager as any of them to cross the shining Crackenback and climb back upwards to return to their barely remembered old home at the Cascades — to find again the great wide valley of springy snowgrass where they could gallop and gallop.

Invisible in snow

Thowra and Storm were naturally very frightened of men and dogs because they had been hunted by them, but they were also very curious.

After they had been some weeks in the Cascades, they gathered up their courage and climbed onto the little knoll where the stockmen's slab and shingle hut stood above the creek. Though it had been empty for a long time now, there were still strange smells lurking round it, and some salt spilt on the ground, which they licked up. Salt was good. There were natural salt-licks in the bush, but not many of them, and sometimes you could find a little left round the places where the men salted their cattle.

Thowra sniffed all round the hut. He was looking for something, but he didn't know what. The cold wind blew a tin billy that had been left hanging under the eaves of the hut. As it swung towards Thowra he jumped backwards and Storm snorted with amusement.

'Let's go,' he said. 'There's nothing here. The sky looks very peculiar, and the others are a long way off.'

The wind rustled the golden everlastings that grew in the grass about their feet, and in the trees close by its low moaning sounded.

'The clouds seem heavy,' said Storm, 'as though they are pressing down. I don't remember a day like this before.'

'You are silly,' said Thowra with a toss of his head. 'You've never lived through a winter before. Mother said we mustn't go too far today because of the weather, but let's just go and listen to the sound the wind is making in the big trees.'

Down near the Cascades hut, there were some tall trees, candlebarks and the first of the great mountain ash, and the two foals had already discovered the fun of playing 'tug-you-last' around the great tree-trunks and up and down the clear glades. Now, as soon as they were in the timber, they could hear the wail of the wind in the tree-tops, far above, and the soughing and sighing of streamers of bark that hung down the trunks.

They felt very small and alone — and very excited.

'What was that?' asked Thowra nervously, as something white and feathery floated down from the dark sky and landed, freezing cold, on his nose.

Storm jumped to one side and shook his head as another cold white feather fell on his ear. They cantered away under a big tree, but, even there, floating so slowly and lightly on the air, the white feathers came, in ones and twos at first, but thicker and thicker till the air was filled with floating whiteness.

It was a long time before they thought of looking at the ground.

'Look!' cried Storm. 'It's even making the ground white. We should go home — it might be difficult to find our way if we don't leave now.'

They had no trouble finding their way back while they were in amongst the tall trees and had the trunks to guide them, but the open valley was a blinding whirl of blown whiteness. The shape of tracks could still be seen, and Thowra jogged along one, his nose to the ground. Storm ran right beside him, almost bumping into him.

'You'll tread on me,' Thowra complained. 'What is the matter?'

'I can hardly see you through this strange white stuff,' said Storm, and he sounded afraid. His own dark coat showed up clearly, but Thowra was almost invisible.

Thowra looked around him then and felt half-afraid too. Nothing could be seen except the swirling, whirling flakes; no contours of hill or ridge, not even the loops of the streams, but the hollow of track still showed just at his feet.

'Quick, we must follow the track before it gets buried,' he said. 'By then we should be at the creek.'

When they reached the stream they stopped to watch the strange white flakes, which almost hissed as they touched the water — and then vanished.

They waded through the ice-cold water and followed the stream on the other bank, knowing they should soon come to the little creek that flowed down from the herd's camping valley.

They kept shaking their heads to try and free their eyelashes and nostrils of the strange white stuff. Their forelocks, solid and wet, hit their eyes with each shake.

When they had gone a little way Thowra suddenly stopped, raised his head and neighed loudly. He could see nothing at all through the white storm, but from ahead came answering neighs and he broke into a canter. Bel Bel and Mirri had come down to the junction of the valley to wait for them.

They could see Mirri from several yards off, but were almost on top of Bel Bel before they saw her.

38

'What's happening to the world, Mother?' asked Thowra, feeling very glad to be safely with her.

'Why, this is a snowstorm, Son. It's heavy for early in the winter though,' she said worriedly, 'especially for down here. We may go hungry before the spring.'

The two mares led their foals back to the herd, who were huddled together in the shelter of some trees. There they spent the cold, stormy night, with the wind howling and the snow lying thick on their warm coats.

By morning the snow had stopped falling but it lay nearly a foot deep on the ground. Trees were bowed down with it, each leaf coated in white crystals. There was no grass to eat unless you scratched away the snow with a hoof.

Disconsolately, the herd wandered down into the main valley.

'The sun will come out soon,' said Bel Bel, 'and then the snow will thaw and we will have grass to eat again.'

When the sun did come out and warm them, all the foals soon found that they could have great fun chasing each other up and down the glittering white hills.

Thowra was no longer invisible, now that the air was clear of the wind-swivelled flakes, but somehow the snow seemed to be his kingdom, and the other foals soon saw that he was swifter and more sure-footed in it than Arrow. Of course if you knew where every hole or little watercourse was, you didn't make any stupid mistakes. Arrow forgot that there was a little tiny stream at the foot of one ridge. He went galloping down, chasing Thowra, and never noticed Thowra's flying leap at the bottom. His forefeet broke through the snow into the creek and, in a wild flurry of snow, he turned a complete somersault, finishing up almost buried.

Thowra saw exactly what happened, and by the time Arrow had got to his feet, shaken all the snow out of his eyes and ears, and gingerly tested his legs, Thowra was rearing and neighing on top of a high rock on the next ridge.

If Arrow had had any sense, he would have taken no notice, but he got in a fury of anger at the sight of the beautiful creamy foal, as he pranced and reared.

With all the foals watching, Arrow made after him, neighing and snorting, kicking and pawing up the snow.

Thowra waited until the chestnut was three strides away from the back of the rock, then he reared up and pirouetted on his hind legs, gave a squeal of joy, and leapt off the steep side of the rocks on to the soft snow, then away down the ridge, bucking and snorting.

Bel Bel and Mirri were at the bottom.

'That's enough, my son. You are making a bad enemy for yourself,' said Bel Bel, but she had enjoyed Thowra's pranks, and there was a gleam of pleasure in her eyes. Her cream colt had looked so joyously beautiful rearing up on the snow-covered rock. He was almost white now, in his thick winter coat, his silver mane and tail gleaming and glittering in the sun. 'Come now,' she went on, 'let's go down the mountainside a little way and see if we can find some food.'

Mirri called Storm and off the four of them went, down the valley and into the tall timber where Storm and Thowra had watched the start of the snowfall the day before. Here Thowra suddenly stopped dead, snorting at the ground. Right at his nose was a set of fresh tracks in the snow, little tracks just like a child's bare feet, but the foals did not know that. Where the snow was very soft and deep there was a gutter, in between the feetmarks.

Bel Bel and Mirri said nothing when the foals began following the trail, noses down. Suddenly Thowra, who was leading, stopped and nearly sat back on his haunches with fright. Only a yard or two ahead of him was the round, furry back of a wombat who was grubbing for food. The wombat took no notice whatsoever and just went on grubbing through snow and mud with his sharp little nose. Bel Bel and Mirri watched, their muzzles twitching a little.

Thowra stood up and stretched out his neck to sniff the thick fur. The wombat turned around surprisingly fast, his beady eyes angry. Thowra nearly sat down again as the wombat waddled on, his round, fat middle making the gutter in the snow.

The horses kept jogging on downwards, nibbling at wattles and odd shrubs. At last, where the snow was thinner, they turned off the spur on to the northern slope where, as Bel Bel well knew they would, they found tussocks of snowgrass.

That night as they camped by a clear singing stream, Bel Bel sniffed the air and looked at the sky. 'There'll be a frost tonight,' she said, 'and another fine day. But I can't help feeling there's going to be a lot of snow, and we'll have to find somewhere else to spend winter — somewhere lower than the Cascades.'

'Well, the nearest lower country with good grass belongs to The Brolga,' said Mirri.

Storm and Thowra both pricked up their ears.

Seeking grass

Heavy frosts made ice on the creeks and froze small, still pools quite solid. In the wonderfully bright days that came after each frost, while some of the more weather-wise mares were worrying about the hard winter that was coming, the foals played and had mock fights with wild exuberance. The biting cold and the bright sun, as Mirri said, had put the devil into them.

Then one day, after an iron-hard frost, clouds came up before the dawn and a moaning, icy wind came from the north. Just as the grey light crept over the valley a flock of black cockatoos flew screaming, crying, to the south, borne on the wind.

'Hmph,' said Bel Bel to Yarraman. 'I don't like it.'

Yarraman looked as if he had not heard her, but as the light grew stronger he started grazing his way into the main valley and then steadily south-east all day, without haste, and never turning back.

The clouds grew heavier and darker, the wind colder. No ice melted that day.

'We haven't seen any other horses,' Thowra heard his mother whisper to Mirri. 'The Brolga must have already decided to go to his lower pastures.'

That night they sheltered in an unaccustomed valley, and at nightfall the snow started to beat down in the wind.

The herd moved around under the trees all night, stamping and whinnying softly. Sometimes a foal dropped down on the hard, cold ground and slept; mostly the sense of disquiet throughout the whole herd kept even the young ones from sleeping soundly.

Thowra did not know what made him feel excited and yet afraid. He did not realise that his mother's anxiety since the first heavy snowfall had been communicating itself to him, or that the strange feeling which all the grown horses had slowly begun to sense — that a hard winter was coming — had somehow made everyone touchy, apt to gallop, kick or bite. He only knew that the howl of the wind and the cold lash of the snow made him want to gallop now, even in the pitch darkness, and leap on to a high rock, rear and neigh loudly to the sky. He could imagine the wild neigh ringing out and the thought of it sent cold shivers down his backbone.

Suddenly he realised that Arrow was passing him and he lashed out with his heels. Arrow gave a squeal of rage and pain but Thowra had cantered off into the storm and the night. Unable to bear his own feelings any longer, he lifted his head to the falling snow and neighed with all his strength. There was a sudden hushed silence in the herd, and then from far to the south-east came an answering, distant neigh.

Thowra stiffened, tingling with a mad excitement, but Bel Bel came up at his side then, and she nipped him on the wither.

'Be quiet, silly one,' she said, not unkindly. 'Yarraman will punish you if you make too much noise. Don't you

43

realise we are no longer in our own country, and that he may have to fight for our food?'

'Are we in The Brolga's country?' Thowra was quivering with nervousness.

'Yes, we are, and we will have to go further into it yet, to get out of the heavy snow.'

'I wish daylight would come!'

'The winter nights are long,' said Bel Bel. 'Sleep while I stand beside you. Tomorrow you may have to fight Arrow for that kick you gave him. We may travel a long way too. You will need your strength.'

When the dawn came, grey and beating with hard, wind-driven snow, Yarraman led off immediately, still south-east, but upwards, over a gap in the hills.

There were strange horse tracks at the mouth of a small valley. Yarraman sniffed them curiously but went on his own way. Bel Bel and Mirri both branched off up the little valley for a few yards, looking carefully at the tracks.

'No more than four young horses, I should think,' Bel Bel said. 'Certainly The Brolga is not with them.'

Just in the few minutes while they looked at the tracks, the herd had vanished into the storm and their own tracks were fast getting covered. Thowra and Storm were both quite bothered, but Bel Bel and Mirri trotted upwards, and kept trotting till the herd came into sight, shadow horses behind a dense curtain of flying snow.

All day long the wind howled and drove the snow in this impenetrable curtain, the sheer force pushing, almost carrying the horses on.

They were getting hungry now, and the only water they had was when they broke the ice on a pool. The foals demanded, and got, milk from their mothers, but there would not be much milk if they had to keep going like this, driven on the storm, and never finding grass. Even the mares were tiring, perhaps because the cold was so intense, but if they stopped they got colder still.

At last, when they had gone a long way down the other side of the gap, Yarraman turned into a side valley that ran across the wind and had plenty of trees for shelter, and there they spent another restless, anxious night.

At dawn the storm still swirled and beat around them. The herd set off again, cold, tired and hungry, and filled with a dread of staying still in one place. They were steadily losing height and both the ground and the air must have been warmer than it was in the Cascades because the snow was wetter and not as thick on the ground.

At last they came to flatter ground in what seemed to be a basin, into which flowed quite a number of streams. Yarraman went several miles downstream and then he started fossicking around for shrubs to eat and the odd patch of grass that might be sticking out of the snow underneath a tree.

'It looks as if this is where we're going to stop,' Mirri said to Bel Bel. Bel Bel was staring at the bank of the stream: snow lay right to the water's edge, but just where there was a crossing there were still the shapes of hoof-marks, half-filled with snow.

'Hmn!' she said, peering more closely and then crossing over and looking at the other side. 'Hmn! I think quite a few horses have crossed fairly recently.' She scratched away some snow from the bank and found muddied, tracked snow underneath.

'Well, what of it?' asked Mirri. 'We've got to eat, and we may eat better here than higher up.'

'Looks as if it will be a quarrelsome winter,' Bel Bel said, and she turned her head towards Yarraman. A hard winter would not worry a horse approaching his prime, like The Brolga, but Yarraman would feel it. The Brolga would not have attained full strength yet, but he must be getting very near it. 'Anyway,' she went on, 'nothing is likely to happen during such a blizzard. Everyone will be too taken up with finding food.'

The blizzard continued for days. Sometimes, down in the low valley, the snow turned to rain, then it would snow again. The horses managed to find bushes which they could eat, and, though they were still hungry, they were not starving yet.

Now that they were no longer travelling, but wandering around trying to find food, Thowra thought he would be able to have some fun, particularly annoying Arrow, since he himself would be almost invisible in the flying snow. But he found it so difficult to see his own mother that he never liked to get far away from her in case he lost her in the blizzard and in the unknown country.

Once, Bel Bel left him with Mirri while she went off scouting further down the stream, and, by her behaviour, Thowra felt sure Yarraman had asked her to go and see what she could see. In that time, he sneaked away from Mirri, crept up on Arrow and gave him a playful nip, but he could not help feeling afraid of the rough weather and the constantly falling snow, and he was glad when his mother came home, even though she had absolutely nothing interesting to tell them.

At last there came a day when the snow stopped falling, and the following night, close on midnight, the wind dropped. Thowra woke because of the sudden silence when there was no longer the howl of the wind, and in that silence he heard a distant echoing of the shrill trumpeting neigh of a stallion. He scrambled to his feet and was just going to neigh in tremulous answer when Bel Bel gave him a swift nip.

'Why, oh why, have I got such an excitable son?' she said, half in anger, half in pride. 'It is not your place to answer that call,' and just then Yarraman's wild cry rang out.

There was an instant electric silence; not one of the herd moved or let go a breath. Then, far away again, but shrill with anger, came the stallion's cry.

'Tomorrow they will start the fights for the grass that we haven't found yet,' said Mirri acidly.

'And the youngest, lightest horse will have an advantage in this snow,' Bel Bel added.

The foals dropped off to sleep again, but there was a restless lack of ease among the mares and young colts and fillies.

Not long after the grey dawn, The Brolga and some of his mares appeared out of the mist and clouds. Yarraman pranced forward from his herd, stepping high, head up imperiously, tail held high and free.

Along came The Brolga, rearing and screaming.

A shock of excitement ran through the herd. The Brolga was growing into a noble horse; yet their own Yarraman was superb — like a sun god against the grey clouds and white snow.

Thowra shivered. The Brolga, like his mother and himself, had that strange quality of merging with snow and cloud, which might prove an advantage over the bright chestnut in a real fight.

He could smell the anger and excitement of the two stallions as they went to meet each other; there was a roar from both horses as they reached within striking distance. Then the snow was flying from their hooves as they circled each other, striking, biting, screaming. Thowra saw blood staining the snow, and the mud beneath the horses' feet.

Yarraman had The Brolga in a terrific grip with his teeth, but suddenly the older horse's hooves slipped in the snow and he was forced to let go. Round and round they circled again. The nimbler, lighter Brolga was certainly better at keeping his footing and when Yarraman slipped again, he managed to get a cruel hold just above the chestnut's withers. Screaming with rage and pain, Yarraman lashed out and missed him, and then with a tremendous effort shook himself free and planted both heels in The Brolga's chest, almost winding him.

The Brolga also had a gash above one eye, where Yarraman had struck. It half-blinded him, but he could still move more lightly and surely than the heavier horse. Now each was trying for the deadly grip on the withers. Yarraman succeeded, but now he was so breathless that the watching herd could see that, even if he defeated the younger horse *this* time, he would not have the wind to give him a real beating.

Thowra looked with horror at all the blood on the snow, and at the two exhausted horses. When Yarraman finally let go, for want of strength to hold on any longer, he found himself hoping that The Brolga would have no fighting-strength left either.

With relief he saw the great, grey horse backing off, every muscle trembling with exhaustion, his one good eye never leaving Yarraman who stood in front of his mares, as a huge, bleeding statue.

New wisdom

Yarraman had won the right for himself and his herd to eat what food they could find when the snow melted. Each mare knew that they could peacefully graze, just as long as they did not trespass on any territory on which The Brolga and his herd were grazing.

Throughout the winter there were several fights between the young colts that ran with each herd, but the two stallions kept away from each other and let their wounds heal.

Yarraman took a long time to get better. Perhaps the food was not good enough to keep his blood strong; perhaps it was just that the snow had got into the wounds; and maybe his age had something to do with it. No one knew how soon The Brolga had recovered, only Thowra saw him once, standing high upon a rock, looking out over a snowy landscape — and, to Thowra, he looked vital, and strong, and terrifying.

It *was* a hard winter. Snow fell often and the great winds roared down from the higher mountains. And there was very little food.

Sometimes Thowra and Storm found a stream that danced and bubbled under its shimmering cover of ice;

sometimes hoar-frost fringed grass and leaves, and made the lovely ice flowers on the frozen pools. Sometimes they heard the song the wind played on the ice-encased snow gum leaves.

Bel Bel and Mirri would not let them wander far away for fear of meeting the other herd; even they themselves wandered less than usual, afraid of bringing trouble on themselves and Yarraman. But when instinct told Bel Bel that a great deal of the snow must have gone from the Cascades, she and Mirri and their foals set off for home without waiting for the others.

It was far from being springtime and the grass was flattened and lifeless, but the two mares and Thowra and Storm felt very happy to be home again. There was still a lot of snow in the Cascades, but it was patchy and mixed with earth and grass. Their usual end of the valley was more heavily snowed than the southern end in which the foals had first seen The Brolga, so they mostly grazed there in The Brolga's country.

Plenty of sunny days came with nights of heavy frost. Once, in a deep cleft in the hills, they found the rustling-leaf snow, and Thowra and Storm descended the cleft magnificently, rolling and wriggling on their backs, the separate, shining icy leaves tossing over them, rising in spume.

'You two are nearly yearlings, but you still play like babies,' snorted Bel Bel, and lay down and rolled herself.

Sometimes the mares' love of wandering would take them far up into the snow on Bob's Ridge and they would all four chase each other downwards, ploughing through the snow, galloping and falling. Then one day they arrived back in the Cascades to find that the herd had returned. Thowra and Storm were not even sure they were pleased to see them — it had been such fun on their own.

Brownie gave Bel Bel a spiteful look when she saw them.

'You two'll turn your foals into lone wolves like yourselves,' she said. 'And each one of you will probably meet a bad end.'

'We'll have had a good life, though.' Bel Bel bared her teeth at Brownie.

It was only a few days after that that Thowra and Arrow had their first real fight and finished bruised and cut, with neither victorious. Thowra came away a little wiser; he knew his mother had been right, that he had made a vindictive enemy in Arrow and that maybe there would be many fights.

'Spring will be late this year,' Bel Bel said, on one of the many days when cold winds swept the valley. 'I'm glad I'm not having a foal this time.'

As it was, only one foal had been born. Then on a day when the breeze was soft and warm, and the sun shone brightly, the mares noticed that Yarraman's coat, and their own coats, were beginning to get a gloss on them again — and they knew that spring had come.

Spring had come and the robin redbreasts were up in the snow, hunting the black insects; the dingoes howled to their mates in the full moon at nights. Then one day there was the sound of a wild stallion screaming, farther to the south.

Yarraman pricked up his ears and listened and when the scream came again, he threw up his head with the lovely cream and gold mane and roared his wild answer. As the sun got higher, he trotted a little way up on to a ridge to watch The Brolga, standing with his head well in the air, and the sunlight glinting on his coat. Sometimes he would call out a challenge, but The Brolga did not come and Yarraman knew he would reign, that spring, undisputed king of the Cascade brumbies.

So the foals became yearlings and, in the good spring and summer that followed the snowy winter, they grew large and strong, and learnt to gallop much faster. It took Arrow a long time to realise that though he was the biggest of them all, and the strongest, Thowra was living up to his name and could travel like the wind, faster than himself or any of the others.

There were no organised brumby hunts that summer, but Thowra learnt to recognise — and dread — the whistling sound of a rope flying through the air. As Bel Bel had known he would, the beautiful cream colt attracted any man that saw him, and, in his strength and vital courage, he did not seek to hide himself in the same way as she did. She tried to teach him all her cunning, but realised she could not expect him to learn everything in one short year.

Storm became a faster mover, too, and the mares were proud of them both — they watched them grow more and more independent throughout the summer and autumn; watched with pleasure how the friendship between the two remained as staunch as ever. They saw, too, the hostility increase between Arrow and Thowra, and wondered what the outcome would be.

In the two colts' second winter the snow did not fall heavily or continuously in the Cascades, and the herd were able to stay there.

Both Thowra and Storm saw The Brolga several times

and knew that he was now a superb horse. Thowra told Bel Bel that he had seen him once.

'With the spring grass and sunshine, and the mating season, he will reach the height of his strength and agility,' said Bel Bel, but she said no more, and left the young horse wondering.

Towards the end of the winter, Thowra saw less and less of his mother, and he and Storm ran more with the other young colts, biting and fighting, galloping, feeling a sudden restlessness. Spring was coming once again and they were almost two-year-olds. Bel Bel and Mirri were both once again in foal, and they went off to higher slopes where they could give birth undisturbed. The young colts went wandering farther and farther afield, sometimes returning to the herd, sometimes spending a night in other country.

There were about six or eight two-year-olds rapidly becoming independent of the herd. Sometimes Thowra and Storm ran with them, and at other times they went off on their own like lone wolves. But they were all together and grazing not far from the main herd up a narrow valley the evening Bel Bel came back with her chestnut foal.

Thowra was beginning to move inquisitively nearer when he heard a clamour that made the sweat break out on his gleaming coat, and he knew that it was the challenge to the leader of the brumbies which, in a way, he had expected.

The Brolga came high-stepping up the valley.

Fight to the death

Yarraman screamed his wild answer to The Brolga's challenge, the rock and hillside echoing it until it rolled in the gullies. Again, on a spring evening, he went galloping, with streaming golden mane and tail, to meet the grey Brolga. But this time The Brolga was no immature young horse — he was a magnificent stallion, just at his prime.

For the third time — and perhaps the last — Thowra watched the grey and the chestnut advancing to within striking distance. He watched their swirling, whirling, purposeful dance, saw the bared teeth, heard the screams of rage. In each fight The Brolga had had the advantage of seeming to melt into the oncoming night or the snowstorm.

The noise of the fight echoed in a terrible way so that the screams of the two horses were doubled or trebled, and only the closest of the watchers could hear the tremendous pounding of their hooves on the ground.

Thowra and Storm had drawn apart from the other young colts, watching fearfully while the two stallions struggled for mastery. There would be no mercy given by either, and, as night drew on, they knew darkness would not part them.

Yarraman was the first to get a deadly grip above The Brolga's withers, but the younger horse managed at last to free himself and at the same time strike Yarraman in the eyes. They fought on and on, not screaming so often now, but their breath snorting through red, dilated nostrils. And all the time the darkness was coming up the valley.

Then suddenly the watchers saw The Brolga get his grip on Yarraman; they saw Yarraman's valiant struggles repeated and repeated; they saw that he could not free himself, and, as night fell, they could just see him beaten to his knees.

Suddenly there was a scream of triumph from The Brolga as he struck blow after blow with his forefeet at the stallion on the ground. Then, in the darkness, they could see the pale shadow of The Brolga and the dark shadow on the ground, and hear the pounding of hooves on flesh.

Shuddering, the young horses drew back; the mares, snorting with terror, took their foals away. Down in the broader valley, by the first faint light of a rising moon, Thowra could see the pale form of Bel Bel. Then there was a thunder of galloping hooves and The Brolga was among them. They could smell his sweat, see his pale outline, all stained with dark blood. Thowra watched him go straight up to Bel Bel, nickering out the greeting of a victorious stallion. To every man and beast her colour — and his — must be attractive. He felt himself sweating with fear again.

Thowra and the other colts turned away and left the herd, heading towards the edge of the tall timber, with no idea where to go, but urgently wanting to escape. They stopped in a little field of snowgrass, just inside the first fringe of trees, and there they spent the night, no longer playing at being independent, but young colts without a herd.

When the moon was high, Thowra slid away through the trees without even disturbing Storm. The moonlight was very bright in the main valley; he looked carefully around before he moved out of the sheltering trees, then he walked into the bright, cold light that made his coat as silver as his mane and tail. A mopoke called mournfully; he jumped, but did not draw back. On he went till he was going up the narrow valley in which they had all been that evening. He climbed on to a high rock and looked round the bend of the valley below him. There lay the great bulk of Yarraman, dark on the ground.

Suddenly there was a noise beside him and another horse came out of the shadows and joined him on his rock.

'Thowra, my son,' said Bel Bel's voice softly, as she climbed up alongside, herself silver in the moonlight, and gazed down on the dead horse. 'What are you doing here? Did you think to gain some of his strength and courage?' And she turned to look at her son and then back at Yarraman. 'You should have it in your blood and bones already; he was, after all, your father. Use his courage and strength, son, and all the cunning and knowledge I have taught you. Come, we will leave him.'

They jumped down and walked away together and at the mouth of the big valley she gave him a playful nip on the shoulder.

'I must get back to my foal. Goodbye!' but Thowra knew that their real goodbye had been said as they left the rock above the dead stallion.

Thowra went down the valley, left the cold, clear moonlight, crept through the trees, and headed back to Storm and the other colts.

At dawn they set off towards the headwaters of the Crackenback River, a small mob of colts bound together only by habit and a common desire to put some distance between themselves and the dead stallion — their father — and to get away from possible trouble with The Brolga, who would now be the leader of the main sections of both herds.

Thowra had led off — really not bothering about any of the others following him except Storm, yet glad, in a way, of their company. However, even one day of travelling showed them that no mob can have two leaders, and Arrow, who had the size and strength to win any fight, would not peacefully let Thowra, the fastest and the one who knew the country best, become the acknowledged leader. He bit at Thowra and kicked him whenever they stopped to graze and drink, but when Thowra, tired of his behaviour, went off at a gallop with Storm, the other colts followed, so Arrow had to go too.

Thowra and Storm had often been in the Ramshead country since they were born there two years ago, and Mirri and Bel Bel had taught them all the good grazing places round the head of the Crackenback. They knew, too, where they could get up and down granite cliffs, where there were tunnels through what seemed impenetrable snow gum thickets, where there were deep holes in the creeks that a young horse could swim in, and easy crossing places in the rough-flowing river.

They led their young mob about, up on the high country among the snowdrifts, and right down in the great mountain ash gullies, where the lyrebirds mimicked their neighing, or sent them galloping off in a frenzy by imitating the sound of a whip cracking or a man whistling.

After the first feeling of being left alone in a very large world had worn off, Thowra would have enjoyed everything if Arrow had not been such a bully. Arrow could not spoil it all because he was not as fast as Thowra, but so often when they were grazing he would lash out savagely with his heels, or strike. Thowra was not afraid to fight him, though he always got the worst of it because none of the others, except for Storm, would take Arrow on, nor would they stay behind with him.

Once, Thowra, remembering the time when he had tricked Arrow and 'lost' him, tried the same trick again. This time Arrow was missing for three days and he was very subdued when he joined them again.

It was then that Thowra began to think they should move over to Paddy Rush's Bogong because the men would be bringing their mobs of cattle again. He started off, early one morning, jogging down through the sun-glistening snow gums, through the mountain ash thickets and tangled woods of the little creeks, to the Crackenback, over it and up the rough country on the other side.

In the weeks that followed Thowra began to understand all his mother's warnings about Arrow making a bad enemy. The fights which Arrow forced on him were never half in fun, like most young colts' battles, which were an exuberance of strength and half-conscious wish to test and train themselves. Arrow was vindictive, and Thowra knew that his lovely silver mane hid some bite scars that he would carry to the end of his life. It also became apparent that Arrow was trying to lame him, for Thowra, if lamed, could no longer be their half-acknowledged leader. Try though he did, Thowra could never defeat Arrow in a fight, and, as the summer wore on, Arrow became stronger and heavier, and more arrogant.

At last Thowra could stand him no longer. 'Let's go,' he said to Storm, 'next time there is a mist. Let's clear for the Brindle Bull country. Maybe The Brolga spends summer there, but if we keep away we'll come to no harm.'

Two or three evenings later, there were black clouds rolling up from the north and the following day rain came with drifting cloud that hid everything. Thowra gave Storm a nip and, without waiting a moment, they quietly wandered away.

There was a long, open glade of snowgrass up which they could canter, barely making a sound, then a little creek running over a sand and mica bed which they walked down, the water quickly filling in the tracks they made. While they were in the creek they heard a whinny through the cold mist, the thunder of hooves on stony ground, and then the crash of a rolling rock. The two colts drew right in under some blanket bushs that overhung the little stream and waited, breathlessly listening. They heard Arrow's imperious neigh, another rock falling, and the crack of a bough. Then the sound of hooves grew muffled in the cloud and Thowra and Storm went back up the stream and cut across country towards the Brindle Bull.

They were determined to stay on their own now, and keep away from Arrow, and they were suddenly filled with excitement. They had never been on the mountain called the Brindle Bull and they would have a whole new world to explore. Even the touch of the cold, wet clouds, or the sting of a wet branch across the eyes, could not cool their excitement.

They did not stop except for an occasional drink, and they kept off any of the usual tracks just in case the others had doubled back in the clouds. Finally they slithered down a smooth, wet rock face into the Crackenback River and stood, tired and trembling, while the water tugged at their legs.

By the time they were clambering up the steep, stony slopes of the Brindle Bull, the wet clouds had turned to rain — heavy, cold rain that felt as if it might become one of those swift flurries of snow in summer that leave the mountains gleaming white in a hot summer sky for a brief hour or two. It was hardly a good day for the start of an adventure, but the colts had been well taught by their mothers to find their way whatever the weather. So they kept on, scrambling up the steep slopes, pulling themselves up on rocky cliffs, forcing their way through shoulder-high heather till they were nearly at the top.

There they stopped where some snow gums grew thickly below a rock buttress, providing some shelter from the driving rain. As they stood there the clouds suddenly blew a few feet apart on the top of the mountain. Trembling with an excitement he did not understand, Thowra saw against the pale rift of sky, as though against a faintly lighted window, a herd of horses pass in ones and twos, like shadows — and they were led by a grey horse who seemed to melt into the clouds.

Man on a black horse

Thowra and Storm were very careful where they went on the Brindle Bull, watching for tracks of The Brolga's herd, listening, smelling. It took them some days to find out the herd's grazing place, and after that they kept well away, down the sides of the mountain, in snow gum woods where there was only enough grass to make a picking for two colts.

There were one or two tiny hanging valleys on the southern slope, where the snow-daisies' leaves made a silver carpet and the daisies, large and white, starred the ground. The colts often grazed in one of these valleys. There were rocky gorges off either side, and a quick getaway if they needed one.

The Brolga and his herd probably knew they were there, and were unworried by the presence of two young colts. Bel Bel may have recognised Thowra's trail and been glad to know that he and Storm were close. She had not forgotten Thowra, as a mare usually forgets a foal after it has become independent and left her, as he was the only creamy foal she had borne. And because she often spoke of Thowra and Storm, Mirri remembered Storm, too.

One day the colts had wandered low enough to see into the Big Boggy Creek. Thowra had learnt how to use all the cunning Bel Bel had taught him when in The Brolga's country, and to keep hidden in the fringe of trees, or in patches of light and shade. Often he only just remembered to look around properly before impulsively leaping up on to a high rock.

This time they peered into the valley of the Big Boggy from some hop scrub. There were a few cattle grazing along the grassy floor of the valley, the sight of which made them very cautious, but there was no sign of anything else. All seemed very peaceful, with no movement, other than that of the head-down cattle. Thowra leapt from one granite block to another till he was on top of a great heap of rocks. There was still nothing disquieting to see. Storm came up beside him.

'It is too open,' said Thowra regretfully. 'We would be foolish to go there, though some of that good grass would be nice.'

They stood for quite a while, looking down longingly, and then moved slowly along the southern slopes, keeping the delicious-looking valley in sight. All of a sudden Thowra stopped and raised his head, his nostrils curling as he sniffed the air.

'Smoke!' He moved to a steep edge to see.

First he looked at the northern sky to judge if the wind had brought the smoke from a distant fire, then he looked closely into the valley. It was a second or so before he saw anything, then it was just a thin ribbon of smoke winding up through some snow gums, on the other side of the valley where a tiny creek came down. Just at that moment a man walked down the creek a few yards, and stopped to fill something with water.

'Man!' he hissed to Storm. 'Let's go before he sees us.'

They slid — one horse a dark shadow, the other a piece of dappled, moving light and shade — through the scrub, heading towards their small hanging valley. And there, in the valley of the Big Boggy, drinking tea from his quart-pot, was a very young man who could think of nothing but the sight of a beautiful cream-coloured colt with flowing silver mane and tail, poised high above him on a heap of granite rack.

The two young horses made their way back to their camping ground. When the young man had finished his lunch, he crossed the Big Boggy and started up the mountain towards the granite rock.

Thowra did not really think he had been seen, or he and Storm would have been far more worried, but he remembered how Bel Bel had shown him how to track other horses, and how not to leave tracks. Instinctively he chose snowgrass or rocks to walk on, wherever possible.

Thus it was that the young man tracked them easily from the granite rocks to the hop scrub, and then had the greatest difficulty in picking up their trail. He lost it so often that as evening drew on, he gave up and lit his fire, boiled his quart-pot, and rolled up in the one blanket he had carried in front of his saddle, and went to sleep.

Thowra and Storm smelt the smoke from their hidden valley. Bel Bel and Mirri smelt the smoke, and The Brolga smelt it, too.

The man's little fire burnt all night long because it was a cold night and he, with only one blanket, kept waking and throwing on another log. His horse picketed close to him, snuffled and stamped throughout the night.

It was only by luck — bad luck — that the man found Thowra's and Storm's hiding-place the next morning. He had failed to find their trail and just happened to ride out on to one of the few places that overlooked their hanging valley. There he sat on his tame black horse, the sleepy-looking man, who suddenly became wide awake as he saw below him, standing on a carpet of snow-daisies, a good-looking bay colt and the supremely beautiful creamy.

The young man sat perfectly still, only his eyes moving as he looked at the valley; trying to find a way in, trying to see if there would also be a way out for the brumbies to take. Just then his horse whinnied.

Thowra, who for a moment or two had experienced a prickly feeling in his hair, knew instantly they were being watched. He threw up his head, the early sunlight like water on his rippling, lovely coat, and saw the man trying hastily to back out of sight.

As though caught in a willy-willy, Thowra whirled round and away, followed by Storm, into the clump of low snow gum and heather that hid the narrow opening into a gorge. But as they went, they heard the crashing of rocks as the man came straight down the cliff on which he had been standing.

'If he gets down unhurt, he'll be after us, pretty close,' Thowra thought, and strained his ears to hear what was happening behind. The crashing of rocks continued, purposeful crashing, as if someone kept forcing a horse down, not as if he had fallen and gone bouncing down among the boulders.

Thowra and Storm burst out of the scrub and up the rocky gorge. Suddenly Thowra turned right, leaping like a goat from rock to rock up the side of the gorge. He had noticed not long before that there might be a possible place of escape up this way, and now was certainly the time to use it. 'No horse with a rider would be able to follow,' he thought.

He and Storm were blowing and sweating when they reached the top of the wall. They turned and looked down and saw the man already following. He leapt off his tame horse and started leading it up behind him. Thowra did not wait to see how he got on, but picked his way carefully over a great slope of wet and mossy rock.

'Keep off the moss, if you can,' he warned Storm. 'Just follow my hooves. If we leave no track from the top of the cliff it will give us a few minutes extra.' His feet slipped, then, with a grating clatter, and he went down on his side on the cold rock, but he leapt up and went on, then across some spongy, wet snowgrass, and into the cover of the trees.

There they stopped for a second and listened. There was no sound. Off they went again, as fast as they could up the steep hill, trying not to set hoof on any soft, wet earth. Then, ringing out through the bush came the sound of a shod horse's hoof on a rock.

'He must be good, that tame horse,' thought Thowra, but he did not guess that he was *extremely* good, nor that he had been fed on oats, and bran, and chaff, on which a horse can gallop much faster than on mountain grass, however sweet and lovely that grass may be.

Thowra began to feel frightened. They were near a great semicircle of rock cliffs that enclosed most evil-seeming bogs — the soft-surfaced, green bogs in which a horse could flounder and sink from sight, black mud bogs that were bottomless, and the squelching sphagnum bogs that no horse really trusted. But both he and Storm knew a track through all this, so, gasping for breath, he made straight for the lower arm of the cliffs.

Thowra stood on the rocks above the great hollow filled with bogs, and then took a flying leap on to a patch that he knew was solid ground. Storm was right behind him, and had left no track to show where they had entered the hollow.

They could not go any faster than a walk, hearing all the time the squelch of water in sphagnum, feeling the awful, unstable surface under their hooves. Thowra was sure he could hear a horse galloping behind them. But he couldn't help thinking if he tried to go faster he might sink in the great, treacherous mud holes. He looked up at the dark, water-stained cliff above him, and knew there was no escape there if the man caught up with them. He started to trot in terror, but nearly floundered into an innocent-looking, green patch, and had to back out.

The other side was not far away, and they reached it before the man appeared. Ahead of them lay some wide, open country where they would have to gallop as fast as they possibly could. All of a sudden Thowra knew why he had come just this way. Sometimes The Brolga and his herd grazed here; and other wild brumbies. Even the stallion that had killed Yarraman would be better company than a lone man with a lasso. And perhaps if there were numbers of horses, the man would not know which one to chase.

But there was no sign of any other brumbies; they must be in a higher grazing-ground. With pounding hearts, the two colts galloped across the wide, open snowgrass, leaping the little streams, galloping with all their might for the trees and cover before the man saw them.

Thowra looked back over his shoulder. There he came, sitting well down in the saddle, leaning forward over the powerful horse's neck. In that glance, Thowra realised that the tame horse was a four- or five-year-old, and therefore much stronger than he and Storm. He was desperate now, and could think only of reaching the herd.

The great black horse and its rider were gaining on them, even though they had a long start. Thowra and Storm stretched their legs even farther with each stride, and made tremendous efforts to go faster. The trees were not far away now — Thowra could see them through a red mist of exhaustion. The sunlight dancing on the leaves seemed like sparks or waves of light. He must reach that line of trees. He was done; he could not get his breath fast enough. Then he felt the vibration on the ground of the other horse drawing closer.

Hiss-s-s came the sound of the rope through the air.

Thowra shied violently at the sound, and the rope struck him a blow on the shoulder and then fell to the ground. Two more strides and the brumbies were in the trees.

Thowra knew the man would try to head them out into the open because he would not be able to rope them in the trees. Somehow they had to stay in timber till they reached the herd's next grazing place. A flock of jays sent out warning cries, but the sweaty and exhausted colts did not hear.

Thowra realised they could hold their lead in timber, particularly if it was thick and low scrubby stuff. Now he was almost sure that he was the one the man was after, and his terror drove him on even faster. He knew this belt of timber went right to the top of the outside rim of a grassy basin — perhaps the herd would be there. The timber was thinner near the top and the man was gaining on him. Just as he reached the crest of the rim, he gave a wild, sobbing neigh for help. If the herd was not there it would be no use going into the open country, but they might be, so it was worth taking the risk. He paused for a second to look down, and saw the startled mob of brumbies below him. Once more he neighed, and then plunged down among them.

There were several shrill answering neighs, and an angry stallion roar, but the man came thundering down right beside him, taking no notice of the mob of brumbies.

Thowra knew that the black horse and rider were coming up almost alongside him now. Soon there would be the sound of the rope. Hiss-s-s! There it was! Again he leapt sideways. Again it struck him on the shoulder.

Then there were horses going everywhere, and Thowra was among them, legs stretching, breath sobbing … and someone was galloping shoulder-to-shoulder with him, pushing him to one side.

He was too tired, his eyes too blurred to see that it was a creamy mare. But even in his exhaustion he somehow sensed that it was his mother, that this had all happened before and he must just go where she took him. He did not see the leggy chestnut foal at her side.

Among the thunder of hooves and the wild galloping there was the different sound, quite close, of the shod horse — the jingle of his bit, the creak of his saddle. He had almost come up with them, and Thowra could go no faster, but he saw that there was some very thick scrub starting on their right and knew that Bel Bel must have somewhere to hide them. So he was ready for her when she swung him round and into a low tunnel of prickly scrub. There she pushed ahead of him into the lead, and for the first time he saw the leggy foal.

The scrub closed in behind them and they were suddenly surrounded in silence, though they could still hear the black horse crashing on over boulders.

Bel Bel led at a smart pace till she stopped abruptly at the steep bank of a creek that flowed in a complete tunnel of wattle, blanket bushes and tree fern. She jumped down into the water and turned upstream, only letting Thowra stop to drink for a moment, and then urging him on and on.

All sounds of other horses were getting very distant, but Bel Bel did not stop. Thowra plodded after her up the stream, sometimes snatching a mouthful of the cold water, still panting, still trembling. He wondered where Storm had gone, but he knew he would be all right because it was he, Thowra, that the man on the black horse had been chasing.

The stream became very narrow and Thowra guessed they must be near the top of the mountain.

'Where we are going, we may find Mirri and Storm,' Bel Bel said; but when they stopped in a little sandy cove that was completely hidden in scrub, there was no one there.

'They will come,' she said again. 'Lie down to rest.' And when Thowra woke, hours later, Storm was asleep beside him.

Mirri and Bel Bel were standing looking at them while they placidly let their foals drink. They led the two colts to a little field of snowgrass, and, before they left to go back to the herd, Bel Bel said to her cream-coloured son, 'Don't go back to where you were grazing. That man will remember you, and remember your haunts. Have you forgotten why I named you Thowra? I knew when you were born that every man would be after you, and you would have to be as fleet as the wind.'

A time to race with the wind

Thowra and Storm moved back on to the main range as soon as autumn began changing towards winter. For a while they stayed in the timbered country below the Ramshead, and often spent the lovely, bright days galloping on the snowgrass between the granite tors. Sometimes there were other young horses near — once Thowra was given quite a beating by a three-year-old stallion who came along with two or three young mares and seemed to want to fight him just because he looked different. But mostly they were on their own, and day after day was filled with a sort of wild joy as the weather grew colder and colder, and they galloped to keep warm, chasing sometimes a dingo, a hare, or a slinking red fox.

The snow was late that year, and in the clear autumn light the rocks looked purple, and the snow gums blended every red and orange and green with their ghostly silver grey. Thowra became lighter in colour as he got his winter coat, and, even more than in other winters, he looked silver rather than cream.

In the early mornings, ice encased each blade of grass and leaf of heather along the little creeks; it crackled where the colts stepped. Often a glaze of ice on a shallow pool shivered and skidded away from their hooves. In the grass, the white frost brushed off on to their legs with every step. It was cold, so cold, but while the bright weather lasted, exciting and lovely, too.

Then came grey, bitter days with the north wind tearing over the mountains, when the young horses vied their speed with the wind's, galloping headlong down the springy grass towards the trees — and the trees were beating and lashing, like the wind-tossed mane on a wild horse.

At night they could hear the wind roaring in the mountains above them, or wailing and howling round the granite tors of the Ramshead Range. Sometimes it was hard to tell whether a dingo howled or whether it was just the wind between the rocks.

Thowra and Storm were becoming — as Brownie had said they would — lone wolves, like their two mothers.

Even the first flurry of snow did not drive them down lower — there was still grass to eat and a snowstorm to race through. Was there ever such a time as this, Thowra wondered, feeling his own strength as something that was his but yet part of the wind and the snow, and the great strength of the mountains. It was a time to gallop and a time to play; a time to race with the wind; a time to sleep below the rocks while the dingoes howled; a time for him and Storm to be alone in all their exciting strength — a time that would soon end. With the spring a new period of the colts' lives would start, but between then and the spring lay this winter. Now the snow started to fall in earnest, and they were driven downwards for grass, at first as far as the headwaters of the Crackenback and the hut on the Gap called the Dead Horse hut, and then on to the Cascades.

Thowra, though still terribly afraid of men, was also becoming very curious about them. If he found any old signs of them he could not keep away — as long as he knew the men had gone — and a hut seemed to him almost like magic. It was, after all, from these huts that their smoke came most often and the fires that men lit were undoubtedly magic.

Dead Horse hut had a roof of loose galvanised iron, and it creaked in the wind just as Storm was trying to persuade Thowra to walk past the hut without stopping to look all round it. Both colts leapt nervously back into the trees as they heard the sound and then, when it was repeated again and again as the cold wind streamed through the Gap, they crept forward once more. Nothing would now stop Thowra going carefully up to the hut to look and smell — and jump with fright each time the iron creaked. Storm stood in the trees, disapproving, until at last he realised that no harm was going to come to them and he too walked up cautiously, with nose outstretched.

A very old saddle had been thrown down on the woodheap under the skillion roof. It smelt of horse, and they were bothered and backed away. Next they inspected the killing gallows which stood, like a windmill, stark against the snow-laden sky. Near the gallows was a newly built stockyard with unusually high fences.

'If they catch any horses that will be where they put them. That's a yard, like Mirri used to tell us about,' said Storm.

'You'd need to be able to jump,' said Thowra, measuring the rails with his eye. 'I could jump in, but I don't know whether I could get out.'

'Don't try,' said Storm. 'The gate is tightly shut.'

'You might be able to get out at this lower corner, if you had to,' Thowra said, but he turned around then, away from the hut. Storm gladly followed him up the next ridge, leaving the scents of man and tame horse behind them.

That night the black clouds massed up against the mountains and they knew that a really heavy snowstorm was coming. Instead of camping near good water and grass they kept jogging along towards the Cascades. They must get into lower country, but they didn't know how many horses were wintering there at present. Thowra felt he could beat Arrow now if he had to fight him, but of course Arrow was not the only colt in the mountains.

By midnight snow was falling. They sheltered under some great rocks until the first grey streaks of dawn came, and then went cautiously downwards, keeping in amongst the trees.

They were right at the northern-most end of the Cascades, where the creek turned towards its great waterfall and the Indi River. This had been part of Yarraman's grazing ground. His scattered, bleached bones might still be lying in a valley which they avoided. The memory of that night, and the nearness to that place, made them nervous and very careful. Thus it was that they saw the group of horsemen, again led by that same splendid black horse, before they themselves were spotted. If they had kept going, they would have met head-on. As it was, Thowra and Storm stopped dead and tried to sneak off further into the timber; but once again the black horse neighed.

Quivering with fear, the two colts still crept as quietly as they could through the bush, but as soon as they heard the black horse and his rider following them, they broke into a wild gallop, heading for the roughest country they knew.

Soon they were tearing down a steep slope of big, loose boulders. This checked their pursuers, who followed cautiously as they dared not risk laming their horses.

Thowra and Storm watched them for a second, trying to get around below them. There were three others besides the man on the black horse, each one on a good, full-grown mount; each wearing a hat pulled down over his eyes, jodhpurs and leather coat that were soaked by falling snow.

As he stood for that one second, Thowra realised it was getting colder and the snow was falling more thickly. Perhaps it would turn into a real blizzard, and he would just fade into the atmosphere, blotted from sight. But he would have to see he was not caught before there was enough snow on the ground and in the air to hide him. Then he thought of Storm — *his* colour would show up unless snow and mist and clouds really enfolded them both.

The men had got around below them, so Thowra began to climb steadily back up the loose, rolling boulders. He saw the horsemen split into two groups. It was time to make a dash for it across the boulders, over the timbered ridge, and down to the creek.

They had a good start on the men, and they went fast across the valley towards the forest near the Cascade hut. The snow fell cold on their steaming coats, thick-falling snow that was beginning to be hurtled, stinging, on the wind.

'We'll play hide-and-seek with them for a while, in the trees,' Thowra said. 'Then, if the snow gets heavier, you can dodge into the timber, and I'll make out into the open and lose them.'

Snow was already starting to coat the leaves and fill the forks of trees. White rosettes were plastered by the wind against the jigsaw-puzzle markings on the snow gum trunks. The ground was becoming white. Thowra knew it would not be long before he would be able to give his pursuers the slip ... but he could hear them galloping. Then suddenly clouds of swirling snow began to fill the forest.

'It's almost thick enough, now,' Storm said. 'I'll go crashing off downwards into the mountain ash, making enough noise for two, if you take to the open.'

'Right,' said Thowra. 'Unless we're caught, we'll meet at the mouth of Yarraman's valley tonight.'

Storm took off, thundering and crashing through the trees and the wild-blowing snow, breaking branches, kicking stones out behind him, giving a snorting neigh. Thowra stood dead quiet in a thick clump of tea tree and hop scrub while the snowstorm grew densely white; then, he, too, gave a joyous neigh and set off for the open valley.

He didn't hear the man on the black horse swear and say, 'That brumby is getting too cunning.' But it was from that day on that a legend began to grow up about the cream brumby, cunning as a fox. Stockmen talked of him round their summer campfires, or sung songs about him as they rode around a restless mob of cattle at night. The cattle went on to tell the brumbies, so that they too knew, all over the mountains, the tales of the mysterious silver brumby.

And Thowra? Thowra galloped down through the trees into the Cascades Valley, felt the springy snowgrass under the snow, listened to make sure that he was being followed, neighed again in joyful triumph and set off as fast as he could go. He led them just the sort of dance he had often led Arrow, leaping creeks where they were narrow, hoping they would blunder in, skirting round deep holes that might throw them, tearing out on to rocky outcrops and jumping off where he knew he had a good landing-place — and neighing if he thought the blizzard had got so thick that they might lose him.

Sometimes he looked back and could just make out the other four horses and their riders, like shadows, galloping through the snow. When he started to get tired, he turned back and quietly let the driving curtain of snow hide him from their sight.

The men had followed at first the crashing, dashing bay that they did not want to catch. Then they had chased a mocking ghost that sometimes showed up as a pale, galloping outline in the snow-filled air, sometimes as a rearing, playing colt on a rock, but was, most often, only the sound of a neigh that echoed through the storm. Now they found themselves in the silence of the snowstorm, with only the distant rush and roar of the blizzard in the trees or round the rocky ridges. There was no sign nor sound of the cream brumby colt.

Thowra heard their voices getting smaller and more distant as they rode back towards the track to Groggin. He had found himself shelter in a few trees up a side valley, and as the day wore on, he went back to meet Storm.

The coming of spring

Spring comes to the Australian Alps like an invisible spirit. There is not the tremendous surge of upthrust life that there is in the lowland valleys, and no wild flowers bloom in the snow mountains till the early summer, but there is an immense stirring of excitement. A bright red and blue lowrie flits through the trees; snow thaws, and the streams become full of foaming water; the grey, flattened grass grows upwards again and becomes greener; wild horses start to lose their winter coats and find new energy; wombats sit, round and fat, blinking in the evening sunshine; at night there is the cry of a dingo to its mate.

Thowra and Storm greeted the first warm, scent-laden breeze off the wattle on the foothills by wandering up towards the Ramshead, where the snow still lay. They were deeply restless and they soon came back nearer the Cascades, where they found that in the few days they had been away, other young colts had appeared, and that the fillies, among them some of the grey daughters of The Brolga, were galloping skittishly about away from the herd.

Thowra and Storm skirted round on the ridges above the main valley, watching.

They had had a rough winter, in a way, finding the other colts unfriendly and against them for being lone wolves. Thowra and Arrow had had only one fight and Arrow could still win. But in snowy weather, Thowra had managed to be the invisible gadfly leading them all into trouble, even once daring to dash right through The Brolga's herd.

The Brolga was still very much king of the Cascade brumbies, but now it was clear that he was taking no notice of the young colts and fillies, just lording it over his own herd in the valley below.

Filled with restlessness and a longing for the company of other young horses, Thowra and Storm went down a ridge to where there was a little group of fillies chasing each other in the sunshine.

Down they went to join in the play and found, to their surprise, that the fillies were just as likely to bite or kick them as to play. But before long Thowra realised they were pleased that he and Storm had joined them, even if they did put up a show of driving them off. So they galloped with them all that day; it was not until evening that they found themselves anywhere near other horses, and that was by mistake.

Thowra simply had not noticed that The Brolga's herd was so near. But when he saw them, he could not leave, for there, amongst the herd, were two more grey fillies like the ones they had been galloping with. Thowra, suddenly knowing that he must gather together a herd of his own, decided that in it there must be the grey daughters of The Brolga.

In the heady springtime feeling of super strength, this did not seem in any way a silly thing to decide — not even when he saw Arrow standing with a few fillies behind him, some distance off, on a little hill.

Thowra noticed that The Brolga himself was not near the two grey fillies, so he squealed and started rearing and prancing in the broad band of an oblique, evening sun ray that came between two shoulders of hill, his long mane and tail streaming like silver flags.

The two grey fillies neighed in answer and came cantering across. The Brolga turned and stared, lifted his head and roared angrily, then came trotting towards Thowra.

'Clear out quick,' said Storm. 'The fillies will come.'

Thowra watched only long enough to see the two fillies coming close to them before he cantered away. The Brolga made a swift charge at them all, driving colts and fillies in front of him. He roared his annoyance, and then turned back to his own herd, stopping every so often to look back, roar and paw the ground.

Thowra and Storm cantered on with six fillies: the three greys, two browns and a bay. They went steadily on, heading for the upland country. They did not see Arrow looking after them and then following with his own herd — one golden chestnut colt with four fillies stringing along behind him.

Arrow had grown into a very handsome colt, still like his father, but his eyes showed their whites, and there was a mean, pinched look about his head, just as there was about Brownie's. The other colts were all afraid of him, not so much because he was far stronger, and a cunning fighter, but because of his meanness. He would be friendly with a horse for a while and then turn on him viciously, and all the young colts with whom he had been running had scars and blemishes on them from his kicks and bites.

Thowra was not afraid of him, but he knew that Arrow would try to maim him if he got a chance.

Perhaps at the back of his head he knew that Arrow would sooner or later want to kill him, and he knew it was better to keep away.

Storm hated Arrow, but Storm too could gallop faster and farther and knew every yard of the country better than the big chestnut did. He knew instinctively that there would be trouble sometime soon, because he could see that Thowra had become so proud and beautiful as he grew up, and the other horse was beautiful too. Though the mountains were vast and wide, Arrow and Thowra might find there was not room for them both as they grew into mature stallions.

But neither Storm nor Thowra were thinking of Arrow now. They went on upwards, feeling proud and happy, stepping lightly on the springy tussocks of snowgrass.

Sunset turned every ridge and hill-top into molten gold, and the valleys below them into long fingers of blue shadow. They stopped to drink at cold, rushing streams, shying away from the floating foam, but the instinct to get further away from the great, grey Brolga kept them moving on till all the light had gone from the hills.

They camped that night in a little grove of snow gums that shielded them from the sneaking cold breeze. Arrow and his herd had not travelled so late into the evening, so they were quite a long way off.

There was still snow below the Ramshead, so Thowra only went as far as the lovely open fields of snowgrass on the ridge above the Dead Horse Gap. It was here, at midday, that Arrow caught up with them.

Heedless, and filled with an unbounded pride in his own strength and beauty, Arrow came trotting out of the trees towards the three grey fillies, whom he had been admiring in The Brolga's herd. His golden mane rippled as he tossed his head, and he carried his tail high. All the sunlight seemed to concentrate on the glittering, golden colt.

The fillies knew he was there before Thowra and Storm did, and watched, fascinated and afraid. Then both the colts saw him at once, and, both roaring with rage, galloped towards him, their teeth bared.

Arrow had never seen Storm enraged before and had not expected him to rush into the attack too. He turned and galloped away with the screaming, angry colts driving him back to his own fillies. The fillies fled too. Storm and Thowra drove the little herd away towards the Cascades, then feeling very pleased with themselves they returned to their group of waiting fillies.

It was three years now since Bel Bel and Mirri had nodded their heads wisely over their two foals, knowing they would run together, knowing they would fulfil the way of the brumbies and run as colts together after they had left their mothers and until they had to fight for a herd of their own. Now had come the time when each one wished to take his herd off on his own, so Storm, with his browns and bay, and Thowra, with his grey fillies, drifted apart, grazing in different directions every day, till each young stallion was left alone with his own mares.

They had weeks before the cattle mobs and the men would come to the mountains, and this year the snow was lying late on the main tops. Thowra, with his love of the high, rocky places, often took his mares right up between the Ramsheads, where there were great drifts of snow in which to roll, and they might spend days grazing on the sweet upland grass. It was most unlikely that any enemies would be there to worry him, and he did not feel he had to take his usual care to keep hidden. The lovely bright days were spent roaming in the sunshine, leaping from rock to rock up in the tors and galloping down the long grass slopes or the lanes between the different Ramsheads. But one day Arrow came.

Arrow was not adventurous, and ordinarily nothing would have made him go alone with his mares into the higher mountains, but he was in a jealous fury with Thowra for having taken the grey fillies.

He came in the morning, quite early, and Thowra and his mares were all four standing up in the bright sunlight on the slabs of a tor, the spring breeze gently lifting their manes, when they saw Arrow below.

Thowra was just going to fly down and chase him but he remembered that this time Storm was not there, and he would have to fight Arrow.

'He can come up here,' he thought, and looked around for the best position. He put the mares behind him, with unclimbable cliffs around them, and then stood facing Arrow.

Arrow did not even stop to think that his superior strength would not be much advantage from below; he came leaping and prancing up the rocks, completely confident of himself — only to get a deadly blow on the head from Thowra's forefoot as he came within striking distance.

He was knocked back and downwards, and was very shaken. He could feel blood trickling between his eyes, but he still did not imagine that he could be beaten. He came up again, angrily — and received the same treatment. This time he stopped to think, realising that he could hardly expect anything else, with Thowra in such a dominant position above him. He decided then that if he waited, just below, where there was a pool of water from which he could drink, Thowra and his mares would have to come down some time; on level ground he could easily win a fight. So he had a drink and then stood and waited in the shade of a rock, while the sun beat down on the four that were on the tor.

It did not take Thowra long to see through his plan, and he could only hope that Arrow would get tired of waiting, but after an hour or so had gone by, he began to get thirsty. Arrow seemed to be making a great show of drinking at the little pool.

'Trust him to be mean-spirited if he could be,' thought Thowra bitterly. Then in a fury he decided it was better to go down and fight before he got too thirsty and too stiff from standing on the rocks. At least he would have the advantage of a downhill gallop, straight at Arrow, but he mustn't go too fast or Arrow would easily sidestep him.

Telling the mares to stay where they were, Thowra sprang lightly down from rock to rock, muscles rippling under his gleaming cream coat, eyes keen, nostrils quivering, ears pricked.

Arrow strutted out into the open to meet him, but Thowra could see he was alert, ready to dodge to one side. Thowra started to gallop straight for him, but slackened speed just a little as he drew close — knowing that he was much more nimble on his feet than Arrow.

Arrow leapt aside, but Thowra swung round, pivoting magnificently on his hind quarters, and struck him furiously with his forelegs. He saw blood spurt again above Arrow's eyes, but then Arrow was coming for him with open mouth and his lips drawn back. Thowra jumped and struck again, and leapt forward too, to try to get first hold on Arrow's withers. He had him for a short time, but his hold was not good enough, and Arrow fought free.

Thowra knew his only chance of success lay in his quickness, so he danced round Arrow, darting in with a strike, a bite or a kick — dancing, rearing, plunging, pivoting, swinging round like a flash. The effort was tremendous, and he was very thirsty, but he could see that the pace was tiring the heavier horse. Sweat was turning Arrow's coat dark, and Thowra could hear his heavy breathing.

On and on they fought, the grass churned to mud underfoot, the smell of blood and sweat all round them, and the sun beating down, then sinking so that its rays sometimes blinded them.

Thowra occasionally saw that same red film of exhaustion in front of his eyes that he remembered when he had had to gallop for his life from the man on the black horse, but he knew Arrow must be even more exhausted because he was making more and more desperate efforts to get a hold or to place a solid strike, so he kept on dancing, and plunging, and pivoting, trying to wear him out as quickly as he could.

There were great bites on Thowra's withers, and he had a gash over one shoulder from a vicious strike — if he kept moving *that* wouldn't stiffen — but he was tired, so tired, aching in the legs, in the shoulders, in the quarters. His heart was pounding, and he could hear his own breath sobbing now, but Arrow's breathing was louder still.

And so they fought until they were both completely exhausted, and neither could beat the other. Arrow had certainly given Thowra more serious wounds, but Arrow was unable to fight any more. When he backed off, Thowra followed him, trying to make a pretence of driving him, but he was too tired even to bite.

Arrow left, and Thowra dropped his nose into the pool of water and drank and drank. There was a soft whinnying from the mares who went to drink and to be with their young stallion. And as the sun sank below the mountains, the light faded and died. Slowly the stars came into the sky, and soon, in the deep blue darkness above the mountains and the horses, the Southern Cross burned.

Thowra lay on the grass beside the stream, too aching and stiff and tired to move.

Legends of Thowra

Men with packhorses, stocking up the huts, came earlier than the mobs of cattle that year. They were at Dead Horse hut before the brumbies got any warning, and Thowra, grazing with his mares on some open snowgrass about half a mile away, knew he had been seen.

He melted backwards into the forest, but it was time to go from the main range, so without waiting a moment, he took his mares with him and set off for the Brindle Bull. That evening they crossed the full-foaming river, fighting through the current, and the red stain of the sunset on the water reminded Thowra of the blood that had run from his wounds into the creek after his fight with Arrow. He wondered where Arrow would spend the summer, and thought probably on Paddy Rush's Bogong, and that he would be better off keeping his little herd on the Brindle Bull, where The Brolga grazed, than too close to Arrow.

Instinctively, when they climbed the mountain the next day, he led his herd towards the hanging valley on the south slope. They would be safe there for a little while. The man with the black horse would more likely look for them at the Cascades in the early summer. He also knew that Storm might go there too. And one bright evening, when the currawongs were calling and the grey, red-crested gang-gangs were chattering in the trees, Storm came down their track, and the two young stallions trotted up to greet each other, whinnying softly.

'Hello, brother of the wind,' Thowra said, as they nipped each other playfully. 'It is good that we should be together again.' For the rest of the summer and the crisp autumn, and during the winter with its snow and cold winds, and while their young mares were getting heavier with foal, the two stallions and their herds ran together.

Neither the summer nor the autumn were quiet. There seemed often to be men about. The man on the black horse chased them several times, but all the cunning that Bel Bel had taught Thowra, and his ever-increasing speed, kept him safe. Twice Storm took the two herds away and left the men galloping after Thowra, as Thowra had more chance of vanishing down a tunnel of scrub or into a deep hole in a stream. But it was never so easy to escape if the men had dogs.

Round the campfires the legends of the cream brumby — his speed, his cunning, his extraordinary beauty — grew and grew. The cattle heard them in the soft starlight nights, and gradually Bel Bel, who was running with The Brolga, heard these tales and was both pleased and afraid. There was one foal she had had that she would never forget.

Some of the stories that were woven round Thowra were strange, too. There was one that Bel Bel heard of how some men were sleeping in the open round a campfire one night, and of how one of the company had woken with the feeling of being watched. Then, in the trees, he had seen a pale stallion vanishing from sight.

There was another tale of two men and their packhorses, and of how they had observed a wraithlike horse appear and disappear in the bush beside their track, keeping pace with them for several miles. All this worried Bel Bel. She kept saying to Mirri that the tales they heard could not be true, but she wondered.

They were true, of course. Thowra was so curious! However, more than once he had saved the two small herds from being hunted by knowing where the men were and which way they were going. As his strength and speed increased he could not help enjoying the excitement and danger of watching the men and their horses, and of pitting his cunning against them. He knew that one of the legends about him was that he had never left a hoofmark by which he could be traced. He knew, too, that many of the stockmen did not believe he really existed. This much he heard from the grazing red-and-white cattle, or from the single beasts he met in the river pools.

As the months went by he even felt less anxiety about Arrow. Thowra had obviously forgotten that Arrow, too, would be growing in strength with each passing day. They did not see each other until the winter, neither having sought the other out. It did not suit Arrow to fight without winning, but his summer and autumn had been less troubled by stockmen — every man in the mountains, whether they believed in the silver stallion's existence or not, was out to catch Thowra — so Arrow had come to regard himself as invincible. However, when the two stallions saw each other in the distance, there was no real reason to fight — there was food enough for all, and springtime was the time to fight for mares — so they went on their separate ways.

The winter's storms came then, and in the whirling, swirling snow Thowra and his herd of three grey mares were mostly invisible, often able to play tricks on the others, and enjoy the wild games.

So Thowra's first year with a herd of his own passed very happily, and he felt within himself the mounting tide of energy and joy which even the intense cold and the great storms could not quench. Then when the first warm, scent-laden winds came, and the warm rains to wash away the thawing snow, Thowra's strength rose with the streams, grew with the grass and with the buds and leaves.

All the mountains, the silent, rolling, grey-green hills, the great, rock cliffs and crags, the rushing streams, and the dense forests, were his kingdom. They were Thowra's because of his joy, his speed, his strength and his beauty, possessed perhaps even more than Arrow possessed them, or The Brolga — possessed, really, because of what Bel Bel had given him, the love of wondering and the understanding of every sign of bird, beast and weather.

Spring was coming to all this mountain kingdom. Foals would be born, young kangaroos, possums and wombats would be snugly in their mothers' pouches. The hawks and great wedge-tail eagles would hatch their young; fat dingo pups would roll in the sunshine; and the wild horses would fight for their mares and gallop over the hills in all the glory of their strength.

Swift Arrow

Bel Bel listened to the trumpeting spring calls of the stallions that were in and around the valley of the Cascades. First she heard Arrow's call, followed by The Brolga's ringing answer, now with a challenge in its sound. Then she heard a different call, and knew undoubtedly it was Thowra's.

All the love of the high, wild places, all the amazing joy in being alive sounded in his voice.

Bel Bel, who was growing old, knew that she would indeed live on in her cream son, and she could imagine him standing high above the valley on a rocky outcrop, the sunlight on his shining cream coat and on the streaming silver of his mane and tail, calling out.

When she heard Arrow's call again it sounded closer to Thowra. Bel Bel started moving in the same direction, with a sudden sense of foreboding. Then she heard her son again, and a clangour of echoes, and knew he must be moving up a narrow valley. She started climbing up a ridge, lithely and swiftly, in spite of her age.

Again she heard Arrow, shriller and more urgent, and by the faint echo, she knew he was entering the valley.

This time Thowra definitely answered him, in a ringing challenge; and now Thowra had risen out of the valley.

Bel Bel started to move faster. She knew the ridge she was on rose to quite a high hill then dropped and climbed again. From the hill she would have a commanding view.

Had the time come when the vast mountains were no longer vast enough for two such stallions as Arrow and Thowra? Bel Bel knew that Arrow had only become more jealous and mean-spirited as he grew up. He had wanted Thowra's grey mares badly enough last year. This year he had probably made up his mind to get them.

She heard their trumpeting, challenging cries as she climbed further up the hill.

Round some rocks she came face to face with a dingo, both she and the yellow dog jumped nervously, and went on their way.

A roaring challenge from Arrow echoed and echoed round the narrow valley, but from far above came the mocking answer, as though Thowra was laughing in the sun.

Bel Bel was not laughing, though. She had seen Arrow often lately and noticed that he was an almost mature horse, heavy and strong, so like his father, Yarraman, in all except temperament. And Thowra was much more her son than Yarraman's, fleet of foot, like she was, and lithe. In this fight he would be fighting for his life.

Up and up, Bel Bel climbed, hearing all the time the wild stallion calls that grew fiercer and more insistent. At last, she reached the top of the hill and stood there scanning the surrounding country. Far away, she could see Thowra and his mares, but Arrow was not yet in sight. She waited and watched. Between her and Thowra there was a stretch of very rough bush country with some great heaps of granite rocks and one or two high cliff faces, but opposite, where Thowra was, there were open fields of snowgrass.

As she watched she saw the three mares disappear from sight into the bush and then saw Thowra rear on his hind legs, almost as though dancing with joy; then he screamed his defiance. Arrow was coming up out of the valley into view.

The big chestnut came slowly, stopping now and then to paw the ground in anger and anticipation.

Bel Bel held her breath. What was Thowra going to do? She thought she knew, she *hoped* she knew.

Arrow's mares were in sight now; and Arrow was advancing slowly, his screams becoming shriller and shriller. Bel Bel, even from that distance, could almost sense his quivering fury. It would have taken a better-tempered horse than Arrow to remain calm against Thowra's taunting. The creamy danced and mocked with unbelievable rudeness, but his movements were quiet and rhythmical, taking none of the energy he would soon need.

Arrow stopped and pawed the ground, then came on again, rearing, snorting, screaming.

Thowra roared a mocking challenge in reply; waited till Arrow got quite close, and then pirouetted and galloped on to some rocks a hundred yards away.

Bel Bel heaved a sigh.

Arrow broke into a gallop and followed, eager to knock Thowra clean off the rocks. Thowra danced to one side, swung round, and struck him a drumming kick in the ribs, one calculated to infuriate more than to damage, and Arrow went flying down the other side of the rocks, pulled up on his haunches, and came back at him.

Thowra waited a moment and then leapt down and away to another vantage point. This time it was only a grassy hillock and he did not let Arrow get close enough to strike or bite him, but, giving a derisive roar, galloped back to the heap of rocks.

Bel Bel saw that he was doing everything to goad Arrow to anger. It was a long time since she had watched Thowra really move, and it was clear that because of his speed he had all the advantages, as long as he didn't let Arrow really come to grips with him. But if it came to a violent fight, there was no question about it, she was sure Arrow would win.

Thowra remained just sufficiently out of Arrow's reach to keep the bigger horse at a wild pitch of anger, and Bel Bel watched him leading the way slowly nearer the bush. Once they were among the trees, she would not be able to see how the battle went.

The sweat was breaking out on her already, trickling from behind her ears. Thowra *must* win, and yet she did not really know how. Supposing Arrow killed him — her beautiful cream foal to whom she had taught everything she knew of the bush!

She saw Thowra gallop through the first of the trees with Arrow close behind. Then there were just flashes of colour as they dodged among the snow gums. Arrow's scream rang out shriller and angrier while Thowra mocked him more and more, until it seemed almost as if the cream-and-silver brumby were laughing aloud.

Then Bel Bel held her breath again. Through the trees it looked as if Arrow had caught Thowra, and was trying to get the first fatal hold above the withers; but she was mistaken. There was Thowra streaking between the trees; there was his derisive cry again, ridiculing Arrow. For one minute she could see him prancing in a little clearing. He was closer to her now, and it was not just in imagination and memory that she saw his beauty.

For a little longer she watched him galloping down a glade, then they both vanished, and she could only hear the screams, both furious and teasing.

All of a sudden Thowra burst into view, galloping straight for the top of one of the cliffs, Arrow fast on his heels.

Bel Bel stood tense and still.

Thowra suddenly stopped on the very edge, stones flying in the air, and then, just as Bel Bel had jumped with him years before, he jumped over another cliff and on to a tiny ledge quite some feet below the top. There he rocked unsteadily for a moment. Bel Bel saw him look up to see what Arrow was doing. And there, flying through space, carried far out from the cliff face by his speed, was Arrow.

To Bel Bel it seemed like ages before Arrow stopped hurtling through the air and crashed on to the ground at the foot of the cliff, lying absolutely still.

Bel Bel only stayed long enough to see Thowra step carefully along the wallaby track, round the cliff from his narrow shelf, and then she set off towards him at a trot. But Thowra had not seen her and she soon saw that he was going to head back to his mares. Bel Bel kept on. She wanted to see what had happened to Arrow. She saw Thowra glance back over his shoulder a few times, and realised then that he had not been able to see Arrow's crash from his ledge, and that now he was determined to get back to his mares before Arrow could find them. She kept on towards the bottom of the cliff.

She crossed a bush-filled hollow and drank at a little stream. A brown wallaby sat gravely watching her, and some gang-gangs threw gum-nuts from the trees.

She went on, looking for Arrow. Suddenly she stopped. Bel Bel remembered that she had seen the same thing before — a chestnut stallion lying in a crushed and huddled heap, with all the tremendous life completely gone from him. In among the shaly rocks at the foot of the cliff, Arrow lay dead.

Thowra had fought for his life using his own weapon — his speed. He had planned his escape, not Arrow's death — but Arrow was as dead as Yarraman had been when the mountains were no longer vast enough to hold him and The Brolga.

She stood looking at Arrow. His head, the only part of him which revealed his mean spirit, was doubled underneath his neck and his golden mane flowed over it. Already a crow had arrived, and was advancing on the dead horse with little hops. A flight of lowries, scarlet and royal blue, flew through the trees, heeding neither Bel Bel nor Arrow. Over the rocks moved a little brown lizard.

Bel Bel shuddered and backed away slowly to start on the steep climb round the cliff. The bush seemed very silent now, after the noise of the two stallions. She began to doubt if she would find Thowra. As he did not know that Arrow was dead, he was certain to take his mares and go right away. Anyway, she would try to find him. But when she got to the top she could not go on without once again going to the cliff edge and taking a last look — perhaps to make sure that Arrow, who had harried her foal from his first day with the herd, was really dead.

She stood on the grey granite edge and looked over. There was the heap of chestnut and gold, and she forgot for a moment that it was Brownie's son. With his narrower, pinched head not showing, he looked the image of Yarraman.

A sound came from behind and startled Bel Bel. She turned in a flash. There was Thowra coming out of the bush.

'Everything was so quiet,' he said. 'I had to come and see what had happened.'

'He couldn't stop,' said Bel Bel. 'He's down there, dead.'

Thowra peered over the edge, his sweat-stained ears twitching nervously.

'Come away,' Bel Bel said, backing away from the cliff edge. 'It is too open here. You must go back to your mares — and Arrow's, if you want them.'

Golden the beautiful

Thowra did not forget that the men had come early last spring, so even when the long fingers of snowdrifts still stretched down the southern slopes and deep snow lay in the gullies, he kept a careful lookout.

He was both proud and embarrassed by the size of his herd now. Besides a rather handsome black mare of Arrow's that he had added to his greys, there were two strange-looking little dun-coloured foals, Arrow's chestnut daughter, and one creamy colt. He did not take much notice of the foals, but he realised that they made his herd slower and less easy to hide.

For a week or more they had been grazing near the headwaters of the Crackenback and Groggin Gap, when late one evening, Thowra heard sounds in the bush. First came the jangle of a bit, and then the *frou-frou-frou* rub of packs on tree-trunks.

He and his herd were not on the stock track, so he told his mares to stay still and he slipped silently through the already darkening bush, closer and closer to the sounds. Then suddenly he stood absolutely still. Walking along the track, her rider leading one packhorse, was a cream filly. There were other packhorses and one stock-horse and rider at the end of the procession, but Thowra could look at nothing else but the creamy, with her proud carriage and swinging stride, the lovely silk of her mane and tail.

For a while, he moved silently through the trees parallel with the track, watching and watching her.

The men seemed to be tired out and swayed, half-asleep in their saddles. They did not even hear her whinnying softly when she looked through the brush and saw Thowra.

Thowra knew quite well that the men must be going to the Dead Horse hut, their packhorses loaded with stores of tinned foods, and flour, and salt for the cattle. He turned back to his herd to put them in a safe place for the night, knowing that he must return to the hut himself. A half moon came up a few hours later, enough to see by and yet not so light that Thowra could not keep himself well hidden.

Before going near the hut, he walked along the horse-paddock fence. He could see the packhorses, moving like restless shadows, but there was no sign of the two riding-horses, neither the creamy nor the other whose colour he had not even noticed. He had thought they would be left in that new yard whose high fences he and Storm had studied more than a year ago.

The timber was cleared quite a long way back from the yard, which stood out on its own against the horse-paddock fence, in front of the hut.

Thowra moved through the trees very slowly, seeking the dark pools of shadow and avoiding any glades where the moonlight shone. A possum watched him with its wistful yet curious, pointed face. It gave a deep, throaty qua-a-r-rk, and he heard the sound of horses shuffling in the yard. He stood at the edge of the trees looking across. Yes, there, silvered by moonlight, was the lovely filly. She whinnied softly again as a man opened the hut door, the light from a hurricane lamp blending with the moonlight.

A voice said, 'The brumbies might be about.' And another voice inside the hut answered, 'Don't worry. The fence is too high for them to jump, but you were a fool to bring her, all the same.' Then they shut the door again and soon the hurricane lamp was turned out.

After waiting a long time, Thowra walked across the open ground to the yard. The cream filly came up to the fence, trembling with excitement, and put her nose through to snuff him.

As she started to whinny, he said, 'No. No. You must learn to be silent, if you want to come with me. What is your name?'

'They call me Golden. You must be Thowra of whom all the other horses speak — and the men even have songs about you that they sing to the cattle, but *they* call you Silver.'

'Thowra is my name,' said Thowra proudly. 'The name my mother, Bel Bel, gave me.'

Just then the bay stockhorse, who had been standing trembling in the yard, let out a shrill, ringing neigh. Thowra was gone in a flash, silent-footed but fast, back into the bush. He was barely hidden in the trees before he heard the hut door opening and saw a man come out with a torch. Thowra watched him go right over to the yard, where the horse and the cream filly stood snorting, and turn his torch on to the ground. When he heard him say, 'Huh, an unshod horse!' Thowra knew it was time to go, and to go on rocks and grass where he left no track.

Last year the men who had brought the packhorses out early had only stayed two nights. These men probably would too — but would they perhaps hobble the horses the next night, or watch over them in turns, hoping to catch him? He decided to wait till later in the night and then go back.

The moon had gone behind a bank of cloud when Thowra next stood on the edge of the bush and peered through the leathery snow-gum leaves towards the yard. He could see Golden moving restlessly about, but the other horse seemed to be asleep.

Stepping from one snowgrass tussock to another, he moved towards the yard again, this time making for the only place in the fence where there was grass and not bare earth.

Golden came up to him again.

'How high can you jump?' Thowra asked her. 'There is one lower place in this fence over there in the corner.'

'I'd never clear that,' said Golden.

'Not even if I jumped in and gave you a lead out over it?' But he eyed the bay horse. With that silly jackass there to bray, the game would be given away before they could get out.

Just then the bay horse stirred; he threw up his head with a startled snort, and then neighed loudly.

'Jump, and come with me,' Thowra said, as he turned to go. Already there was a clatter in the hut and a man's voice cursing.

Thowra bounded away over the grass. He looked back, but Golden was not following, and just before he reached the trees he heard the door open. He was hidden by the time the man appeared but it had been a close call. Thowra watched the man prowling around, saw that he

100

could find no more tracks and that he was puzzled. He went back inside, but there were still sounds of him moving about, and then came the smell of smoke as it poured out of the hut chimney.

Just then the dawn wind came, stirring the darkness of the night, touching with cool, long fingers Thowra's coat, his ears; whispering through the snow-gum leaves. Daylight would soon come, and he must not be seen, but he could not tear himself away and he remained, never taking his eyes off the yard. The man came out with a mug of tea in his hand and leant on the yard fence. He called Golden. To Thowra's amazement he saw her walk over to him and take something out of his hand and eat it.

Thowra tossed his head and turned away into the thick bush. He made no sound as he went back to his herd, but Golden's whinny followed him. He stopped for a second and listened, not understanding how she could whinny to him and yet accept something from the man. But the whinny sealed his determination to get her for himself.

Thowra came through the trees and found his herd in a glade that was filled with the liquid gold of early morning sunshine. They looked beautiful, his greys with their tiny odd-coloured foals, and the one lovely cream one. It was then that he realised how risky it was, trying to free Golden. He must not take the chance of being chased by the men himself, and his herd being found — but how wonderful it would be to have her there with the greys.

That morning he led the herd up towards the Ramshead, and put them in a gully that opened to the north-west where there was no snow. Then he turned back to the hut, going carefully and quietly through the thickest bush, and leaving hardly a hoofmark.

All his senses were alert. He heard the faintest rustle made by an early-moving snake, saw its beady eyes. He felt the gang-gangs looking at him, and saw their red crests up. When two kangaroos quickly hopped by he trod even more carefully. Then, in the distance, he heard the sound of a shod horse. Thowra slid farther into the thick scrub, and stood waiting.

He heard two horses approaching, and when he knew they had passed, he drew closer. There were the two men riding Golden and the bay horse. The pack horses must have been left behind, which meant the men would stay another night. He followed for a while to see what they were doing. They were wandering without direction, looking for something — and, if it were his tracks they were looking for, they were wasting their time, because they were not going to find any.

He turned back to the hut and had a look around. The packhorses were grazing in the horse paddock. Everything was as he thought. He headed for the Ramshead and the herd.

That night Thowra went to the hut again, stepping proudly through the dark forest before the moon had risen. Leaves brushed his shoulders and there was the lovely damp scent of the bush at night. He kept thinking of what Bel Bel would say to such a daring expedition as this — and yet he knew she would understand. She was creamy herself and could appreciate how lovely the cream filly was. It was Storm who would really consider him a fool.

He kept watch from the edge of the trees for a long time, slightly surprised that Golden showed no sign of knowing he was there, but he had been even more silent than before, and Golden's senses were not as sharp as a wild horse's.

The fire and the lamp were both out in the hut, and all was quiet. He could see nobody watching over the horses, and the horses were not hobbled. Still suspecting a trap, he came out of the trees slowly, thankful that the moon had not yet risen. He reached the fence, his skin pricking with nervousness, but nothing happened. The bay was sound asleep.

He measured up the fence again, and in the springtime surge of strength and spirits, he felt sure that he would be able to jump out and lead Golden away.

He backed off, speeded up as quietly as he could, and jumped.

'Now, come on and follow me!' he said to Golden.

The bay woke with a startled squeal. A man burst out of the hut, shouting, 'Got you, my beauty!'

'Come quick!' said Thowra, and with only the very short run available in the yard, he took three strides and made a huge leap. His knees rapped the top rail, yet he still seemed to lift higher. A rope whistled through the air and fell short. Thowra felt his heart almost bursting with fear and effort, but he was over the fence. The other man ran towards him with a rope, and Thowra swung wildly as he felt it hit his flank. Golden called, but she was still in the yard. He called in answer, but she still did not come. Thowra didn't realise that the first man had roped her. He galloped towards the trees, hearing the men getting saddles and bridles. But a brumby stallion who knew the country would get a good start while they saddled up. He raced away towards the Cascades, taking the opposite direction to where his herd lay, the one the men might easily expect him to take.

He galloped through the night, darkness like a curtain around him. A white owl flew, crying, from a tree and he shied in sudden fear. He could hear the men close behind, so he branched off the track and down a rock gully; the men, when they found they could not easily capture him, soon gave up. The owner of Golden had no wish to lame her in a midnight brumby hunt, and anyway it was obvious that Golden might very well bait a trap for Thowra, so they decided to stay at the hut another night.

In the morning they built up the rails on the lowest side of the yard.

Thowra watched the track to Groggin and knew that they had not gone down from the mountains; he watched the sky, too, because he could see that bad weather was coming, and sensed that it was coming very quickly. When the men had not gone by mid-afternoon, he hastened off to his herd and took them lower down the Crackenback, where, if there were snow, they would be sheltered. Before they had reached the glade, the wind was howling over the mountain-top and bringing with it biting flakes of snow. The foals were frightened and kept getting under their mothers' feet. Thowra felt responsible and stayed with them in the gathering storm. His knees were bruised and stiff from their rap on the fence, and he was glad to be with his mares.

All night long the cold snow fell. The men at Dead Horse hut gave up hoping for the cream stallion to come, and worried about their own horses. The packhorses were better off than the two riding-horses because there were trees in the paddock under which they could shelter.

Golden's owner was particularly worried. There was not room for even one horse to stand in the skillion; it was full of wood and bags of salt.

At midnight they decided to turn them out of the yard into the horse paddock. Already the snow lay inches deep on the ground; covered rails and fence-posts; slithered with a soft thud off the trees. The cream filly and the bay horse walked gladly through the gate and towards a clump of trees.

The men sloshed their way through the snow back to the hut, shook the flakes off their coats, threw more wood on the fire, and settled down again for what remained of the night.

It was in the heavy, dark hours of the early morning, when the blizzard was at its height, that Thowra came.

He had to walk right to the yard before he was sure it was empty, then he went, silent-footed in the snow, right up to the skillion. But there was nothing there. He went back to the horse-paddock fence and followed it till it went through some trees. Here he could hear the snuffling and shuffling of quite a number of horses and guessed Golden would be with them.

He retreated a little way until he found a panel of fencing over which he thought he might be able to jump — it was not so much the height of the fence that bothered him, but rather where it was and where to jump — in the blizzard it was difficult to see anything clearly. He cantered towards it, making an enormous leap.

The snow beat in his eyes, hit his legs, chest and belly. He was flying through the blizzard, waiting for the terrible pain of biting barbed wire if he had miscalculated his jump. But there was no pain. He slithered a little on landing and drew a huge breath of relief. He was safely over!

Thowra jogged down the fence line until he came to the trees, then sneaked in, moving silently from tree to tree, conscious of every sound, feeling the cold touch of the snow on his coat. It was easy to see the dark-coloured horses, as he drew close to them, but Golden, like himself, was invisible in the snowstorm, and it was Golden he must find.

He had circled right round the group of horses before he found her, standing on her own under a tree by the fence. Straining his eyes, he could just see her outline, sensed that she had become suddenly tense, and he knew then that she had seen him. She stood quite still.

'Will you follow me, now?' he asked. 'I will jump the fence and stand beside it so that you can see where it is. This fence is not too high for you to jump.'

He could tell she was trembling with nervousness, but he did not understand that she was torn between her desire to go with him and her instinct to stay obediently where she was.

He moved off and she followed, back to the panel in the fence which he had jumped before. He took her to the fence and told her to make certain she knew how high she must leap.

The snow was driving behind Thowra this time; the wind almost lifted him, and he was so excited that he felt no fear of jumping too early or too late, or not high enough. When he landed he turned back and stood by the fence, neighing softly. For a moment he thought that Golden would not come; then she came, invisible — though he could hear her galloping — till she was right at the fence and taking off in a wildly high jump. She, too, was over and free. He led her off through the bush.

Challenge and escape

Thowra led Golden through the snowstorm. He was so wildly elated with his success in freeing her that he could hardly stop himself from jumping up on a high rock to trumpet his victory, and to set the echoes ringing in the hills. When he heard a dingo howl close by, he longed to roar back at him — and never realised that Golden was shaking with fear at the sound of the wild dog. He led her steadily back to the herd and got there as the first eerie, snow-filled light of the dawn came over the hills.

All the mares snuffled Golden curiously, while she stayed nervously by Thowra's side, but he would not let them waste time getting acquainted. As soon as the men missed Golden they would be after her. There was no time to lose; they must go as fast as the foals could travel, over to the Brindle Bull.

It was necessary to cross the Crackenback much higher than usual because it was foaming full. Even then the first place he tried was too deep and swift for the foals, and they had to go higher still — and nearer to the men. Then Thowra found a crossing that he decided would have to do.

The snow was still falling, hitting the water and vanishing away. The anxious mares whinnied as he went across, the water foaming above his knees and nearly to his girth — white foam and grey, swirling water. He called to his mares. Golden had followed him closely, but those with foals stood and looked. Then the grey mare with her creamy foal started in, keeping the young one on the upstream side. She went very slowly, anxiously nuzzling at her foal and urging him on as his long legs slipped and stumbled among the slimey boulders. Then the force of the current hit them and the foal fell. He neighed with terror as he struggled to his feet. Thowra went in to try and help.

'Go back,' Thowra commanded, for the first time feeling a compassionate interest in his sons and daughters, but realising what a problem they could be if there were a real hunt for him and Golden. He could dimly remember — or remember from the tales Bel Bel had told him — the great brumby drive on Paddy Rush's Bogong when he himself was little bigger than his own foals.

They trekked up the bank of the river, drawing ever closer to the men. At last, Thowra found a place that was a possible hiding spot, and escorted each mare and foal across, the little dun foals, all wet and bedraggled, looking more mousy than ever.

They had only just reached the safe covering of the bush when something made Thowra look higher up the stream, and there, through a thin curtain of falling snow, he could see a man, the one who usually rode Golden, sitting on the bay horse. Obviously he hadn't seen them or he would have been after them already, but he might see them if they started to move.

'Stand still!' he told his herd. 'Don't move at all!' But it was all very well to say this; there were tired, fidgety foals to be considered. The dun-coloured ones would not show up, but restless little creamy would, and Golden, if she did not understand. But Golden was staying very quiet; she began to tremble violently as she recognised her master.

Again Thowra did not understand how torn she was between her loyalty to the man who had trained and fed her; and her longing to be with him, the wonderful silver stallion of whom all the horses, all the cattle, all the men spoke.

Just then the snow started to fall more heavily. Thowra drew his herd further into the bush while they were hidden by the snowstorm, but he could hear the man coming. He thought how, if he had been alone, he would have remained absolutely still and silent so that the man could have passed quite close and never seen him, but a herd of ten was not easily hidden. The only thing he could think of was to act as a decoy himself, lead the man off away from the herd.

He turned to Boon Boon, the creamy's mother, and told her to take the herd up to The Brolga's grazing ground, near the very top — knowing that The Brolga was still in the Cascades. Then he told Golden not to leave Boon Boon for a minute, and he went off silently, taking a direction that would bring him just ahead of the man, although he would still have the shelter of fairly thick timber. He wanted to be seen, well enough for the man to see he did not have Golden with him.

He faded through the bush and listened. When he heard the horse quite close, he walked quietly through the trees so that he was just in front of the man.

There was a clatter of horse's shoes on rock as the man spurred his mount. Thowra bounded away. He knew he must keep his pursuer close enough to think he had a chance of catching him, and yet he must not let himself be caught — he must lead him right away from the herd.

It was madly exciting to see how near he could let the man come, and still allow time to dodge him. The rougher the country, the better he could dodge; the bay horse was not much good on steep, stony places.

To the man, Thowra must have been like a dream leading him on through the storm, sometimes just visible — a creamy flash, or two creamy flashes. Sometimes there was just the sound ahead of branches swishing or of hooves on stones. The man could never have told, in that beating snow, if Golden were there or not. Once, Thowra deliberately neighed twice, as though he were calling Golden and she answering.

At last, he was approaching the place he had been making for — a long, steep gully that went right down one side of the mountain and dropped off into sheer space. This gully was full of boulders and small stones. Thowra had only been down it once, with Storm, and had thought then that it might be a good place in which to escape from a man hunt. Very few tame horses carrying a heavy load could get down it without laming themselves, and, even if they did, there was no track leading off. He and Storm had found a way through huge rocks and dense heather to the foot of a waterfall, but it had taken a long time to find it, and there was nothing to mark the place.

There it was, the top of the gully; the storm was slackening slightly, and a faint tinge of blue was in the sky. He must hurry because the falling snow would help to hide him.

Down the snow-slippery rocks he went, slowly at first, to make sure the man was following, but keeping himself partly out of sight. Then, when the bay horse was quite close, he charged off, leaping and flying, almost trusting the air more than the slippery leg-breaking rocks. He gave a mocking neigh. This was like leading Arrow on! Even if the man discovered now that Golden was not with him, he must be made to follow.

Down, down he went. Sometimes he felt a sickening shudder in his legs when he did not land squarely on a rock, or when a rock rolled, but it was not for nothing that Bel Bel had taught him to fly like the wind through the roughest country.

Down, down, down, and the snow was still blowing in blinding flurries. He checked his speed because the man had dropped back. Now there was no sound of a horse clattering behind him, so he stopped and looked around.

The man was on the ground; he was looking at the bay's leg, at the hoof, feeling the tendons, feeling the knee, even running his hand over the shoulder.

'Looks like the end of him for a while,' thought Thowra, and went steadily on downwards, until he found the way through the waterfall. He had a drink and crossed the stream, then went silently and tracklessly up the mountain towards the very top, to the camping grounds of The Brolga, where the herd should be grazing in safety.

The snow stopped, but an ice-cold wind blew the already fallen snow like sharp pebbles that stung against his coat and in his eyes. He kept in the trees as much as possible. It was nearly evening when he reached the grazing ground. There, in the grassy basin, he saw his grey mares and his foals, his black mare, and the lovely creamy filly he had stolen from the stockmen.

Of them all, perhaps Golden was gladdest to see him. It had been an anxious day for her, though Boon Boon had been friendly enough and had explained what Thowra was doing. But the others had ignored her, or sometimes given her a nip. She had also found it hard work to keep up with them and to stay quiet, as Boon Boon insisted she must, and leave no tracks. In fact, it was almost impossible for her to leave no hoofmarks because of her shining silver shoes, though one of these had already come off on the rough rocks.

Now, when she saw Thowra, she whinnied and trotted over to him.

Thowra nuzzled her, relieved and thankful to find her there; he had been afraid that she would not follow the herd without him.

Thowra, of course, never bothered himself about how the man would get back to the hut, or how the two of them would leave the mountains with one horse vanished and one lame, but he did think that it would be quite a long time before anyone bothered them again.

With no snow on the lower mountains, they grazed for days on the Brindle Bull and enjoyed the lovely summer weather. The foals played and learnt to eat grass. Golden lost all but one front shoe, and tried to learn to be quieter and to keep herself hidden in the trees. But the ways of the wild country need a lifetime of practice, and she had only been trained to carry a man on her back and do as he made her do.

112

Away from the main range, Thowra did not know what was going on, and did not see the first small mob of cattle come early to the Cascades. Late one evening, about two weeks after he had captured Golden, he was amazed to hear a tremendous stallion roar from the rim of the basin above him, and see, standing silhouetted against the blue-gold sky, The Brolga.

Thowra, like The Brolga had once been with Yarraman, was too full of his own strength and vigour to run away. He turned to Boon Boon and told her to take the herd to Paddy Rush's Bogong, then he went prancing and high-stepping forward to meet the great grey horse.

He did not notice that his own fine herd had only withdrawn to the rim of the basin, or that The Brolga's herd were lining the opposite rim, forming an audience for the big, green amphitheatre in which he was going to fight. He kept prancing forward, and The Brolga came rearing and screaming towards him.

The green basin in the hills was filled with the last of the sunlight as the two horses, the enormous grey and the lithe, swift creamy, met. Spears of light shot from Thowra's tossing mane as the two wheeled and danced round each other without placing a blow.

It was natural that The Brolga should feel completely confident, just as it was natural that Thowra, in his first pride of being a stallion with a herd and foals of his own, should feel unbeatable. But in those few moments of dancing and dodging The Brolga's forefeet calmed Thowra down enough for Bel Bel's teaching and her cunning to reassert itself. He realised that only his swiftness of movement was going to save him.

If The Brolga had not caught sight of Golden he might easily have got tired of trying to fight a nimble, flashing

113

tease, but he had seen the beautiful creamy filly and wanted her for his herd.

He made a dash at Thowra, teeth bared; but Thowra was no longer in the same place. The Brolga pivoted on his great, powerful hind legs and struck rapidly with both forelegs. But Thowra had gone again and, in going, placed a resounding kick on The Brolga's big, grey rump.

This time Thowra backed off and waited for The Brolga to make his next move. He was annoyed that Boon Boon was letting the herd stand and watch. Now he would have to lead The Brolga in another direction. The Brolga could sense Thowra was distracted and hit him on the side of the head. Thowra shook his throbbing head, jumped to one side and charged The Brolga himself, with a well-placed forefoot. Then away again.

The Brolga, unlike Arrow, did not waste his energy in rage, or in galloping after him. He followed slowly, rearing and snorting. Thowra knew he might never tire him, but he could lead him on to the rim of the basin, timing their arrival there for the fall of night. In darkness he should be able to escape and, he hoped, join his herd. Surely Boon Boon would understand what he was doing and get the herd away.

The Brolga saw what he was doing before Boon Boon did, and suddenly the big grey stallion left Thowra and started trotting to where the grey mares and the beautiful creamy were still outlined against the evening sky.

Boon Boon remembered how her father, The Brolga, had valued the creamy mare, Bel Bel, above all his herd. As soon as she saw him coming she knew that he was after Golden, and she hustled the herd away, down into the timber.

The Brolga broke into a gallop, but Thowra was catching up, then racing past, placing a thundering kick on his shoulder and foreleg. For a while The Brolga took no notice of the madly galloping and kicking, creamy stallion, but pursued the disappearing herd.

Thowra was desperate. It would be awful to have risked his life capturing Golden from the stockmen, only to lose her to the same stallion that had killed his father. He knew he could gallop faster and dodge more nimbly than The Brolga, so after another really fierce kick at his chest, he raced past him and then turned to confront him.

The Brolga gave a cry of anger, rose on his hind legs, and struck. Once again Thowra dodged his blow. The Brolga rushed forward after the herd, but Thowra was back in front of him. This time the grey came quietly and steadily onward, the whites of his eyes showing, and his mouth open. Thowra danced away. The light was fading, and he would be able to escape to his herd if only he could keep 'playing' The Brolga for a little longer. He danced, he dodged, he kicked, while the big, grey stallion kept forcing his way in the direction of the herd, but all the time it grew darker.

The grey of The Brolga's coat was beginning to fade into the oncoming darkness, and sometimes, when the big horse moved swiftly and came from an unexpected angle, he was like a ghost, without substance in the night. For a few minutes, The Brolga had all the advantage. It was almost completely dark, but Thowra's light colour still showed more clearly, and The Brolga came at him to give him a real beating. Thowra received some tremendous blows but always he just managed to avoid The Brolga's bite. When he reckoned his herd must be well away then he started to dance off in another direction.

The Brolga suddenly gave up the idea of catching Golden that night, and when a ringing neigh echoed round the basin, he stopped chasing Thowra to listen. It came again from the direction of his own herd. Thowra recognised that it was Bel Bel, his mother, calling The Brolga away. The galloping hooves behind him stopped, but Thowra kept on until he reached the rim of the basin. There he threw up his head and neighed once to Bel Bel. When he was sure he was not being followed, he galloped down and swung in the direction his herd would have taken for Paddy Rush's Bogong.

Thowra in flight

Now that Arrow was dead, Thowra could be undisputed king of any other stallions who spent the summer with his herd on Paddy Rush's Bogong, and there was more room there than on the Brindle Bull. Pleased to be going there, he led his mares to the old grazing ground where he had been with Yarraman's herd when he was as small as his own foals.

It was exciting, too, going over all the country that he and Storm had explored; finding some scrub grown far thicker, some burnt and offering no cover at all; finding again the rock paths and the ravine where they had lost Arrow.

He examined very closely the cliff that Bel Bel and Mirri had once made them jump down to avoid the man hunt, and realised it still offered a good place of escape. He showed it to Golden and taught her how to make the twisting jump that was needed, then showed her the way into the scrub. Always he was teaching her to be quiet and to try and leave no track, and at last she had lost the fourth shoe.

Boon Boon, with her cream foal, might become the object of a hunt, too, so she also practised jumping down the cliff, and then took her foal over it.

Every day, Thowra went to a vantage spot where he could look out over the Crackenback towards the Dead Horse hut, and spent hours watching. Somehow he was sure the owner of Golden would soon be back. And only about five days after they had reached Paddy Rush's Bogong, he saw the faraway specks of men on horseback heading towards the Brindle Bull. Just for a moment they were visible, then they vanished into the bush. He went back to the herd and took them off into some thick scrub, the snow gums and heather closing around them and covering their tracks.

There was a tiny clearing on the banks of a creek, inside their hiding place; and the foals lay there, beside their mothers, while the mares and stallion listened all day long.

At night they all crept out to feed with the shy wombats and wallabies, and listened to the mopokes calling. Just before dawn, they were hidden again in the silent, aromatic scrub. Another day started to pass very slowly. The sky had become a milky grey, and the black cockatoos were crying in the trees. The still air in their clearing became very oppressive. Thowra felt his coat pricking uncomfortably. It was too still, and the cockatoos' cries were full of foreboding. He wished he knew what was happening on the Brindle Bull.

The wind started to blow, hot and menacing, and the silence was broken by the roar it made through the trees, by the groaning, lashing boughs. Thowra was now feeling really uncomfortable. Through the torrent of sound made by the storm he thought he could hear movement on the mountain — not galloping, but animals creeping, hiding.

He ordered the herd to stay absolutely quiet and made his way cautiously out through the dense scrub, working

118

this way and that so that he could be sure no enemies were approaching through the cover to their hiding place. He saw nothing until he reached the very edge of the belt of timber and heather. The long, clear glade beyond was empty. But moving along through the next belt of trees, he could see, in amongst the bending, wind-contorted limbs, a file of horses, with small grey foals beside their mothers, and there, in the lead, just behind The Brolga, was his own mother, Bel Bel.

Something must have made Bel Bel look in his direction. He was sure he was hidden from sight, but it was as though she looked through all the leaves and heather hiding him, and saw his eyes. She moved her head in a nod of recognition, but made no other sign.

Thowra went back to his herd. That night he would not let them go out to graze. Tremendous rain started soon after dark, and they took shelter under the thick trees, but they were all getting hungry and restless. Thowra himself wandered to and fro through the scrub.

At last, after midnight, he saw Bel Bel coming through the rain and the darkness, through the grotesquely moving trees.

'Well, my son of the wind and the rain and the storm,' she said, 'it would seem as if you have brought more than a little trouble on us all through stealing this filly from the men.'

'What has happened?' asked Thowra.

'The Brolga is very angry,' she said. 'The men came searching, trying to find you and this filly they call Golden. There were men everywhere. At first they did not bother about us, but then perhaps they were angry that they did not find you, and they started chasing and roping. That's why we left. Next they will come here. You will have to go farther away.'

'I know this mountain and all its hiding-places very well,' Thowra said.

'Yes, my son, I know you do, but there are a lot of you to hide. You will have to go farther down the river. The country is rough there and the grazing is not good, but it would be better to have a summer of poor food and to remain free.'

As she spoke Thowra saw the fire and sparkle in her eyes. She was old now, but the courage of the 'lone wolf' mare was undiminished.

'Where is Mirri?' he asked suddenly.

'Mirri died,' Bel Bel answered sadly. 'It will be my turn soon. My great wish is that my bones should bleach up high on the Ramshead.'

'And mine, too, some day,' Thowra said. 'What does The Brolga mean to do now? Stay here, or go back to his grounds on the Brindle Bull?'

'I don't know. He may fancy this mountain and hunt you out.'

'Hunt me out!'

'Yes. You couldn't beat him in a fight. He'd like Golden, too, you know that.'

'Oh well,' Thowra said. 'I'll wait and see where he goes, and what the men do.'

'I wouldn't wait. I'd go before the men come after you for your and the filly's beautiful cream hides, or before The Brolga kills you for both.' And Bel Bel was gone as silently as she had come, fading into the dark and the storm, vanishing behind the beating, wind-twisted boughs of the snow gums.

Thowra thought over what she had said. His mother knew so much, and all she had taught him had been good. He knew it would be better to go now, taking his herd away under cover of the night and the wild rain.

Ghost-like, he flitted back through the scrub; his herd followed him out. All through the night they travelled, up and down steep slopes, over rocks, across streams, along the soft, snowgrass glades, around the top of Paddy Rush's Bogong and down the other side; up and down and along rougher and rougher country.

Dawn came, and across a break in the stormy eastern sky a flock of brown teal winged their way. There was water close, plenty of water in the Crackenback River and many small creeks, but the grass grew only in odd tussocks, and the herd was very hungry.

Thowra led them on and on. 'There must be better grazing than this somewhere,' he thought. Down on the river there might be more grass, but men came there. The only thing to do was to cut away from the river, and see what lay in the hills.

In the weeks that followed, Thowra taught Golden all he could about the bush, about keeping herself hidden, about making no sound, and leaving no track.

One night, Boon Boon came to him.

'There is not enough food here for mares that are feeding hungry foals,' she said. 'We are getting thin and weak, and our foals do not grow enough.'

Thowra, too, was tired of the rough, uninteresting country, and of always feeling hungry.

'We'll go then,' he said, 'back to Paddy Rush's Bogong.'

When they got back to the mountains, he did not lead his herd straight to the grazing grounds. He left them hidden some distance away, and went up himself, late in the evening, examining the ground, the grass, the shrubs, all the way for any tracks of other horses, wild or tame.

The only signs he saw were weeks old. When he carefully peered into the grazing ground, there was no one there, and as he walked all over it, looking and sniffing with the greatest thoroughness, he realised that no horses had been there for at least three weeks.

He went back for the herd.

After the sparse grazing on the hills down the river, the mares never lifted their heads from the sweet grass. They fed all day without ceasing. Thowra and Golden, too, were very hungry, but not with the urgent hunger of the mares with foals at foot, so when Thowra started off to have another look round, Golden followed him.

Only scattered cattle could be seen over on the main range, but down on the crossing of the Crackenback there was a small mob of horses.

'Storm!' said Thowra excitedly, and started down to meet him, as usual going where he could leave no tracks and in timber where he would be invisible from the other side of the river.

It was late afternoon when the two horses met. Red sunlight gilded Thowra as he playfully ran to meet his half-brother, his brother of the wind and the rain.

Storm reared up, too, a magnificent bay horse now, and they nipped each other joyfully, cavorted and danced. At last, when their greetings were over, Thowra asked:

'Are you coming to the grazing ground?'

'For a night or perhaps two,' Storm answered. 'The men are looking everywhere for you and Golden. And anyway, there will be too many of us.'

As they climbed up the hill, Thowra reflected how his theft of Golden had made life very dangerous and uncomfortable — how everyone said so, and yet no one seemed to blame him for taking her. He remembered that night at the Dead Horse hut, when he had first rubbed noses with her through the rails, and knew he would steal her all over again if he had to. He looked back at her, saw her putting her neat hooves carefully where he put his, saw her outlined in burning gold by the setting sun. She was lovely, and she was his.

Storm had four mares and foals with him. It would mean quite a number of them on the grazing ground if they all stayed together. Storm was probably wise not to stay long, but, now that they were together, he realised how much he had missed his company.

'Where have you just come from?' he asked Storm.

'The back of the Brindle Bull.'

'What's going on there?'

'Well, men are always appearing everywhere. They don't usually bother about us ordinary-coloured horses, but you can never be sure. Also, there's no room for anyone else but The Brolga.' Then, as he walked along beside Thowra, he added, 'I didn't really expect to find you here. I wouldn't be surprised if The Brolga doesn't come over and fight you for Golden — and, anyway, the men will come here soon.'

'I couldn't find enough good grass anywhere else, but I like this country,' said Thowra, 'and I know all the hiding places.'

They went steadily on up the hill, not hurrying the mares and foals, and keeping well inside the timber. They did not see a man sitting absolutely still on a chestnut horse high up on a rocky crag. The man stared and stared at the movement in the timber, then he, too, went on up the mountain.

Only a man who had begun to know something of the silver brumby's cunning would have guessed that he was there in the trees — that the faint suggestion of movement in the timber meant horses led by 'Silver'. This man was Thowra's old enemy, the man on the black horse. The last of the daylight went, then, but the man had seen enough.

About an hour later, an almost full moon rose over the eastern hills, throwing its eerie light into the clearings and long glades, making strange shadows among the trees, leaving pools of darkness in deep hollows or gullies. The wild horses went on up through the timber, never having to move in clear country until they were nearly at the grazing ground.

As a matter of course, Thowra stopped and looked cautiously out through the trees before he led the other horses into the bright moonlight. This time the man was well hidden, and he clearly saw the beautiful cream stallion step out of the trees; the man held his breath when he saw, just behind the stallion, the filly, Golden.

The horses went through the moonlit clearing and into a gully filled with black sallee trees and were lost to view again, among the long, drooping leaves, the dark boughs and trunks, the festoons of old man's beard.

The man waited a while and then rode across the clear ground into the black sallees and followed the horses up the hill.

The herd was peacefully spread out in the wide valley when Thowra got back to them. Little foals lay asleep on the grass, sleeping mares standing over them. But Boon Boon was wide awake and neighing softly. When she saw the number of horses with Thowra she moved nervously around and stood over her little creamy foal. When they were all down in the moon-filled valley there was quite a mob of horses.

It was Thowra who first heard the jangle of a bit. He looked up and saw the horse and its rider.

'Go!' he urged. 'Split up! Don't stay together!' When Golden tried to come with him he bared his teeth and turned her in another direction. A man by himself might get confused in the moonlight, and be unable to make up his mind which horse to follow. If he chased Golden, Thowra thought he might manage to cut in and confuse him — and he felt extremely confident of evading a rope.

The man did chase Golden, of course. He had made up his mind to go for her, thinking that perhaps if he caught her and tied her up, he might get her brumby stallion later. He was gaining on Golden, and had got his lasso ready, when there were suddenly two creamies galloping ahead of him, and, as soon as the second one was there, they began to twist and weave, and dodge in a way that made it almost impossible to keep them separate in his mind. But this man had learnt a lot since he first used to hunt Thowra. For one thing, he had become skilled with the rope. Several times, as they galloped, he could have lassoed Thowra — and Thowra knew this — but it was Golden he really wanted.

Just before they reached the trees would be the danger time. Then, Thowra knew, the man might rope either of them rather than lose both.

Thowra's heart was thudding with fear and anger. The line of trees, black in the moonlight, was still some yards off. The man was almost alongside.

'Stop suddenly and swing right round, then towards the trees again,' he told Golden as he stopped and ran straight across the front of the pursuing horse.

The man thought very quickly and decided that he would not get Golden before she reached the timber and its concealing shadows. The rope went whistling through the moonlight and round Thowra's neck.

With a squeal of rage and terror the stallion galloped faster than he had ever galloped before, straight for the trees, and instead of being able to hold him, the man and his horse were dragged with him in his crazy gallop.

Thowra, maddened by the cutting rope on his neck, and the sudden, desperate fear of being caught, could only think of the trees, and the sheltering darkness underneath them. With branches stinging his face, his flanks, and whipping down his rump, he raced in amongst them. He was too frightened to plan, but without thinking lowered his head, and shot down a tunnel in the snow gums.

He could hear a great crashing behind him and the man's voice. Then the rope went slack. For a while he barely understood that the man was no longer holding him. The rope was still round his neck, terrifying him.

Often the end of it caught on something, and pulled him up with a jerk. He did not realise his danger, but kept on in his wild flight. At last he calmed down; there was no longer a horse following him. Slowly he slackened speed and stopped. By a miracle the trailing end of rope was still hanging free. Now he tried to get it off, but the noose had pulled tight around his neck and he couldn't loosen it. He tried desperately to shake it off, not wanting to waste time in case the man followed him again. Also, he wondered where Golden was.

He struck across the hillside through the timber, but by now he was able to understand from the snagging of the long rope that, for once, he would be safer in the open grass country. Out in the long glade he trotted in a direction he hoped might lead him to Golden. He knew she would stay in the timber and wondered whether it was safe to neigh softly — otherwise he might miss her.

He neighed and stood still to listen. There was no sound, no sound to the side or in front of him, and no sound from behind where the man must be.

Trees threw long shadows across the glade. Within the timber there was heavy darkness, but on the outer fringe each tree danced silver in a soft breeze, like living things, the moving legs of a hundred creamy horses dancing to mountain music.

Thowra trotted on. Before he had gone very far he stopped and neighed again, his ears trembling forward to catch the faintest reply. Then it came on the breeze, and it was definitely Golden answering, and then he heard the deeper call of Boon Boon.

With a snort of relief, Thowra broke into a canter, though not so fast that he would be brought up with a terrible jerk if the rope caught in a bush.

He neighed again, once, and they answered him; then at last he was with them. Boon Boon propped and shied away as she saw the rope trailing from his neck, but Golden nibbled at his shoulder for a second and then began to work on undoing the tight slipknot with her teeth.

It didn't take long for Golden to remove the rope. Thowra was free! The scent on the breeze was sweeter, the cold glitter of moonlight on the free-fluttering leaves was thrilling, the touch of the snowgrass underfoot, and the sweet taste of the creekwater — all perhaps better than they had ever been before.

Thowra drank and drank, as though he would fill himself with the freedom he had so nearly lost.

Horse hunt: man hunt

That night Thowra's herd did not gather all together, and in the morning he went back to the grazing ground to see if he could find them.

The air was fresh and clear, renewed by the night. Thowra felt his old urge to leap on to the top of a crag and trumpet out his joy in being alive and free. He saw little curls of mist rise up from the river and puff away into nothingness in the breeze; he heard lyrebirds calling in the thickets round a creek, and his heart seemed to stop for a second when one mimicked the crack of a stockwhip. Then he lost his panic as the mimicking voice whistled and then barked like a dog. The man had never had a dog; it was just Menura, the lyrebird, having fun in the early morning.

He moved so quietly and carefully that a dingo mother playing with her fat puppies in a patch of sunlight did not hear him coming.

'Never mind, old woman, I won't hurt your beautiful children,' he said to her. 'Tell me, have you seen sign of man near here?'

'A man on his own two legs went towards the river a mile from here, leading a lame horse, late last night. You might be able to smell his blood. He had cut his head, and his horse, too, bled from the shoulder.'

Thowra nodded his thanks, snuffed at the pups, and said again, with much politeness, how beautiful they were. Then he went on his way with more confidence.

He came on the man's trail, and shied with sudden fear at the smell. A jay mocked him from the trees above.

There was still no sign of the three missing mares and their foals, or of Storm and his herd.

A silent gang-gang threw a gum-nut down on to his back. Thowra jumped and then shook himself with annoyance. Up above him, from the direction of the grazing ground, he suddenly heard a sound that made his coat prickle and the sweat break out behind his ears. He went on with far greater caution than before, circling round a little so that he could look into the grazing ground from the dense cover of some scrub.

The green valley lay below him, filled with early morning sunshine — and with a mob of horses. Running excitedly to and fro, sniffing at every trail, was The Brolga.

Thowra stood absolutely still. He must have time to see if his own mares were there, and think what to do next. He knew he was hidden by snow-gum branches, and so peered through the thick leaves and saw that his own mares were not there. He also saw that Bel Bel was not with The Brolga's herd and wondered if she had gone to warn him, or simply remained at the Brindle Bull.

Then he saw The Brolga pick up the trail he had made with Golden the night before, the trail of the man chasing them. Now he knew he would have to move, and very quickly, or The Brolga might find what remained of his herd. He hurried away, as fast as he could go without making a noise or leaving a trace.

He went in as straight a line as he could towards the place where he had left Golden and Boon Boon, and all the time he listened, he looked, and he sniffed the keen air for any strange scent that would tell him The Brolga — or anyone else — was near. Twice, a long way ahead of him, he thought he saw something moving, but he decided it might be a silver-grey kangaroo, or perhaps just a shadow. Then he saw it again. He looked at the ground; there was no track. He stopped and listened; there was no sound. He sniffed and just then the breeze blew back to him. Unmistakably came the scent, a scent he knew well, a scent that rose right out of his eternal memory. His nostrils quivered, his top lip curled right back. Who was it? And then, of course, he knew. Bel Bel was ahead of him. He went on, faster, to catch her.

He saw her, fairly clearly ahead, saw her suddenly swing round and listen. He showed himself, and they trotted to meet each other.

'Where are you going, little old mother?' he asked.

'Searching for you, my son, to bring you warning.'

'I have seen The Brolga,' said Thowra, 'and he is already onto the trail that Golden and I left last night when a man chased us. I'm going to join what is left of my herd, and I must waste no time.'

'I'll come with you a little way.'

They trotted on together through the trees and through the mint bush that was starred with pink-mauve flowers. Here the trees' bark was splashed with red and green. There it was pure silver where a clear creek crossed their path, and where there was a spongy swamp over which they must not leave a track.

'Soon I must turn back,' said Bel Bel, 'but, before I leave you, tell me, where are you going to take your herd?'

'Over to the hanging valley on the Brindle Bull, and when The Brolga goes away from here, we shall return.'

'You must not fight him again this year,' Bel Bel answered. 'Wait until next year, when you will have reached your full strength.'

'I am already faster than he is,' said Thowra.

'Next time you fight him,' Bel Bel said, 'it will be either you or The Brolga, so before you fight again be sure you have all your strength and all your cunning. I must go now.' She nuzzled him briefly on the wither, and then went off through the trees.

Thowra looked back over his shoulder several times and saw her still trotting on and then vanishing from sight. It did not seem strange to him that he and his mother had never forgotten each other. Other mares forgot their foals, foals forgot their mothers, but Bel Bel, the creamy mare, had never forgotten her cream colt foal, nor had he forgotten her, though he was now a stallion almost at his full strength.

He hurried on. The Brolga, with no need to hide his tracks, might go faster than he — and The Brolga must not find Golden and Boon Boon. Bel Bel was right; if he and The Brolga fought now for Golden, The Brolga would surely kill him.

Thowra did reach Golden and Boon Boon before The Brolga found them, but up the hillside he could hear the big, grey stallion, still following the trail.

Thankfully, he saw that the rest of his herd were with the two mares. Without wasting a moment, he mustered them and drew them back up the hill and round on to the Crackenback Fall. He had to risk their movement through the bush being seen by any men over on the main range, rather than risk passing too close to

The Brolga and having him pick up their tracks immediately.

It was just bad luck that one of the foals started a rock rolling down a long, stony slope, and worse luck that the rock kept going and gaining speed and collecting other leaping, skipping stones with it so that there was quite a clatter. There was more than enough noise to make The Brolga stop and listen. Just then a gust of wind blew sharply from the northwest and carried their scent straight to the trembling, sniffing, grey nostrils.

Thowra heard the snort of breath being drawn through those back-curled nostrils, and knew The Brolga would be after them. He looked around for the best line of country, and saw a long rocky spine, tree-covered and precipitous — a place where the nimblest-footed horse would have a big advantage. A hawk was gliding over it.

'The Ridge of the Hawk,' thought Thowra. 'That is the place for me.' He turned to the mares, 'Now go,' he said. 'Go quietly but fast. Go to the hanging valley on the Brindle Bull and wait there for me. I may be a long time. I will stay here and try to get The Brolga to follow me, or I will fight and run to stop him from catching you. Go!'

He watched the mares and foals fade away through the bush, watched the creamy filly, Golden, as the sunlight dappled her in glory. Then they had gone, and he waited till he heard the sound of The Brolga coming. When he knew he was close, he went very quietly and hid in thick trees on the first knoll of the Ridge of the Hawk.

The Brolga cantered into view, fierce grey head up, ears pricked — listening, not watching the tracks.

To stop him looking down and possibly seeing where the herd had gone, Thowra kicked a rock and sent it bounding down the ridge.

The Brolga swung towards the sound. Thowra moved just enough for his creamy hide to show through the trees — to show twice — then he stood still.

The Brolga gathered himself into a grey curve, like an iron hoop, and shot towards the rocky ridge.

Thowra watched him, deep-chested, powerful, the great, strong legs stretching over snowgrass and bushes. Then he went tearing down the ridge, making enough noise for ten, not just for two.

He could hear The Brolga crashing down behind him, the heavier, older horse not managing to take the rough, steep ridge so fast. Just then, he saw that the ridge split into two a little distance below, and he determined to wait, where it divided, and see if The Brolga would go headlong past him.

He hid in a cleft between two immense rocks, having first kicked a collection of boulders down the northernmost ridge. The boulders bounded down as though a small herd of brumbies were flying down the ridge. The Brolga came, and then hurtled past. Thowra was just going to move out of his cleft in the rocks and go down the other ridge, when all of a sudden he heard The Brolga's headlong gallop slacken and stop, and, before he could get more than a few yards away from the division in the ridge, The Brolga, in a fury, was charging upwards, again.

For a second, Thowra heard the echo of Bel Bel's voice in his ears — 'it will be either you or The Brolga' — but he could not run away, because then The Brolga would soon guess that Golden was not with him, and start looking around for her tracks again. He would have to dodge and hide, take up as much time as he could, while the others got away, and lead The Brolga as far as possible from any tracks they might have left.

Quiet as a ghost, he moved among the rocks, always being careful to leave a way of escape behind as well as in front. Then he stood, trembling with excitement, his beautiful silver-cream hide streaked darkly with sweat. The Brolga was near the top. There was quiet for a minute, perhaps for two minutes, and Thowra did not dare move over to see where The Brolga was.

Something that was half a sound, or a sound he half heard, seemed to be very near him. Then all of a sudden he was staring into The Brolga's fierce eyes from behind the rock. He just had time to notice the red, fiery flesh inside the dilated, grey nostrils before he had sprung backwards into thick heather scrub, turned round and away. Only his speed could save him now.

The Brolga was right behind him. Thowra felt his breath, hot, scorching like a north wind, but he also felt his own strength surge through him.

To the hawk that had returned and was hanging in the air above the ridge it might have seemed a flashing second in which either horse could have won the desperate race — either the enormous, powerful grey, or the silver-cream, so lithe and swift. That second, though, which flashed past the hawk, was one of wild effort to the two horses. The Brolga was straining every ounce of his great strength to get close enough to Thowra to bite or strike. Thowra was calling up reserves of energy that he had never used before, trying to leap away down the rocky slope — to leap away and live. To each horse perhaps that second seemed an hour, or a day, or a lifetime.

Suddenly Thowra felt himself, as one steel ball, his legs beneath him filled with an immeasurable power. He sprang, cleaving the air, almost from underneath the bounding grey, gathered himself together as he landed on a rock and sprang again. He was out of reach. A snow-gum branch whipped him across the flanks, he smelt the tang of the leaves. Just behind he could hear The Brolga's breath, but each leap took him farther out of reach.

He knew it was no use getting too far ahead. Soon would come the moment to stop and offer fight, to keep drawing The Brolga farther and farther away from the herd's tracks, lower and lower down the steep slope so that it would take him hours to climb back.

The Brolga was too angry to stop and think that it was really Golden he was after — or perhaps he felt in all his pounding blood that it was better to kill Thowra *now*. The screams of jays in a snow gum only made him angrier. He went plunging down after Thowra, crashing and stumbling over the boulders.

Thowra, nimble and swift, kept just ahead.

Right down to the Crackenback they went, Thowra in the heat of the chase forgetting all about his first and oldest enemy — man. And there, on the opposite bank, listening and watching, alert and on fairly fresh horses, were two men.

Thowra had seen the shining water and wanted to be in it. He had seen white sand stretching to the water at the crossing, and heather and the big white-flowered pimelia bush dipping to the water from the banks, but as he saw them he saw the men, and everything was instantly blurred by the horror of the situation. All he knew was that it would be better to go down-stream for a while, rather than try to get back uphill where the fresh horses would undoubtedly catch them very quickly. This all happened in one second — he saw the river, he saw the men, he forgot The Brolga, and he turned and fled.

The Brolga saw the men, and he turned, too, and followed Thowra as fast as he could go.

Clouds of white spray splashed up in the sunlight, as the men forced their horses fast through the river. Then there was a fantastic chase, a chase that became a legend among men, with many of the other tales of Thowra's extraordinary feats.

Thowra knew the country along the river well, and knew, too, many of the little valleys that stretched back into the hills where he and his herd had tried to find grass early in the spring. He thought he would keep to these valleys where trees, ferns and logs had fallen, where tea tree grew, covered with hanging moss and creepers, and the creeks wound invisible through this tangle of dead and living bush. He felt certain that he, so sure-footed and without a heavy man on his back, should be able to race even the far fresher horses through that leg-breaking, neck-breaking country.

When he was being chased by The Brolga he had not thought about the men, and now, chased by men, he forgot about The Brolga. He went at truly breakneck speed along the banks of the Crackenback, waiting till he found the particular creek and fern-filled valley up which he intended to turn.

He clattered perilously around a rocky outcrop that overhung the foaming water, he forced his way through and over a mass of fallen trees and driftwood left by floods, and all the time he could hear the crashing and clattering behind him of the pursuit. Not much farther, and he could turn away from the river and into the dark cleft of the valley where the Christmas bush and tea tree were flowering and where there was the hot, steamy smell of rotting fern, and wood, and leaves in the unmoving air.

His heart was thundering. How long it was that he had been galloping he did not know; he was tired, but at least Golden should be safely away by now, along with Boon Boon and the other mares and foals.

The men were very close as he turned into the valley. He heard a rope whistle, and leapt into a great thicket of tree ferns.

In all the layers of rotten logs and the old fern-trunks that were interlaced, back and forth, over the creek and across the valley floor, even Thowra stumbled and crashed, but he knew the men, with their tame horses, would never get through it as fast as he. There was hope now. He looked back once, just before he plunged into a tangle of the dark-barked swamp gum that was hung with green vines, laced with blanket bush and bracken, and he saw the men, on two bay horses, saw the vivid colour of their check shirts — and then he saw The Brolga. How was this going to end? If he got away from the men, could he ever get away from The Brolga? Would he escape only to be killed?

It was impossible to go very fast. Often he had to leap from one log to another; often he broke through rotting timbers into water or squelching black soil and steaming leaf mould. The heat was oppressive in this valley where no wind stirred, and Thowra had been forced to gallop twice for his life; first last night, when he also had the terror of being roped, and now, almost all the day, and he could feel his strength ebbing. But the sound behind him of the men and The Brolga was still there.

The sweat streamed off him. He knew he must drink soon. He made an enormous effort to get ahead enough to have time to stop and drink. He looked back and could see only one man behind The Brolga and both he and The Brolga were sufficiently far behind to give him a moment at a deep, dark pool. As he drank he wondered where the other man was. If he had tried going higher up, in the hope that the country would be so much clearer that he could race ahead and get right around the two brumbies, Thowra knew he was going to be disappointed; the sides of the valley were all deeply cut by tiny gorges and creeks, each one filled with a tangle of fallen timber or with rock, rubble and creepers.

Thowra drank with gasping gulps and then went on and on, and anyone watching him — seeing the lovely cream stallion leap on to a log, change feet and leap again, dance through a trap of branches lying this way and that — would hardly have known how exhausted he was. But, though he gained more distance from his pursuers, they still kept on coming. The chase was like a fantastic nightmare, slow-moving because none of the horses could go fast through the immense tangle.

At last he knew that there was much less noise behind him. He looked around, standing for a moment with heaving flanks, nostrils dilating with every shattering breath. There was only The Brolga to be seen, and he was still following.

Thowra knew another valley half a mile further on, that came in from the south. If he followed that it would give him a good short cut on the way back towards Golden and the rest of his herd on the Brindle Bull — but he was not going to let The Brolga follow him forever. Exhaustion rose through him in waves, and anger at The Brolga for having kept up the chase for such a long time.

He came to a small, peaty clearing. There he stopped and waited, his head thrown up proudly, even though he gasped for breath — at least he could snatch a few minutes rest while The Brolga plunged on up the valley through all the entanglement on the ground. As he stood waiting, the last glittering gleam reflected from the sunset died out of the valley.

Then a strange green glow began to flow through the deep valley; only the tall, slender ribbon gums stood out of the greenness in white majesty. Thowra looked around him, aware of the strange light, not knowing that he, too, stood out in pale splendour like the ribbon gums — the silver stallion indeed, as the men who had first seen him at night, by the light of the campfire, had named him.

There he stood, in the little clear patch of ground by the creek, surrounded by the interwoven green bush, with the tall white pillars of trees, and the green light. There he stood, waiting for The Brolga.

The Brolga came, striving to gallop towards his enemy, but slowed down by all the tangle on the valley floor. His breath was rasping in and out, and Thowra had had time for his own breathing to have lessened to deep, pounding breaths. The Brolga was exhausted and so was Thowra, but here, below the white ribbon gum pillars, with the flowing green light becoming deeper and deeper as evening approached, they must fight.

It was not the fight Bel Bel had predicted — that was still to come. It was a weird fight between two horses that were too tired to hurt each other, a fight that went on, in silence, till they both dropped down at the farthest corners of the clearing, unable to move. Night came then, and the green light became grey, and then darkness covered the two stallions where they lay.

A fox barked nervously, and suddenly, from above, there was the chattering bark of a great, black flying phalanger silhouetted high up on the white trunk of a

139

ribbon gum. The phalanger took off and went gliding right across the exhausted stallions. A mopoke, disturbed by his noise, gave his first call of the night, 'Mopoke, Mopoke' echoing in the dark-enclosed valley.

Gradually, there came all the creeping, rustling sounds that are heard in the stillness of the night, as wombats climbed out of their holes and padded softly along a tree-trunk that formed a bridge across the creek, as possums climbed among leafy branches, as the snakes — the evil ones — wriggled along the ground.

Thowra lay so still that a possum passed quite close as it went from tree to tree. The exhaustion of the horses soon changed into deep sleep and they lay there, their feet still gathered underneath them, as they had dropped.

The slow hours of the night passed, the stars moved across the sky above the net of leaf and branch that was the ceiling of the valley, and even though Thowra was fast asleep, Bel Bel's training of cunning did not leave him. Before too many stars had disappeared above him, Thowra woke and got stiffly to his feet.

He looked over towards the heap in the darkness which was The Brolga, then moved silently away, turning up the southward valley that would take him on the first part of his journey towards the Brindle Bull and his herd. Like a pale, floating apparition he went on and on through the night.

In the first grey dawn The Brolga woke and found himself alone, with no track to show him where Thowra had gone; alone, and far away from his own country.

Now Golden is the prize

Slowly, through the bright, hot summer, yet another legend began to grow up round Thowra, a legend the men started to feel was true — and one that the horses believed absolutely.

It was said that bad luck came to everyone, either man or horse, who chased the silver brumby stallion. Hadn't plenty of men been hurt and their horses lamed? Hadn't one lost the beautiful filly, Golden? And Arrow, the horses said, had been killed. Surely this Thowra had a magic quality. Not only had he escaped from two men on fresh horses when he was exhausted, but he had vanished.

And just like the wind in a blizzard can twist and turn even wild horses until they are almost lost in the swirling snow, Thowra had twisted and turned The Brolga as they galloped, and The Brolga had woken in the weird first dawning, quite uncertain where he was.

Every horse was sure that Thowra, though a horse, was, in some magical way, part of the wind after which his mother had named him.

The men felt that something would surely happen to them if they chased him, but they could not resist trying to catch him. The Brolga felt that Thowra would defeat him, in some very unusual manner, but he longed for revenge — and he longed to make Golden the pride of his herd.

All summer the stockmen and The Brolga hunted Thowra and, if they saw him, they chased him. Thowra and his mares and foals were chased, but they always vanished. Sometimes they were heard, and yet not seen. If they left some tracks, these tracks would abruptly cease, as though they had all melted into the air. It was the mysteriousness of Thowra that made each stockman feel as if he must catch him.

Of all the horses running in the mountains, Bel Bel alone thought she knew the secret hiding place that enabled Thowra and his herd to disappear from all their hunters. When she heard how Thowra and his mares vanished, she wondered if he had rediscovered the deep valley that was like a cleft in the hills at the back of Paddy Rush's Bogong, the valley with the grassy Hidden Flat that could not be seen from the top. The valley where Yarraman and his herd had hidden after the men's brumby drive so many summers ago when Thowra and Storm were foals.

Old as she was, she decided to go off and see for herself if this was where he was hiding.

As she jogged along purposefully through the bush, she came on fresh tracks and recognised them as Storm's, so she followed him and found him with his mares, grazing peacefully. She whinnied and he lifted his noble bay head with a swift movement that reminded her of Mirri. Then the big stallion rubbed his nose on her neck.

'I'm looking for Thowra,' Bel Bel said.

'I also came this way feeling that I might find him,' said Storm, 'and yet I don't know why.'

'If you come with me, I think you will remember why

you have come this way.' Bel Bel nodded her old head. 'You have been here before, but you were very young. Mirri and I brought you and Thowra here when you were foals.'

Storm set off with the old creamy mare, carefully following her trackless way, because he knew they must not lead either The Brolga or any wandering stockmen to Thowra's hiding place.

Bel Bel scrambled down the cliff into the valley rather lower downstream than the grass flat, and she and Storm walked together up the rocky creek bed, or along narrow banks above the green water.

As she walked, Bel Bel was thinking that when autumn came she must go to the Ramshead Range, and there perhaps she would stay, for the time had come for the wild snow to cover her body. It was impossible that she should live as long as her cream and silver son. Perhaps, if she found him now, this would be the last time she would see him; perhaps they would meet again, high on the range, before the snows came.

When they rounded a bend in the rocky, foaming river, just where there were great high cliffs, they came on the Hidden Flat, a long, quite wide, green valley. Above it were high, steep sides where the ribbon gums grew, white and slim, among the grey-green peppermints, the tree ferns and the blanket bushes.

Bel Bel stopped and looked back at Storm. Storm was standing with one forefoot raised, his ears pricked, and with a puzzled expression in his eyes.

'I don't remember it,' he said, 'but I know I've been here before.'

Then into view, between two white ribbon gum pillars, stepped Thowra, followed by his herd.

Bel Bel stood, arching her neck with pride, looking suddenly like a young mare with her first foal — so beautiful was Thowra, his feet stepping high and gracefully, his head held with such majesty as he led his herd to water.

'It's no wonder,' she murmured, 'that man and horse are after him.' Then she and Storm went forward to greet him.

Thowra threw his head right up, his nostrils and eyes wild, as he heard their steps, but when he saw them, he neighed happily, and trotted towards them.

'Well, little old mother,' he said, rubbing her withers, 'you knew my hiding-place?' Then he exchanged nose rubs with Storm. 'And you, brother of the wild wind, did you know as well, or did Bel Bel bring you?'

'I brought him,' Bel Bel said. 'But, like you, he would have known the way in memory; long ago Mirri and I brought you here to hide.'

She walked over to greet Golden, because once Bel Bel herself had been the only cream mare in the mountains; she had been the one that was beautiful and sought after by stallions for their herds, and by men because of her colour and her strong, sure legs, which would have carried a stockman many miles over the mountains — but which never did. Now Golden was the prize, the famous and glorious mare, and Bel Bel must greet her and be proud that her son had captured — and held — her.

Thus it was that Bel Bel and Storm kept Thowra's secret of how he vanished from his hunters, and when they heard horses — or cattle — say, 'He is like wind — he must be partly a child of the wind — he comes from nowhere, he vanishes into nowhere,' they would smile to themselves. Yet they, too, half-believed that Thowra had become almost magic, even though Bel Bel knew that it was she who had woven a spell over him at birth, and given him his wisdom and his cunning, all that made him seem to have the wind's mystery.

When Bel Bel and Storm at last left Thowra at his Hidden Flat, Bel Bel said something that stayed in Thowra's memory.

'Maybe,' she said, 'I will see you up on the Ramshead before the snows come.'

As the days grew shorter, with summer turning to autumn and then to winter, he kept thinking of what she had said, and at last he set off to the face of Paddy Rush's Bogong that overlooked the range where he watched to see if the cattle mobs had gone, and when he saw no sign of man or beast, he collected his own herd and led them down, over the Crackenback and up on to the range.

He was so glad to be back in his own country that he almost forgot his feeling of uneasiness about Bel Bel. But as he was climbing up above the Dead Horse hut, one single hoofmark that he knew to be hers caught his eye. He didn't really go looking for her, he just had a feeling that if he visited all his old haunts he would surely find her. So he climbed up the range, stepping happily up the steep laneways of snowgrass between the tors and then climbing from rock to rock in the tors themselves, to some high rock from which he could survey miles of the lovely country. His coat shone, in spite of getting thick for winter, and his muscles rippled beneath it.

Everything he saw — every cliff and crag, every rock or grassy glade — he recognised from the past, and yet he saw them now with a new intensity. He had trained himself never to forget any feature of the country through which he travelled, and now each tor, each weathered rock, was stamped on his memory like a photograph, and if he had to gallop through that photograph — escaping from either man or horse — he knew exactly where he could place each hard, strong hoof, exactly where he could leap, exactly where he could twist and turn.

All the world was very quiet, high up there on the range. It was rare that any other horses, except Storm and his herd, ever came as high, and most animals were already heading lower, anyway, before the snow came.

They saw dingoes, and occasionally a red fox, whose thick coat was ready for winter and stood out against the grey-green grass. Thowra noticed how busy the scurrying insects were, from the tiny ants to the great bright blue and red mountain grasshoppers — but he, too, knew that it was going to be a heavy winter. A great deal of snow would fall to cover the bones of an old creamy mare if she chose to die up there among the high-lifted peaks of the range.

Though the sun was shining, the first day they were up on the range a faint, milky haze was spreading over the sky the next morning. Already there was the winter hush of expectancy in the air.

By the second day Thowra had still not found Bel Bel, so he headed up yet higher, leading his herd through the chill dawn. The quietness was intense up there — there was no bird call, no rustle of leaves, not even the sound of a creek. Nothing moved except the silent-footed herd.

Into this still, quiet world, through an opening in the rocks, high above and to one side, burst Bel Bel, galloping for her life.

In a flash, Thowra knew that a man, or men, were

after her and that she had taken the rough way through the Ramsheads, hoping that she would not lead her hunter to himself.

Quickly, Thowra and his herd made themselves invisible among rocks, and from his hiding place Thowra watched. He could only see one man, on a big chestnut horse, a well-bred looking horse, and Bel Bel — Bel Bel galloping like the old mare she was, tired and not so nimble, depending on her own cunning and courage, rather than on her speed.

Then Thowra did something that no wild horse could be expected to do and which all the stockmen for ever afterwards spoke of as just another example of the mysteriousness of Thowra — he left his hidden mares and went off swiftly and silently on a line that would take him just below Bel Bel. He aimed to reach a certain clear snowgrass platform among the rocks before she did.

He stood in the centre of this clear snowgrass and when he knew the man on his galloping chestnut would be able to see him clearly, he reared up and screamed the wild, triumphant scream of a stallion glorying in his own strength.

The man pulled up his horse on its haunches and stared at the gleaming stallion. Then, just as Thowra knew he would, he forgot Bel Bel, dug his spurs into the chestnut's flanks, and went after him at racing speed.

Thowra switched round and led him right away from Bel Bel — and away from Golden and his other mares, too.

Perhaps that stockman had recognised Bel Bel as the mother of Thowra, but he could not have hoped that Thowra would try to save her as he had, because no man would have believed — till then — that a full-grown brumby stallion would remember his mother. Quite certainly that stockman would not have expected Thowra to draw him off and then lead him on such a terrifying gallop — a plan that could only have been devised by the most cunning of minds.

Thowra was enjoying himself. This rock and snowgrass world was his world. Not far from here was the great granite overhang under which he had been born. This was the country Bel Bel and Mirri had loved so much, the country in which he and Storm had romped as foals, and later, as irresponsible young colts.

He knew it all so well, the wild, high land, where wedge-tail eagles planed overhead, and dingoes howled to the moon at night, where a silver stallion could leap from rock to rock right to the top of a granite tor, and scream his defiance at the pursuing man.

So Thowra raced ahead of the man and mocked him as he had once raced with Arrow and mocked him. Up and down the ribbon lanes of snowgrass that lay between the tors, he went leaping through tumbled rocks, or up a tor, jumping from block to block. By now, Bel Bel had stopped to watch. She saw her son, as she had once known she would, galloping free and wild, with his silver mane and tail foaming in the cold sunlight, like the spray of a gleaming waterfall. She saw him in all his perfection, poised on the top of a tor, noble, cream head thrown up, as his defiant cry rang out, a great strong-shouldered, deep-chested stallion, not a fault in him, not in his powerful quarters, nor his strong, clean legs; a silver horse against the sky, free and wild, never marked by saddle, or girth, or spur, his speed never checked by a bit.

For a while she lost sight of them, but after some minutes she saw Thowra galloping along a narrow, rocky ledge below the South Ramshead, then along a ridge against the skyline, mane and tail streaming out like spun silver.

Bel Bel trotted across the mountainside. Again she lost sight of them and, tired out, thought she would make towards the sandy cave where long ago she had put her cream foal to shelter from the storm. On and on she trotted until suddenly, as she was getting near the cave, she heard the thundering of hooves. Quickly she hid herself in among some rocks. Outlined against the milky clouds was the great overhang of granite under which Thowra had been born.

As she watched, Thowra, all cream and silver strength, cut the air above that granite rock, leapt, and landed twelve feet below, on soft snowgrass that had been his first bed, and went galloping on.

Bel Bel saw the man on the rock's edge, trying to pull his horse back on its haunches and stop, but his speed was too great. The chestnut hurtled over, stumbling and grazing himself badly on landing. The man somersaulted off and the horse went madly on. Stirrups flapping, reins trailing, he vanished into the trees below.

The man lay still for awhile and then got slowly to his feet and started down the mountain. Bel Bel moved towards the cave, making no sound, leaving no track, and feeling supremely happy. The winter snows would come now, to cover the bones of an old mare. She had seen Thowra as she had always known he would be — a king of mountain horses.

Thowra's search

The winter snows came in a wild and tremendous blizzard. Thowra knew the storm was coming and he moved his herd down to his end of the Cascades.

As he led them through the wind-moving snow gums — hearing the continual tree murmur, the word of a storm coming — he thought that this might be as heavy a winter as the one when he was a foal, and Yarraman had had to take his herd farther south. If he, Thowra, had to go south for grazing country, he would have trouble with The Brolga. Bel Bel's warning was still strong in his mind. He must not fight The Brolga till next spring, so when he had to go lower, he took them down into the western foothills, finding little patches of grass country.

It was an unusual winter. Snow fell deeply, in almost every storm, but on the lower levels, it was often followed by warm rain that melted the snow, and all the foothills were filled with the sound of roaring streams. Up on the range, snow lay thick and white, drifting across the mouth of the cave, covering in a blanket the place where Thowra had been born.

Thowra had expected Golden's owner to come looking for her when the snow kept the wild horses low in the mountains, but as the rivers rose and stayed high because of frequent rain, he knew there were uncrossable barriers on every side — either rivers in flood, or deep snow. He remembered the story of the four people wearing long narrow boards on their feet that carried them over the snow, but these people had come so long ago ... and Golden's stockman had not looked as if he could even walk far; perhaps he could only ride a horse. Untroubled, Thowra found plenty of patches of grazing country for his hungry herd over towards the stockmen's track from Groggin to the Dead Horse hut.

For months the great winds of winter blew, the rivers roared, the snow fell in silent flakes. Trees, bowed with the white blanket, sometimes snapped and broke in the night. The black cockatoos flew crying through the mountain ash forests and up where the snow gums bent and twisted in the wind.

Once, when the snow was packed hard by the wind, Thowra left his herd and went up into that great world of white, where even the rocks were plastered with glittering ice patterns, and the leaves on the snow-gum branches were encased in ice so that they rang together, as the wind blew, and played wild music to which a silver stallion could dance on the snow.

Golden had wanted to go with him but he had refused fiercely to take her. He knew that she was getting restless — but he had seen Bel Bel and Mirri get restless and go off from the herd before their foals were born.

All the same he did begin to worry about the way she had started to wander, for he knew she was not sufficiently bush-wise to be alone — also she was too beautiful, and his greatest prize.

Thowra knew he would not be able to bear to let her be far from the herd, or far from him. He still had no understanding of how Golden was often torn between all the training and security of her former life, and the freedom of the wild life with him. Nor did he understand that, as the time for the birth of her first foal drew close, Golden began to think of her old master and his kindness, of the food he had given her, and the safety of yards and well-grassed paddocks.

Gradually the long, roaring blizzards of winter, the wailing winds, and the short days, the bright frosts, and the bitter cold, changed to the swift-swinging spring storms, a hotter sun, and daylight remaining longer on the hills. The sky, on a fine day, was a deeper colour, and no longer had that glass-blue, brittle look. There was the first faint upthrust of growth on grass and shrub, the first soft, scent-laden breeze from the lower slopes. It was getting near the time for the young animals to be born. Two little dun-coloured foals arrived. Then one morning Golden had gone.

Thowra called the rest of his herd together and led them off to follow her tracks. He was amazed and pleased to find how little track she had left. She hadn't got the printless hooves of Bel Bel, but she had learnt her lessons in bush wisdom better than he thought.

Golden was heading for the high country, and after a while her track led them on to the stock route to Dead Horse hut. Then Thowra saw the clear track of two shod horses and, in sudden, unbelieving panic, knew this track was a little older than Golden's. The men were ahead of her and she was following them.

He hardly stopped to wonder how the men had crossed the deep, rushing snow-waters in the river. He could not know that this year Golden's owner had left horses in a paddock on the mountain side of the river and that the men had constructed little wire bridges over which they could walk. Golden's master had got across on foot to his horses and come out to the mountains earlier than ever before.

The little foals made the herd's pace slow. At last, Thowra became so worried that he decided to hide his mares right off the track and go on quickly to find her.

Soon after he had left them it began to rain heavily, and in a short time all tracks were washed away — even the tracks of the shod horses. No scent lingered either. By the time that Thowra, dripping wet and muddy, was near Dead Horse hut, he knew that Golden could have left the track in many places, and he set out to try and find her near the hut.

There was no sign of her, no sign at all, and when he got too close to the hut, both the man's stockhorse and packhorse neighed wildly and raced in excitement. Twice, Thowra saw the man come to the door, but probably the driving rain kept him from coming farther.

Thowra searched all day, taking care not to go so close to the tame horses again, but he never found a track nor a sign of Golden.

After midday he went back down the stock route, looking for her on either side. Just at evening, the rain stopped and an odd mixture of watery blue and pink appeared in the grey sky. The track still ran like a little creek, the bush dripped dismally and there was no trace of Golden. Thowra was feeling both concerned and miserable when he went back to Dead Horse Gap.

All through the night he searched near the hut. Once he felt sure that Golden's scent came to him on the light breeze, and he went in the direction from which it came, but still he found nothing. Every time he got near the yards the other horses neighed, and he knew the man came out several times to see what was upsetting them.

At last dawn broke and as the light came Thowra was standing, hidden by trees, on a little knoll not far from the hut. Suddenly he was sure he heard a faint whinny. The man came out of the hut and stood looking up the Dead Horse Ridge. Then Thowra saw a movement in the trees above the hut.

In a tiny clearing he could just make out Golden standing with a little cream foal at her feet.

The whinny sounded again — this time he was sure of it. He saw the man walk slowly and quietly towards Golden. Then Thowra could keep silent no longer. He threw up his head and gave the great cry of a stallion to his mate.

The man hesitated once and then kept walking slowly forward, extended his hand towards the lovely cream mare. Thowra watched in bitter silence. The man drew closer and finally put his hand on Golden's neck, petting and stroking her. Golden seemed to be nuzzling him with her soft nose. Then she bent and nuzzled the foal as though showing it off, and the man bent down to it but did not touch it. Presently she nosed the foal on to its trembling legs.

As the man put his arm round her neck and started leading her towards the hut, Thowra gave another despairing cry. Golden raised her head and looked once in his direction, and then let herself be led on by her old master, the little foal wobbling beside her.

In the greatest anguish, Thowra saw her go with the man into the high-fenced yard in which she had been that first night, and heard her grateful whinnying as the man came out of the hut with a tin of food.

Thowra took one last look at the lovely mare with her foal — his foal — and went off quickly, silently back to the herd. Through the bush he went, a proud-stepping, beautiful stallion, in the prime of his life, cream and silver, dappled by light and shade as pale shafts of sunlight from the cloudy sky fell onto him through the grey-green gum leaves.

He found the herd where he had left it, the mares rather troubled at the length of time he had been away — and astounded when he told them what he had seen. But at the end of his story, Boon Boon nodded wisely and said, 'She might want to go to her old master out of care for herself and her new-born foal, but she'll want to come back in a few days. Let us find some grazing on a sunny slope not too far from the Gap, and you can go back and see.'

Thowra nodded, but all he could think of was the high fence. 'She might be able to jump out again, but she'll never leave her foal,' he said.

Realising that the man knew he was about and that he would be trying to get Golden again, Thowra understood that his usual great care to leave no trail must be doubled. But he could not bear to stay away from the hut for long in case the man tried to lead Golden and her foal straight to the lower country.

Thowra felt sure bad weather was coming, so he found some better grazing for his herd, lower down, and facing the sun so that the grass was already getting its spring sweetness.

At dark he went back to the hut. Golden was still in the yard. He did not go up to the fence, but simply waited until morning to see if the man was making preparations for going out of the mountains.

The man only caught his stockhorse, not the packhorse, and Thowra saw him fix a lasso to his saddle. So that was the day's plan — a hunt for the silver stallion! Thowra knew that he must now really act like a ghost horse. He moved away, leaving no trace to tell that he had ever been there.

Each night he went back, hoping Golden would show some sign of wanting to escape, but Golden only noticed her foal or, when the man appeared, showed gratitude to him for food and water. Her coat was beginning to shine; the foal was getting stronger.

Then, out of a fair and sunny afternoon, the black clouds began to roll up with speed and force. Thowra went up to the hut to see what was happening. Would the man forget he wanted to catch the silver brumby and take his mare and foal and race the storm to the lowlands?

But the storm was going to race everyone. A lashing wind was already bringing snow, when Thowra hid himself in the trees above the Gap and watched. The man came on his horse, hurrying down from the direction of Bob's Ridge where he must have been watching for him. Suddenly great swirls of snow almost blotted him from sight. The wind began to roar through the Gap, and the sound of it in the trees higher up was menacing.

Thowra shivered. This was going to be a bad storm. He saw the man stand looking in the direction of the wind, saw him glance back to Golden and the foal who were racing nervously round the little yard. Then the man walked over to the yard and turned Golden and the foal through the gate into the horse paddock where there was shelter.

All at once, the noise of the storm filled the air completely. It was as if nothing was left but its enormous roar, for the wild-driven snow hid the ground and the groaning trees hid all the world, blotted out everything but the immense noise.

'For the wind I have named you,' Bel Bel had said, and Thowra, thrashed and torn at by the great storm, moved out of the trees and felt his way to the horse-paddock fence. Just as he reached it it seemed that he was going to be blown from his feet; he knew then that he would not possibly be able to jump the fence in this blinding storm. The wild force of the wind lifted him and threw him against a fence post, and the roar was louder still and filled with a new sound of crashing trees and branches.

Thowra felt choked with terror, but he heard Golden's scream of fear quite close and he answered her and started moving towards the sound of her cry. He went slowly, afraid to let himself be carried by the wind in case he was lifted again and thrown against a tree.

For just a moment, the snow cleared enough for him to see that a tree had blown down and pushed the fence flat on the ground. Then the blizzard closed in again. He felt his way across the fence and was in the horse paddock.

He neighed to Golden to come, but she was there already, almost beside him, with her little foal.

'Come!' said Thowra, and with the foal sheltering between them, they went out over the fence.

Thowra led them a few yards into a little scrubby gully where they were safe from falling trees, and protected from the main force of the wind. There, the trembling little foal had a long drink, getting from its mother comfort and warmth, and relief from fear. Thowra saw that it was a filly, with a mane and tail as silver as his own. She was beautiful.

'What have you named our foal?' he asked. 'She should be Kunama, which means "snow".'

'Kunama,' said Golden, nuzzling the foal and then nuzzling Thowra, 'Kunama.' And the sweet filly wagged her furry wisp of a tail.

By then the tornado had passed over them and there was only the steady roar of the storm — no more trees were uprooted, and the day became lighter again. For a horse that knew the country well it was safe to move.

'Come!' Thowra commanded.

Golden looked at her little foal and then in the direction of the storm-enfolded hut; she gave Thowra a playful nip on the shoulder and followed him up the gully and away around the back of the hut. It was wisdom to choose the safe care of her old master when a first foal was going to be born, but when Thowra's great call came through the spiralling storm, her only wish was to follow him.

Thus Thowra returned to his herd with his creamy mare and his lovely silver daughter. Thowra had won his prize for the second time, but a faint idea crossed his mind, perhaps something had to be won three times before it was freely owned.

King of the Cascades

In that lovely spring, Thowra's full herd was becoming fairly large — large for a cream-coloured stallion who depended on speed and ghost-like movement for his safety.

Golden had Kunama, each of the three grey mares had yearlings still with them, and two had foals at foot, and there was also Arrow's black mare and her yearling. A herd of this size could not really move about without trace or track, but that hardly mattered. In the spring Thowra had only one thing to fear now, and that was man — men could not follow a track as well as wild horses could, and there was no living horse that Thowra feared.

Perhaps there had never been a time when Thowra was so happy to be alive. This happiness was different from the happiness he and Storm had felt, up there on the Ramshead before they gathered their herds. This time it was a joy like owning the world, as though — and perhaps he was right — there never was and never would be again a mountain stallion like him, Thowra.

Even the danger of Golden's master still being in the mountains and out to capture her again only seemed to add excitement. If there was only one man after him, he knew he could lead that man on a chase to end all chases! No, until the stockmen and their dogs were in the hills there was nothing really to fear, and many men and dogs could not come now even if they wanted to — the snow was getting deeper in the mountains above and the rivers running wildly.

At the top end of the Cascades the grass was good and the sun shone, warm and life-giving. The foals grew, and the coats of all the horses became shiny.

Several times Thowra went back to Dead Horse hut to see if anyone was there, but each time nothing moved but the wind through the Gap, swaying an old strip of green hide that hung outside the hut, rattling a piece of galvanised iron.

It was while he was up at Dead Horse Gap, one glittering spring day, that The Brolga came looking for Golden.

Boon Boon heard him first, heard his excited scream a mile away. She immediately gathered the herd together and started them uphill where banks of snow still lay, all molten gold in the sunshine, to the place where Thowra would surely be coming soon. But The Brolga had already picked up Golden's tracks, and though he did not hurry, stopping to prance and snort, he could easily catch a herd with young foals in it.

'You yearling colts will have to aggravate him,' Boon Boon said to her own yearling. 'But don't get too close. Draw him off, annoy him, but only a little or he may kill you.'

Filled with importance, the colts trotted back to The Brolga, dancing and showing off, trying to scream like stallions — but The Brolga soon got tired of chasing these little sons of Thowra, and he went after the herd again.

When Boon Boon saw him coming faster, she said to the other mares, 'It's better to hide the foals in the thick scrub; we can come back for them later,' and she led them to a patch of dense heather. Only the mares with foals went through it and planted their young ones, the others galloped around the outside; then they all joined up together again, and galloped across a flat square of snowgrass and upwards to a belt of trees. There they stopped because The Brolga was very close and they knew they might be able to dodge him in the trees.

Boon Boon was pretty sure he would not bother about any of them except Golden, whom he would try to drive back to his own herd.

'Dodge and dodge!' she said to Golden. 'And don't let him drive you back.'

The snow gums were tall and there were a few candlebarks among them with high, straight trunks. There were plenty of opportunities to dodge and move about — but, of course, that could not go on for ever. Unless help came The Brolga would win in the end — and Golden was worrying about Kunama, her lovely foal.

A fast, light mare could swing and turn neatly round the trees; and without much effort, Golden managed to keep a thick patch of snow gums between herself and The Brolga. Twice the great, grey horse tried to break through and come straight for her, but each time she had gone and was behind some other barrier — Thowra had taught her well.

The Brolga was screaming with excitement, and Thowra, way up in the snow on top of Bob's Ridge, heard him at last. When he got down, it was Golden that he saw.

Thowra gave one shattering, tremendous roar of rage, and The Brolga stopped, ears pricked, the breath snorting

161

through his nostrils. Then Thowra charged down like a furious storm cloud.

'Go!' he said to Golden, and as The Brolga tried to follow her, he sprang on him with flailing hooves and bared teeth, and when he reared up under some tall candlebarks, his great mane and tail looked like a foaming waterfall in the flickering, moving light and shade, as Bel Bel had once thought they would.

Here was the most beautiful stallion the great mountains had ever seen, in his full strength, fighting for his mate, and it was as though everything around was hushed and still: no wind blew, and the leaves held themselves in perfect quiet. Even the sound of a little stream was muted, and neither the red lowrie nor the jays flew by. There was nothing but the pounding hooves and tearing breath of the two huge horses.

The herd knew that it was not just for Golden that the two stallions fought, but for their lives. One must die so that the other could be the supreme ruler of the Cascade brumbies.

This time Thowra had no fear of losing.

A year ago he would have used every snow gum to help him dodge. Now he drove his old enemy into a little open space under three tall candlebarks, and there fought him, not only with his usual weapon of nimbleness, but his new-found mature strength. The Brolga was the first horse he had ever seen fight — it was he who had eventually killed his own father.

Thowra remembered seeing him and his herd go past that cloud window on the top of the Brindle Bull on the day Yarraman was killed. He remembered the feeling of cold foreboding and fear at the sight. Now, as he fought The Brolga below the candlebarks, it seemed as if his whole life had been leading up to this moment of destroying the grey stallion. Hadn't Bel Bel told him to wait until he reached his full strength? Wasn't it the way of the wild that the old king of the stallions must be killed?

While they fought, the mares came drifting back to watch, peering through the snow-gum leaves at the two powerful horses — Thowra's mares, and three of them The Brolga's daughters. The sun passed below the hills, then sunk behind the lower ranges of the Murray Valley, while the two horses strained and fought, hooves thudding on damp ground or on hide and flesh and bone. As darkness came The Brolga was beaten to the ground.

It was Boon Boon who neighed first, and then Golden — Golden who had no instinct to tell her that the old king should be killed. And Thowra, knowing his enemy would never trouble him again, left him, defeated but still living, below the shadowy trees. He had won his prize for the third time!

Thowra, half-bucking, half-kicking, shook the foam from his glorious mane and cantered over to Golden and Boon Boon, his two favourite mares. Then he called all his herd away and they travelled by the bright light of the moon down into the Cascades. A mopoke called them, sitting white and stiff on a dead branch. Possums peered at them out of the trees, and a dingo went trotting past. Later they heard him howling, the answering call from his mate echoing round some wooded hollow.

The ghostly herd — all its light-coloured horses whitened by the moonlight — trotted in single file down the narrowing valley that led into the Cascades.

163

Thowra stepped out proudly in the lead, head and tail held high, gleaming silver. Golden followed, with Kunama's tiny head close to her side and the little foal trotting feet keeping up with her swinging strides, and Boon Boon came next with the other grey mares and their foals after her, all silver-white and pale, made mysterious by the moon. Arrow's black mare, like a dark shadow, followed with the yearlings. On and on they went, at this swinging, proud walk — the king of the Cascade brumbies and his herd.

Four kangaroos stood still to see them pass, and some brown rock wallabies watched from below the moon-gleaming snow-gum leaves. The slow, old wombats saw the proud herd and knew a fight had been fought and won. But even the wild little bush animals knew that a horse of that unusual colour was nowhere safe. They themselves were the soft colour of the bush — able to merge into their surroundings at the first sound of an enemy, be it dingo, dog or man — but Thowra and Golden, Boon Boon's colt, and now Kunama, were only invisible in a snowstorm.

Just for a night of moonlight, just for a month of spring, while the rivers roared and the snows still lay thick, Thowra could be the proud and wonderful stallion, like no other brumby stallion ever seen before — lord of all the herds, lord of all the grey, green hills and valleys, of the shining streams, and the great rock tors. Later, when the men returned to the mountains, he would have to gallop again with the wind, his brother, but for this short time he could live in all his wild joy and strength.

The ghost herd went down to the Cascades, one after the other, and ran into The Brolga's herd, who had come to

Thowra's end of the valley, looking for their stallion. As soon as they saw them coming they knew The Brolga had been beaten.

In silence Thowra came stepping downwards till he was quite close to them, then he reared up and screamed his triumph, and the valley rolled the echoes back and forth. Thowra waited till the sound had died on the night air, and called again. This time, after the echo faded away, there was absolute quiet; no mopoke called, no dingo howled, there was not even the rustling sound of a bush animal going home — all was still. Thowra, the silver stallion, had entered his kingdom.

The spring that year was shining and perfect. Thowra roamed with the big herd of brumbies up and down the valley of the Cascades, safe and unworried. But he knew two things — that he must cut back the size of his herd because with them he could not escape from men; and that he must find out if there was more grass country higher up the stream from his wonderful Hidden Flat so that he and Golden and Boon Boon and their foals could escape there from any man hunt.

One day, Thowra went off on his own to explore above the Hidden Flat. For hours he trotted along through the bush, watching with joy every magnificent sign of spring — a robin redbreast catching insects on a drift of snow, a lowrie flashing red and blue across a glittering pool, the foaming streams, the new growth in the grass and buds on shrubs. Down by the Crackenback the wattles were in flower and the golden balls fell on to his back and stuck to his mane. Underfoot were the little dark brown and purple black-eyed Susans. The bitter pea scrub was flowering, brown and gold, nearly shoulder high to the cream stallion. The mountain world was bursting into flower, everything filled with the joy of living.

Thowra crossed the river and jogged on, up on to Paddy Rush's Bogong and down the other side — careful to leave no track as he neared his Hidden Flat.

Down he dropped into the valley and then started to force his way round the cliffs at the head of the grassy flats. The sun was already dropping into the west when he found a steep and dangerous way round, and moved cautiously along a wallaby track that hung perilously above the bright, glittering stream.

At last he got round the rocky, great bluff, and below him there was a narrow gorge with towering cliffs on either side. The wallaby track led on and Thowra followed it, creeping ever so slowly. It became wider, and though there was still the tremendous drop below, he could walk freely. The gorge ended in another cliff, but there was still a good track round it. Thowra went on. Suddenly he found himself on quite a wide, rock platform looking into a wonderful valley that was big enough to graze a dozen horses for several months, and cut off all around by enormous tiers of cliffs.

This was exactly what he was looking for, if only he could find a way down. Here was a beautiful valley, and, by the way the cliffs rose, it would not be looked over from above.

He searched all round the lookout platform, but Thowra could not find a safe path down. At one place a few turpentine bushes clung to the rocks below the track, and it seemed to Thowra that a faint path went through them. Wondering if it was safe, he braced his forefeet carefully and pushed his head through. He could still see a tiny path. He stepped cautiously forward between more bushes — the path was there all right. He moved forward again, and still the path went faintly through the bushes and turned down towards the cliff.

Soon the bushes ended, and Thowra was on a narrow ledge. He realised that it passed below the lookout platform.

In half an hour he was in the valley, drinking at the stream, nibbling the grass. In the morning he would examine the cliffs for any place that he could jump down if he was ever hard-pressed to escape. He wished Bel Bel was with him, but Bel Bel must have stayed on the range for the snows to cover her.

At last, Thowra had found a home for himself and whatever mares he wanted to bring.

Black man: shod horse

It was evening when Thowra went home, and he travelled by the southern end of the Cascades. He was listening and watching — not for man, but to find someone whom he wanted to see. However, he found no tracks or signs of a single horse, let alone a herd. He trotted on, enjoying the feel of the springy snowgrass under his feet, and at last he came over a little rise and saw below him a number of grazing horses — and among them was the one he was looking for. He neighed, and his neigh was without the challenging sound of a powerful stallion, and was not the cry of a horse to its mate. The big, bay stallion in the valley below heard and knew who he was and what he was saying.

Storm threw up his head and neighed in answer, then started trotting towards Thowra, while Thowra came down the slope to greet him.

'Well, brother of the wind,' said Storm, 'what news do you have for me? I know you fought and beat The Brolga, that was good, but what else have you been doing?'

Thowra told him of Golden's recapture by her master, and of her return with him to the wild horses.

'We are both brothers of the winds and of the storms,' Thowra said, 'and I must indeed be brother to the wind itself, because it was the wild tornado that uprooted the tree over the fence and freed Golden.'

Storm nodded his beautiful, bay head.

'Yes,' he answered, 'the winds and blizzards will always protect you — it is in the bright months of summer that you are in danger.'

'That is why I have come to speak to you,' said Thowra. 'Why don't you graze your herd near mine, here in the Cascades, and later, over on Paddy Rush's Bogong? Then if Golden and Kunama and I, who the men will surely hunt, have to go, you will be there to look after the others.'

Storm nipped Thowra on the neck.

'Even Mirri and Bel Bel would not have believed that we would remain brothers all our lives,' he said. 'Come on, we'll all go together until you leave us near your herd, and when the time comes for you to go over the river for summer grazing, we'll go too, and I, brother, will always be near your mares and your foals.'

So it was that Storm and his herd grazed in the Cascades almost alongside Thowra's herd, and the valley seemed almost filled with wild horses.

Fortunately, there was plenty to eat that spring. Days of sunshine made the grass grow thick and fast, sweet and fresh, and made tremendous growth on the shrubs. There would be food for all until it was time to move; and over on Paddy Rush's Bogong the grass would be untouched and would provide good grazing for the summer.

The warm sun and good food made the horses sleek and shiny. The little foals played just as Thowra and Storm had, four years ago. Kunama grew in size and beauty every day. Instead of Golden teaching her the wisdom of the bush, Thowra, who knew his silver daughter would have to grow up as wise as Bel Bel, taught her himself. He taught her to leave no track with her tiny, neat hooves; to hide herself in trees and shrubs; taught her to read the tracks of other horses; to know how old they were, how fast they were going. He showed her the tracks of the sleepy wombats, the dark wallabies and the sweet silver-grey kangaroos, and he showed her where the wedge-tail eagles nest.

It was Thowra who taught her to recognise all the weather signs, just as Bel Bel had taught him — how to understand the voice of the wind and the story of the clouds in the sky, how a strange, fermenting green heart to storm clouds meant wind-driven ice that could cut through a horse's hide.

He was surprised to find that Kunama was far easier to teach than Golden had been. Golden's mother and father had both been tame horses, living with men, and he supposed that, having been brought up by men, her instincts were not developed.

Kunama reminded him of Bel Bel, with her inborn wisdom. Perhaps, she would be even wiser than Bel Bel, because with a cream coat, she, too, would lead a hunted life, and must be wise in order to survive. Thowra knew that mares with foals to look after often had a special understanding of the bush and weather. If, like Bel Bel and Mirri, they were 'lone wolves', their wisdom, knowledge and cunning could become very great — that was why Bel Bel had been almost as much a leader of the herd as Yarraman. Thowra now understood that it was because of Bel Bel's skills that Yarraman had seemed magic to the other horses and to the men. Anyway, he knew as soon as he saw Kunama prick her small ears, then shiver, as seven black cockatoos cried and flew overhead that she would need everything he could teach her as well as all her own inborn wisdom, if she were to remain free and wild, and live her life in the mountains.

Boon Boon, who had become fast friends with Golden, looked after the little foal sometimes, and Golden was very pleased to see her leggy filly cantering after the big grey mare.

There was one other thing in which Kunama took after Bel Bel and Thowra — she loved to wander, and this was dangerous in a foal, unless, like Thowra and Storm, it had a wandering mother. Boon Boon watched her carefully. Later, when she was weaned and could gallop faster, she would be able to go off with Thowra on his travels, but not now.

That spring the rivers were kept high for a long time, simply because there was never a great spring flood. No actual rain fell in the high mountains; there was only ever a snowstorm or frost and bright sunshine. The bright sun melted the snow and kept the rivers high, but if warm rain had fallen, the snow would have been washed off in a big rush and caused an enormous flood, and after that the level of the rivers would have dropped.

When Thowra and Storm decided to leave the Cascades, they crossed their herds so near the source of the Crackenback that they did not realise how high the river really was. They were surprised when they were quite some time on Paddy Rush's Bogong before they saw the first mobs of cattle, but once they had seen the red-and-white beasts dotting the grassy slopes of the Ramshead, Thowra, at least, became doubly watchful. Though it was a great safeguard for all the mares to have

Storm near, it meant a large number of horses were very close together — and the more horses, the more difficult it was to keep them hidden.

Among the yearlings in Storm's herd was a beautiful, spirited, black colt with two white feet and an unusual splash of white on his flank. Thowra noticed him, and noticed his mother, too, a coal-black mare. He studied her closely, thinking that she didn't look like a wild horse, so he asked Storm about her.

Storm seemed worried by the question.

'The black one?' he said. 'Yes, I call her Lubra, but she tells me her name is Highland Lass. I'm afraid she and her yearling colt may bring trouble, too. She's an escaped tame horse. I didn't steal her from the men. I took her from a stupid stallion, way up past the tin mine, near the headwaters of the Indi River. I only found out later that she had escaped, or maybe I would have left her alone. I thought that by the time I got her back here we would be far enough away for her owners never to follow us — now I'm not so sure.'

'It's a long way,' said Thowra.

'Mmm! But I've since found out that she used to run in races, with a man on her back, a man wearing a bright striped coat. I think the men may value her, just like they value Golden.'

'She's not bad to look at,' Thowra said, 'and the colt is a handsome young thing.'

'Oh, she is,' said Storm, 'and she can go like the wind, but I've never been able to teach her any sense the way you've taught Golden. Of course, being black, she's not so difficult to hide, but as for making her take care to leave no track — it's impossible! The colt, Tambo, isn't bad at all — very intelligent in fact.'

It was a lovely morning — a bright dawn with pink wisps of cloud streaking the sky. Thowra left Storm and was returning to his herd when he was seized with the longing to be on his own, galloping through the cool air, up as high as he could get. So he swung round and headed off for the topmost rock-covered hill on Paddy Rush's Bogong, galloping through the sharp-scented eucalypts, over silver banks of snow-daisy leaves where soon the big white flowers would star the slopes.

He leapt from rock to rock to the top of the hill and stood there in all his glorious strength and beauty, gilded by the eastern sun, silver tail and mane streaming in the breeze. He looked out over the land that was his kingdom — right out to the main range which he loved best of all, the range where a horse could roam, wild and free. He wondered suddenly whether he would be allowed to let his bones bleach up there, or whether his burial place would be chosen for him by some younger stallion, just as he had forced The Brolga out from cover to fight under the three great candlebarks. The only promising colt in the herds was Tambo. His own handsome, dun-coloured sons and the one creamy, who had grown darker as he got older, would probably wander far away.

He leapt down off the rock and started to gallop for joy, back towards his herd, when suddenly he saw a mark on the wet earth. He pulled up short on his haunches and looked again. There, straight across the damp ground, was the track of a shod horse.

To his astonishment he could find no continuous trail. Whoever was riding the horse was almost as cunning as himself. Without wasting time he went straight back to the herd where he found the mares very disquieted.

Boon Boon trotted over to him as she saw him coming. 'There was a man on a horse watching us,' she said, 'a *black* man, black as that mare, Lubra.'

Golden had joined her, and Thowra saw that she was deeply troubled.

'I have heard the men talk of the cleverness of the black trackers if cattle are stolen,' said Golden. 'Perhaps he has come because of Lubra. I am sure she is a valuable mare. Let's go and ask her if there were any black men where she came from.'

Thowra had become more troubled as Golden spoke. The very fact that the shod horse had been ridden so that he left almost no tracks now made sense. Anyway, there were all the stories that Bel Bel had told him about the Aborigines. The Aborigines were wild, too, and really belonged to the bush even more than the brumbies, they owned it like the possums did and the kangaroos.

He made the herd disperse in amongst the snow gums and went off himself, silently, through the trees and scrub, to find Storm and to go with him to question the black mare, Lubra.

Storm was surprised to see him again so soon.

'What is it, brother?' he asked anxiously.

'A black man on a shod horse is on the mountain,' Thowra answered. 'Golden thinks we should ask Lubra if there were any black trackers where she came from.'

Lubra and Tambo were standing by a pool in a little stream when they found her.

'A black man,' she said, looking fearful. 'Yes, there was. He was clever at finding any beasts that had wandered. I think he will be looking for me.'

'She's a foolish mare,' said Storm, as they went off, 'but I think she knows there was a black man all right.'

'I had better take a good look around late this evening,' Thowra muttered. He was troubled. It seemed it was not only Golden who was going to bring danger.

All day the brumbies remained under cover of the trees. Thowra felt a little better by the afternoon because all the bush animals and birds behaved quite normally, which they would not have done if there had been men about. He saw a dingo go slowly along a track as though he had no thought in the world except his next meal. Even the jays gave no warning sounds, only chattered at a poor, inoffensive echidna. Then just before sunset, Storm appeared.

'I have seen the black man,' he said, 'and *he* has seen Lubra. He appeared just like a shadow between the trees — his horse dark brown, his own clothes grey, or green, or dirty, so that they did not show up.'

'You look after the herds,' Thowra suggested, very worried, 'and I'll go off now and see if there are any other men about.'

The bush was quiet as he went on his scouting expedition. The only sounds were the normal rustlings and movements of evening, as the wombats came out to sun themselves in the last pleasant rays, as the animals who fed by day went off to their homes, and those that fed by night started to stir. He knew no possums would come till that strange moment that belongs to no time at all, when it is neither dark nor light. Then their pointed faces, that are both curious and wistful, would peer down on him from the gum trees, and he would smell the strange possum smell, more pungent than eucalyptus, but very like it.

Though Thowra searched and searched through the country that he knew so well, he could find no sign of the black stockman, or of anyone else. All was quiet. Down by the Crackenback crossing, the river moved, black and silver in the starlight. The sand was unmarked by anything except the bush animals and the receding flood levels. A tawny owl hooted softly. It seemed that all the bush was at peace except for Thowra, with the restless mind and the skin that prickled.

He went back to the herd, still feeling that somewhere in that peaceful bush there had been eyes watching him.

The next day everything was absolutely quiet and the bush creatures moved about just as usual. Thowra wandered around several times, and again at dusk and during the early part of the evening. He saw nothing strange, heard nothing strange, and this time he felt nothing strange. He was less worried by the time he got back to the herd.

The night was very calm and still. The Southern Cross hung, bright and clear, above all the country around the headwaters of the Indi. It was not possible even to imagine any lurking danger in the friendly bush.

Thowra and Golden went to drink together from a moss-fringed pool at the head of a long glade. The water in this particular pool was very good and they were drinking it slowly, relishing its flavour, sucking it through their teeth, letting it lap gently into their nostrils. A puff of wind came from the south. Thowra lifted his head. All at once he became tense. There was a sound borne on the wind, a sound he had never heard before — as if wood was knocking against wood, but he could not guess what it was. Following the sound, the wind carried a scent to them. Thowra sniffed and listened.

'It is the scent of man,' he whispered. 'They are close, and I don't know what they are doing.'

A legendary leap

Thowra and Golden moved silently back to the trees where Kunama was sleeping. Boon Boon was nearby, her head up so she could smell the air, ears pricked forward.

'It's time for Golden and Kunama to hide,' Thowra said. 'You come, too, Boon Boon, and I will show you the track in and out of my secret valley. We must hurry. I'll send your colt to tell Storm we've gone, and that I'll come back when you and Golden and the foal are safely hidden.'

Golden stirred the little filly and they all four set off in the night, walking silently at first till they were well away from the men, then trotting, keeping to the snowgrass lanes where they would leave no track. In the starlight each creamy was just a hint of a pale horse moving, but Boon Boon was invisible.

They had quite a long way to go, and would have to hurry. Over the top of the mountain and down, along on a gently dropping grade, silent-footed over the dead leaves of peppermint forest, they went; sometimes using the rocks of an old watercourse as a road on which they would leave no hoofmark. They trotted, on and on.

Suddenly alongside them hopped three silver-grey kangaroos.

'Hello!' Thowra said, startled. 'Why are you travelling at night, and where do you come from?'

'We come from the other side of the Crackenback, and we're travelling at night because there is going to be trouble on the mountains.'

'Trouble with man?' asked Thowra.

'Yes. In all the lore of the kangaroos — all the tales that pass from kangaroo to kangaroo throughout the country — it is told that when the white men get the black men to help them catch animals, their traps are made with the craftiness of both black and white.'

'Traps!' said Thowra, thinking of the sound of wood striking wood.

'We were camped near the Crackenback when you came down last night. We saw you, but we don't know if the men who slept there did.'

Thowra felt his coat prickling again. After all, eyes had watched him.

'No one moved,' the biggest kangaroo went on. 'They watched for a long time, waiting in case you came, because the black man had not seen you, and they wondered where you were — but they must have gone to sleep by the time you came down to the water, because no one moved.'

'You heard them talking, then?' Thowra said. 'I never smelt or heard their horses.'

'Their horses were left in a hollow a mile away. Yes, we heard them talking. The man who owned your mare, here,' he nodded towards Golden, 'wants her back, and when he and his friends met the black tracker who had come looking for a big black mare, they all got together, planning a big brumby drive into the yard they have made. But they won't get you!' he looked knowingly at Golden. 'Well, goodbye, we must be going.'

The three kangaroos hopped on their way.

'Come on,' said Thowra. 'There's no time to lose.'

On through the night they went, cantering now, wherever possible, and the smell of the peppermints was sweet and strong. At last they reached the Hidden Flat and dropped down into it, then, Thowra told them to follow him closely while he led them round into his Secret Valley.

It was a perilous journey in the dark. When Kunama heard a stone start down, knocking against other stones, and then bouncing from rock to rock, down, till the sound of its falling was lost in the darkness and the depth, she started back in fear, but Thowra said, 'Come on!' and Golden said 'Come on!', and Boon Boon, behind her, said, 'Go!'

Down they went, following Thowra, their rockhard hooves clinging like goats' feet. At last they were at the bottom, standing by the starlit river, with the looming cliffs above them, and only the memory of their breathless descent.

'I must go back to the others and warn them,' Thowra said at last. 'Hide here. When daylight comes you will see plenty of grass. I should be back by tonight.'

He turned to go, the pale shape of him showing against the cliff, then swung back again, starlight reflecting in his eyes. 'If I get caught,' he said, 'I will free myself, somehow, and return to you.'

Then he went up the cliff, leaving the two mares and the filly foal behind in the strange Secret Valley.

This time Thowra really hurried. He thought of his mares and of Storm and the sound he had heard of a trap-yard being built. The men would probably wait till midday or afternoon to start their brumby drive. They would know that the horses went out feeding in the cool early morning, and would be harder to find. At the back of his mind, like a dream, was the faint memory of galloping beside his mother, one oppressive afternoon, when the men had built a trap-yard and were driving all the wild horses through the bush.

On he went. Dawn came slowly — silver-coloured and fresh. A little grey thrush burst into song right beside a stream where he stopped to drink. Thowra, sweating and breathless, hurried on.

As he drew near to the top of the mountain he moved with even greater caution, but there was nothing to suggest danger, nothing to suggest the group of stockmen and dogs that was already waiting at the foot of the mountain, ready to close in on the horses and drive them towards the trap-yard.

He hastened first to find Storm, and if he didn't know his brother of the winds and the blizzards so well, he might have missed him, but as he looked along a band of snow gums, he seemed to see among the leaves and the boughs the shape of a noble horse.

Storm looked in amazement at the sweating Thowra.

'What's happened?' he asked.

Thowra told him what he knew, and added, 'All the horses must try and get through as best they can. They'll have more of a chance if they travel in ones and twos.'

Storm nodded.

'It's no good going south, though. That's where Lubra and the black tracker came from.'

'That's true,' Thowra agreed. 'Better to go into all that wild tangle of valleys off the Crackenback, for a while, where I hid with my first small herd. And I've just come up that way and seen no one.'

180

'Lubra is foolish,' said Storm, obviously wondering what trouble she might bring. 'Well, we must go.'

Thowra stretched his creamy nose forward and nipped him on the neck.

'I hope we meet again after today, brother,' he said.

The two stallions went off through the bush, each to warn their mares — the superb silver horse, and the noble bay with the strong head, and the great, kindly eyes.

'Go!' they said to each mare with her foal at foot. 'Go!' they said to the yearlings. 'Don't stay together — a foal with its mother, yes, but otherwise each of you has a better chance alone.'

And soon there were flitting shadows moving through the bush, hiding here, hiding there, but all travelling north-eastwards — mares with little foals, sometimes two dry mares together, colts, fillies, and, alone but watchful, the bay stallion and the silver one.

The first thing that made Thowra realise that the men were already closing in was when he noticed two wallabies hastening nervously towards him, and then a dingo close behind.

'Man!' the dingo snapped, and went hurrying on.

Thowra knew it was too late, but seeing his other two grey mares he joined them, and led them to a deep creek bed he knew. He told them to make their way silently along it until they thought the men had gone, and then at nightfall, if all was well, to aim for the Hidden Flat.

Just then a blue heeler cattle dog came trotting up the creek.

Thowra leapt up one of the rocky sides.

'Keep going,' he neighed to the mares. 'The dog will follow me.'

The dog did follow him, but in the long years since the first brumby drive Thowra had learnt how to deal with one dog, and he waited and kicked out at him. The dog knew better than to let himself be hurt, so he kept his distance, and barked.

Thowra went at him with teeth bared and ready to strike. As the dog leapt to one side, Thowra was after it. But the dog's master had heard the scuffle and was rushing towards them, cracking his whip so that other men and other dogs would come to his assistance.

Suddenly, all was wild movement below the great mountain ash trees. There were men, horses, dogs. Whips were cracking, voices shouting — and Thowra had to turn and head up the mountain again, as almost every other horse in the two herds would shortly have to do. The men were everywhere on the mountain — men from the Murray, after Golden, men from Benambra after Lubra, men from all the Snowy River country who had come to join in the hunt. Some of the men were among the very best riders of the mountain land. There were men on blood horses, men on nippy stockhorses, men with splendid dogs. And they were all after Golden and Highland Lass whom Storm had named Lubra.

Thowra thought it was worth trying to drop quietly into the top of the deep creek bed and hide himself until the chase had gone by. There was a thicket of snow gum and hop scrub ahead, leading right to the edge of it. He dived into the scrub, pushing through it quickly, and down a rocky crag to the creek. He stopped amongst the scrub and rocks at the bottom, trying to breathe without sound.

There was no escaping! Two dogs came barking madly after him. Thowra stood his ground and struck at them, but again there came the sound of a whip. With a parting splash at the dogs, he leapt out and up the creek. A rope whistled and fell short; the man was quite close. Quick as a thrown knife, Thowra wheeled round in an attempt to get away downstream, while the man coiled his lasso again. The dogs closed in. He bit one and kicked the other — then saw another man and his horse standing in the creek below him. He bounded up a rock rib. There, at the top, was a third man coming towards him.

Thowra went galloping on through the bush — the great creamy horse with his mane and tail foaming out behind, galloping, and being edged upwards by the men all the time. Now that his freedom might be lost again, he felt more tremendously alive than ever before. He was aware of every cream hair in his coat, as though each one was tingling, feeling and listening. He was aware of his ears pressed back, his nose, his keen eyes. He was aware of the hardness of his hooves, of the immense strength in the muscles of his legs, his quarters, his shoulders. He was aware of all these things, and of himself as one great, powerful, silver stallion leaping up and up the mountain, harried by dogs and by men.

'Strength, and power, and all Bel Bel's cunning, don't fail now,' Thowra thought, and once again Bel Bel's voice seemed to echo through the bush, ringing in his ears above the sound of hooves. *'For the wind I have named you ...'*

'Swiftly, swiftly,' he thought, and all the time the noise of the drumming hooves grew louder, coming from all around, echoing off the rocks, sounding through the snow gums. There were horses galloping up the mountain from every direction, all the wild horses being driven by many mounted men and their dogs. Soon they would be driven along the grazing grounds. In a sudden flash, Thowra thought of the direction from which the sound of the men building their trap-yard had come. Yes, they were being driven towards it.

He shot into some thick snow gums, and the touch of the leathery leaves on his hide made him feel the size and strength of himself once more. There was still one possible line of escape — the craggy ravine in which he and Storm, as foals, had hidden from Arrow. He felt sure the trap-yard was just close to it.

A man on a fine black horse was coming up close to him now. He heard the whistle of a rope, and desperately propped and swung away. The rope clipped him on the ear and fell to the ground like a dead snake. The pounding of hooves was greater than ever. Now six horses were running with him, galloping, sweating, straining, blowing, their flanks touching his flanks, their hot breath mingling with his. He could see the wildness of their eyes. The mare he had taken from Arrow's herd was there — and the foolish mare, Lubra, with Tambo alongside. He wished he could see Storm.

Now they were at the grazing ground and another mob of horses was galloping to join them. The noise of hoof-beats was like the roll of thunder — and as terrifying. Thowra could feel the terror running through the mob.

More horses joined them all the time. Storm must be somewhere, but there were too many, all bunched together, madly galloping, for Thowra to see him.

Suddenly he noticed — with eyes trained to pick out anything unusual — a long fence hidden in trees and bushes. The mob were racing alongside it already. It must be the wing of a yard, like the wings on the yards the men built for their cattle. Even now, the horses were as good as caught. Thowra strained his eyes to see the yard. He guessed it must be hidden by a patch of scrub ahead. The only way of escape was for the whole mob to break when they reached the scrub.

'Swing west!' he urged. 'Tell every horse, swing west!'

All the men who were not behind the mob of horses were riding that western flank, shouting and cracking their whips. It would be difficult to break through them.

'Come on! Come on!' Thowra called. 'Swing west and break through them!' And he swung himself, forcing the others on his flank to swing with him, and led them off at a tremendous pace. The others followed.

The men from the rear immediately galloped towards the flank, trying to head them, and those out on the wing already redoubled their shouts and whip-cracking.

Thowra galloped towards them as he had never galloped before, and heard the mob pounding along with him. But the men were racing across, and there were so many men that there seemed to be no space between them.

Thowra suddenly screamed to the mob, and charged one man on a lightweight, liver chestnut, knocking him flying. Just then he got a blinding cut across the eyes with a whip, and even if he had succeeded in passing one man, it looked as though there were twenty more closing in on him. He charged again with utter desperation — aware of the hesitation in the mob behind him — but the whips cracked and then two ropes came flying, and he knew that the men wanted him more than any of the other brumbies except Lubra, now that Golden was not there. He turned before another rope could entangle him, and found the mob had turned already.

For a moment despair seized him, but then hope followed. He was now running straight towards the long fence instead of beside it — and could, therefore, jump it. The ravine was on the other side ... there was still a chance.

Once more he was almost in the lead, though he was careful not to get right out in front, careful to see that his cream hide was partly hidden by the madly fleeing bays, browns, blacks and chestnuts. The smell of fear rose all round him. He must keep calm. There was the fence looming ahead. The leading horses had seen it and were trying to slacken speed, and there were men trying to swing them away from it in case they all crashed through it and into the deep ravine.

Thowra prepared himself to jump, hoping that no horse would dash into him as he took off. He shortened his stride, gathered himself together, and sprang with all his great strength. Forelegs bent close to his body, up he went.

'Higher, higher!' he told himself, as it was a very high fence.

He heard a shout ringing out above the thunder of hooves and the general shouting and whip-cracking. The men had seen him, but he knew he was clearing the fence. He was away, even though he could see that the landing was rough on the other side.

He landed neatly and safely, and in two paces was at the edge of the ravine. He knew exactly where he was and how to get down. As he jumped over the edge he heard a crash. The brumbies had dashed into the fence and broken it.

How much they had broken of it he did not know because no horses came into the ravine while he was there. As he hastened away to safety he neither saw nor heard the men trying to force the brumbies away from the lip of the cliff, and round up those who had quickly broken through again.

Thowra went down the ravine a long way, even though it led in the opposite direction from the Secret Valley, until he came to another deep cleft that ran into it from the eastern side. He turned up this, often looking behind to see if he was being followed. When he got to the end of the cleft, he took off cautiously through the bush. Even though he could see no one and heard no unusual sound, he was convinced that he was being followed. He felt that prickling in the coat ... Unless he was sure he was safe he did not want to go straight towards the Secret Valley.

An hour passed, and there was still no sign of man. He turned slightly in the direction of the two valleys. Soon it would be evening, but he could not rid himself of the feeling of being watched.

He stood still in a clump of peppermint and blanketwood and waited. After a while he saw two horses coming quietly, so quietly through the trees and heading for the Hidden Flat. As they got closer he recognised them — it was Storm and Tambo!

He was so pleased to see Storm, but there was no time to hear anything about the rest of the herd, because Storm said, 'I hoped we'd find you. Lubra is caught, and Golden's master saw you escaping and has got the black tracker with him to try and find you. You'd better go to your Secret Valley, but be sure to leave no tracks. Tambo and I will go much lower down the stream and work our way up into the Hidden Flat. Goodbye, brother.'

'Goodbye,' said Thowra, going off alone, swiftly through the bush.

He could not help wondering if this was the last time he would glide like a shadow through the tall trees, and for a moment he felt as if he were another horse, seeing himself in all his silver magnificence.

He had gone about five miles when he heard a sound. Someone was close! Then he saw them — Golden's master, the black tracker, and the man on the fine black horse, and with them four dogs.

Thowra stood perfectly still, melting into the scrub, but a dog whined and he knew he must fly like the wind.

He was determined he would not lead them towards the Secret Valley, but there was no choice really, for that was the way they drove him.

The men were well mounted, but Thowra had no weight on his back and he could go faster. If only he could lead them on till evening ... Men could not see in the dark ... He kept on trying to dodge and twist, to turn them away from the route to his two valleys, but it was all that he could do to keep ahead of them.

As he galloped, he knew suddenly that he could not bear to let them catch him, he would rather be killed trying to get away. If they drove him on and on towards the Secret Valley he might or might not reach the cliffs. But if the men were close behind he would jump, anyway, not waiting to find his safe way down.

Thowra had barely a chance to look back but he was sure one horse went lame, the big black, and that there were now only two following him.

The light was fading. Soon it would be the possum light, the timeless area between night and day — the light that might be Thowra's light, too. A wind came from the north, quite suddenly, *his* wind, and there was the smell of rain. The tiredness from the day's galloping dropped away from Thowra; he felt renewed. This was his hour as well as the possums'. The light was almost gone and there was rain coming to cover tracks. He galloped and galloped and was well-enough ahead to choose his own line over the cliffs.

There were the two candlebarks that marked the place to jump. Thowra gathered himself together, keen-eyed in the darkness and the wind enfolded him. He came to the edge of the cliff and he leapt — leapt through the light that was neither light nor darkness — on to the grassy platform he had tried as a landing place before, felt it firm beneath him as he landed, and took off again instantly for the next leap. And all that the men saw was the pale ghost of a horse hurtling through space and wind, and when they reached the edge, there was nothing to be seen at all; just the sound of a stone falling a long way off.

Even the black tracker saw no way a horse could have made it down alive, nor did he imagine that there might be a beautiful valley below, where Golden and Kunama and Boon Boon were hidden. The men turned back through the darkness, saddened by the thought that they had chased a beautiful horse over such a cliff. In the night, there came rain to wash away all signs of tracks, and in the morning the black man took Lubra and left for the south.

Golden's master looked for her all through that summer, and even in the summers that followed, but he saw no sign of her. And though he often told of how the silver stallion had hurtled over the cliff to his death, there grew up around the campfires stories of a great silver stallion seen galloping over wind-packed snow way up on the Ramshead Range; of a ghost horse that drank at

the Crackenback River; of a horse that all men thought
was dead appearing in a blizzard at Dead Horse hut and
vanishing again; of the wild stallion cry that could only
be Thowra's. But no man knew where the son of Bel Bel
roamed.

Glossary

BLACK SALLEE TREE: A small eucalyptus tree with dark green and black trunk and narrow, dark leaves. They grow thickly in damp places and are often hung with a grey-green fungus called Old Man's Beard.

BLANKET BUSH: Tall shrubs with a woolly leaf. Mostly grow around creeks.

CANDLEBARK: A tall, beautiful eucalyptus tree, with cream or white bark that is splashed with red in summer time.

CHRISTMAS BUSH: There are a lot of native shrubs called *Christmas Bush* by bushmen because they flower at Christmas time. This one has a white flower with some mauve spots inside it.

FLYING PHALANGER: A possum that has large folds of skin between the forelegs and hind legs that enable it to glide from tree to tree or from a tall tree to the ground.

GANG-GANG: A small dark grey mountain cockatoo. The male has a scarlet head and crest. They are very fond of the gum-nuts (the fruit of the gum trees, containing seed) and come down to the valleys in bad weather.

KILLING GALLOWS: Looks rather like a windmill and is used for raising the bullock when killed for beef.

CURRAWONG: A big black bird with a white flash on their outer wing — sometimes they are grey. They are known as the mountain magpies, and have a clear, bell-like call as well as a harsher one.

LOWRY: Any parrot rosella. They are very bright in colour, often royal blue and scarlet.

LYREBIRD: A large dark-brown bird which lives in the damp, thick bush around creeks. The lyrebird has a magnificent tail which it spreads in the shape of a lyre. The lyrebird can mimic any sound.

MOPOKE: A little grey-white night bird of the owl family. His cry at night — 'mopoke' — can often be heard.

SKILLION ROOF: A roof built out from the main building, making a sort of lean-to shed.

SNOWGRASS: Grey-green, springy, tussocky grass which grows in the snow country. Lovely grass to run on.

SNOW GUM: Also called a White Sallee. It is a eucalyptus that usually grows quite high up in the mountain and sometimes is twisted to very strange shapes. Its bark is frequently marked like a jigsaw puzzle in green, grey, white, red, pink, yellow and orange.

TEA TREE: Many different sorts of shrubs and trees, generally with a papery bark and a small white flower. Tea trees usually grow near creeks. They have a leaf rather like a tea leaf, hence the name.

TOR: In the Ramsheads, a tor is a tall, bare rock or cluster of tall rocks, sometimes surrounded by smaller boulders.

WHITE RIBBON GUM: The eucalyptus tree that the native koala eats, known as ribbon gum or manna gum. In the mountains they grow very tall with white trunks, and perfectly straight like marvellous pillars.

WILLY-WILLY: Wind that goes round and round and upwards, and can bluster along at a tremendous pace, whirling everything round and up. When really fierce it is called a tornado and can uproot trees in a few seconds.

Wild Echoes Ringing

WILD ECHOES RINGING is the last story ever written by Elyne Mitchell. This story takes place some time after *The Silver Brumby*, but still has the magic and adventure of all the other Brumby stories.

We first meet Socks and Lightning in *The Thousandth Brumby*. Socks, the black brumby with four white legs, was a loner until the day Lightning, a blue heeler, left his dead master and followed him. It's not long before they are great friends and the combination of horse and dog is unbeatable ... time and again they help each other outwit those men who want to catch the dog, and those who want to catch the brumby. And when they find a special pup called Miss Dingo — a dingo — blue heeler cross with a blue-tinge to her ruff — she soon becomes part of the family.

Together Socks, Lightning, Miss Dingo, and Miss Dingo's and Lightning's pups travel the mountains together. Although they do not run with Thowra or Son of Storm's herds, they don't fight with these brumbies. Rather, they are all friends, and work together to outwit man.

We hope you enjoy *Wild Echoes Ringing*.

Chapter One

Socks, the black brumby with the four white feet, was half-waking even though he was warm and comfortable in the hollow tree above the Ingegoodbee River. He kept thinking he heard a strange whisper in the sound of the river — a message? A warning? Something that the river was saying?

At last he got up and moved quietly to the tree opening. He walked to the stream, the faithful blue-black heeler, Lightning, a pace behind. He listened to the message that was in the river's song.

Socks could tell by the quizzical expression on Lightning's face and his half-cocked ears that Lightning was also hearing the song of the stream, and perhaps wondering, sadly, if it were any word from his old dead master.

Yet there was nothing clear in the whispered song, and something puzzling because it seemed to be about faraway streams and mountains, and yet about the thousandth brumby catcher, and about Thowra, the Silver Brumby. Socks listened and listened, and began to feel that he and Lightning should be near Thowra to warn him of danger. Lightning kept starting off in the direction of Thowra's Secret Valley, and then coming back, as though to say, 'Come on! Come on!'

It was clear that Lightning felt there was something amiss, too — some great danger — to Thowra.

Without Socks even having to pull Lightning's ear, they set off northwards in the dark — northwards to where the snow was probably falling, and where the wind that was already blowing down by the Ingegoodbee was surely howling with blizzard force.

Socks could only imagine the Ramshead country, and the snow gathering into a whirlwind — a whirlwind that circled round and round, hiding the snow-packed rocks then suddenly taking the shape of a silver horse.

There was something haunting about Thowra; Socks knew he must go to Son of Storm's Hidden Valley, just downstream from Thowra's and to where he could get to Thowra's Secret Valley, and make sure that they were all safe — Son of Storm, Thowra, and Thowra's favourite mare Boon Boon.

Lightning seemed to feel the same urgency to go and find Son of Storm, and to check on Thowra and Boon Boon. They simply kept going northwards into the blizzard.

Slowly the peppering pellets of snow became bigger pellets borne on the wind. Horse and dog, they bowed their heads to the biting cold and kept the snowflakes out of their eyes.

Socks felt a deeper dread claiming him, as the wind and snow gusted in his face. A robin redbreast, carried on the wind, fluttered helplessly past them.

The snow was gathering on the ground on the north side of bushes and grass tussocks. There was a feeling of dread — increasing with every blast.

Socks imagined he could hear the sound of the hoof-beats of the Brumby Hunter. What was the Brumby Hunter doing in the high country in winter, anyway? Such a foolhardy action could mean only one thing, the Brumby Hunter was having one last crack at catching his Thousandth Brumby, and what better horse than the legendary Silver Brumby? This time he would not go home without his ultimate prize. So would it only increase the danger to Thowra and Boon Boon if he and Lightning went towards the Hidden Valley? They might lead the Brumby Hunter towards Thowra's Secret Valley. They kept on going, and the higher they got, the more the snow fell and whirled around.

Suddenly Socks stopped, with one forefoot in mid-air. There in front of him — just for a moment — was a ghostly silver horse all misted around in wind-tossed snow. Lightning gave one bark and then was quiet.

The ghostly horse vanished away and Socks and Lightning lingered on, but Socks heard the sound of cantering hooves more plainly, and he and Lightning slackened their pace. They also heard the howl of the wind more loudly.

Socks rubbed his head on Lightning's. There was something rather weird about this storm, and it was comforting to rub against Lightning; Lightning was such a loyal and faithful friend — ever since Lightning had left his dead master's side and come with Socks — the two loners walking together.

They both listened for a few seconds to the sound of the advancing hooves, and then, without Socks's urging, they both backed into thick scrub together and waited to see what would happen.

The hoof-beats slowed down and then stopped.

Socks peered through the tea tree's small white blooms and saw something that made him gasp. There was the Brumby Hunter and suddenly, too, there was a twisting whirlwind wrapping around the Brumby Hunter's horse. Then just as suddenly, the whirlwind was gone, and the Brumby Hunter's horse was standing, trembling, as though it had seen a ghost — which indeed it may have.

Socks, himself, felt a cold touch creep down his spine, and he looked at Lightning and saw him shiver slightly, too. Yet he knew that they must go on and warn Thowra — if he did not already know — that the great Brumby Hunter was on the search again.

But how to warn Thowra without leading the Brumby Hunter right to him? It was best to do nothing at all for a while and see what happened.

Socks and Lightning stood absolutely still, feeling that even to breathe might give their position away. As they stood, they saw the Brumby Hunter press his horse onto the bit and move off.

They followed — slowly — until, all of a sudden, as though he had heard something, the Brumby Hunter veered a little to the east.

Socks and Lightning veered east, too, but cautiously, for the easterly direction led to the Secret Valley. Socks corrected the course a little, and kept a careful watch ahead and all around.

The Brumby Hunter kept trotting on slowly, as if uncertain whether he was on the right track.

Socks was uncertain, too, but he and Lightning had to keep the Brumby Hunter in sight.

Hours passed and Socks and Lightning were both feeling very uneasy. They had travelled so far so quickly — maybe some of Thowra's magic was indeed rubbing off on them? In fact, they must be getting nearly level with the Secret Valley, and what was the Brumby Hunter going to do?

The Brumby Hunter turned harder to the east.

Socks and Lightning were worried. Soon the Hunter would come to the edge of the cliff above Thowra's Secret Valley. There was no way into the valley except through Son of Storm's Hidden Valley.

They kept close, watching, yet nothing seemed to happen. Then, some low, dark clouds thickened around the wide-spaced candlebarks which fringed the cliff edge, the snow began to fall more thickly, coming down in great, tossed gusts, masking the Brumby Hunter, even masking the black horse with the four white socks, so that Lightning pressed closer to Socks' legs. This early winter fall of snow caused Lightning's skin to rise with fear of he knew not what.

Somehow he was sure there were spirits about that night. He was sure he heard his old master whistling, but as he started to bark his reply, Socks gently rubbed his head for silence and for watchfulness.

They watched the snow whirling round the Brumby Hunter as he reined in his horse and sat looking into the chasm which contained Thowra's Secret Valley. The snow masked both him and his horse, then cleared, came in swirling gusts and then cleared again.

While they watched just for one moment, the snow ceased and in that clear, grey second, there was Thowra cantering towards the two big candlebarks which were surely markers for him, and always had been.

Socks held his breath as he saw Thowra tighten the muscles in his quarters as though he were going to jump.

The snow closed in again and suddenly whirled in a dancing cloud around the stallion, and even Lightning was not entirely certain that he was contained in that whirlwind, or willy-willy, of snow.

Socks knew, in his heart, that Thowra had jumped into the Secret Valley — maybe onto one platform and then another, as legend had it he had done once before when he escaped the men who were chasing him.

The great Brumby Hunter rode his trembling horse between the two candlebarks. Socks and Lightning walked a little closer to the edge, trying to see what had happened, though Socks was certain he knew that Thowra had jumped.

Apparently the Brumby Hunter could see no way down, and turned up the big cleft of the Secret Valley to try to find a way in. Socks and Lightning crept closer to the edge.

There, right on the edge, Lightning sniffed out the hoofmarks where Socks thought Thowra had jumped. His excited sniffing around alerted Socks, and Socks knew for certain that this was the place from which Thowra had taken off, and that the legend was true. He heard a sound rising up from below, and a picture formed in his mind of a silver horse jumping through space and landing on a platform, then taking off again through the flake-filled night.

As long as the Brumby Hunter thought Thowra had jumped to his death, there would be no more hunting and Thowra could live in peace — as long as Thowra could content himself with staying quiet and not trying to tease *any* brumby hunters, far less appear as a silver whirlwind, or a hawk.

The best thing to do, Socks and Lightning both thought, was to go down to Son of Storm's Hidden Valley and, from there, creep up the cliff to Thowra's secret place and make sure he was there — and alive.

Chapter Two

Socks and Lightning stood there, well hidden in heath bushes by the cliff edge, watching the Brumby Hunter riding up and down the edge, waiting to see what would happen next. And all the time they waited, the snow floated down more and more thickly, covering up tracks that told of Thowra's strong jump through empty space; but sharp-cut indentations were there, even if masked by snow, that told of Thowra's leap — that told that the legend was true, and that Thowra knew of a way of jumping down the cliff.

And Socks knew in his heart that Thowra had floated, like the snowflakes, down, down and down, into the safety of the Secret Valley.

Lightning knew, too, though sometimes he wondered if it were just a cloud that he had seen — a cloud of snow?

But clouds did not jump, clouds did not hold the shadow of a fine horse's head, or of its fine legs. Lightning, too, felt convinced that Thowra was safely in the Secret Valley with Boon Boon.

Then suddenly through the snowflakes, there rose up, as though dancing, a white hawk. It danced through the floating, spiralling flakes, and brushed against the eyes of the Brumby Hunter's horse, driving it away from the cliff's edge, and the white hawk called once, its voice saying, 'Go home, go home.'

Far away, in the distance, both Lightning and Socks heard a dingo howl, followed by a faint whimper.

'Home! Home!'

Both Socks and Lightning turned their heads towards the Ingegoodbee and the hollow tree that was home. Had not the white hawk called 'Go home!'? That white hawk could be Thowra; it might not be, but both Socks and Lightning were sure it was.

Lightning leapt in the direction of the whimper, and then, as there was no other sound for a moment, he stopped still, listening. He knew, and Socks did too, that a bark would bring the Brumby Hunter after them, so he made no sound. There it came again, an echoing howl and a soft whimper that said plainly to him, 'Lightning, Lightning! Come quickly. Come to me!'

Lightning moved silently, one blue-black paw after another — tiptoeing, tiptoeing — as silently as the snow flakes falling into snow. Socks walked silently, too, the pair of them ghosting along through the night.

Then the whimper came from a little closer, an almost silent whimper that surely would not be heard by the Brumby Hunter.

Lightning began to quicken his steps, still tiptoeing, for nothing must tell the Brumby Hunter where they were. Both Socks and Lightning felt fairly sure that the Brumby Hunter might be rather cruel — just as well not to be seen by him, not to lead him to the hollow tree by the Ingegoodbee River.

Yet Socks still wondered about the Silver Brumby, but it was no good wondering. Really, he was certain that

Thowra was safe, with Boon Boon. He knew the cloud of snow was Thowra, also the white hawk — hawk or whirlwind of snow — the Spirit of Thowra, or ghost of the Silver Brumby.

Then suddenly the whimper sounded near their feet. Both the friends stopped in their tracks; they saw at once what Miss Dingo was whimpering for.

Socks stiffened and Lightning let out a low growl, for there was Miss Dingo crying over a pup — her own dog pup, and he was dead.

Poor Miss Dingo; she whimpered and whimpered and licked the dead pup, but nothing could bring him to life. He was bitten all round the head and in the throat, and had been dead for several hours. Miss Dingo had scratches and bites all over her face, too, and she had the smell of another dog all over her. She had obviously tried, with all her strength, to fight the other dog off, but had not succeeded. Lightning began to feel fury rising up inside him. A dog had undoubtedly been violently bullying *his* Miss Dingo and had killed her male pup — his son. Lightning was beginning to feel very angry indeed. Now it was time to seek revenge.

Lightning and Socks followed the track of the dead pup's blood.

Soon they realised that it was leading them in the direction of the Ingegoodbee, and they hurried more.

Lightning's hackles were rising as they got nearer to the hollow tree; Miss Dingo was hanging back and occasionally whimpering with fear.

Lightning was beginning to feel very angry. Suddenly a very strong smell of dog came from the hollow tree, and Lightning went mad with rage, ran towards the tree, and straight into the hollow.

Noise and dust erupted, the noise magnified by the hollow tree. Socks put his head inside to see who was winning — and perhaps to get a mouthful of dog!

No dog was going to hurt *his* Lightning or even Miss Dingo, and he had a picture in his mind of the Brumby Hunter's cattle dog.

So Socks stayed there looking at the dog until he managed to get between his front legs and escape out of the hollow tree, with Lightning after him and Socks after them both.

Miss Dingo, seeing Lightning chasing the dog, howled and howled, then went inside the hollow tree to make sure the other pups were all right. She looked at the place in the hollow in which her dog pup always curled up and slept, sniffed all around, sat down in it herself, and howled and howled. Finally, she put her head on her front paws and whimpered over and over again.

Lightning and Socks came back and found her still crying, but Lightning had fought and beaten the dog in a fierce tussle, and Socks was very proud, feeling that Lightning had avenged his family. Lightning licked Miss Dingo's torn ears and curled up beside her, then quietly licked her until she went to sleep.

The savage dog might have been beaten by Lightning, but he was not finished, and he started back through the night, limping towards the hollow tree on the Ingegoodbee River.

Socks woke later, feeling that perhaps the marauding dog might return. Everyone else in the hollow tree was sleeping the sleep of the exhausted, so he walked up towards the Ingegoodbee Pools, and there he saw the dog drinking. Socks blew a warning snort through his nostrils. The dog saw him and jumped nervously. The dog knew that Socks and Lightning were great friends and would protect each other to the last gasp — fight each other's battles. He turned back, but not before Socks had decided to follow him to see where he went.

Socks kept himself well hidden and silent, especially when he realised the dog was going north — into the driving snow, north towards Thowra's Secret Valley.

The snow was falling more heavily. Socks was aware, too, that he was getting further and further from Lightning and Miss Dingo, and he felt very uneasy — yet somehow he had to go on. He had to find out if the dog would die after the hiding Lightning had given him or if he would slowly recover? Somehow he thought that heelers were very resilient — tough as tiger snakes. Still, there was an intermittent trail of blood from the wounds Lightning had inflicted and he followed that. The snow fell in larger and larger flakes, thick on the ground now, thick in the air, thick on Socks' eyelashes, matting his mane. He began to wonder if Lightning had woken and missed him — to wonder if he might follow him? They had left the Ingegoodbee Pools a long time ago, and were going south and east from Dead Horse Ridge.

They were, Socks knew, in the area leading to Son of Storm's Hidden Valley, and that meant, eventually, to Thowra's Secret Valley.

Socks was worried, though he had seen no sign of the Brumby Hunter.

What was the wounded dog doing in this country? And why wasn't he with his master? Didn't he have a good master? Perhaps he was undisciplined and a bit of a wanderer.

The only thing to do was to keep following the trail of blood and hope that perhaps Lightning would wake and come after him.

It was lonely without his companion, his blue-black heeler who had been with him ever since the dog's stockman master had died.

Chapter Three

Then everything began to happen at once. The silence of the snowy night was broken by Lightning's bark and a whip crack, and, suddenly, the snow-muted sound of cantering horses — the sound and the half-vision of Thowra through the falling snow, his marvellous strength — the wonderful Silver Stallion — there then not there, alive and yet vanished.

A furious curse rang out, the Brumby Hunter's voice. It was time for Socks to send a disturbing neigh, and for Lightning to add a wild, distracting bark.

A neigh came again, this time from behind Socks. Somehow, the ghost of Thowra was now behind him. The Brumby Hunter was in front of him — no shadow horse was between them — Socks should charge the Hunter!

He charged! Through the falling snow, even though his eyelashes were matted with snow, he saw the Brumby Hunter's horse before his charge carried him chest-on into it.

He felt the bite of the whip that had cracked a moment earlier. Then his teeth closed on warm flesh. He had the Brumby Hunter's horse by the neck, above the withers, and he hung on.

He hung on all the fiercer as he realised that Lightning was in the fight too!

Then a cold blast of air swirled the snowflakes. Socks let go his mouthful to get a better grip. The Silver Brumby had come to fight his own battle! *And in his own way*, using all the help the weather would give him — the whirling snow flakes, the soft-feathered birds of the air to brush their wings in his assailant's eyes.

Most of all he would use the magic of a whirling dervish pillar of snow to confuse the Hunter — a pillar of snow that somehow could be a rearing horse, or sometimes just a cloud blown hither and thither.

Socks let go his second grip so that he could rear up and strike with his forefeet.

He got in one blow with his off forefoot, then a cloud of snow came around the Brumby Hunter and his horse, and the Hunter was puzzled. From inside the cloud, the Brumby Hunter shouted a rather muffled shout.

Socks could barely see what was happening, but he knew that the Brumby Hunter was turning tail and going, pursued by a cloud of snow, and that cloud was suddenly the shape of a great, strong, silver stallion. There was a rush of wings and the white owls came again and beat their soft-feathered wings against the head of the Hunter's horse — by then he was galloping.

Socks galloped after him, and a white hawk joined in harassing the Brumby Hunter. Suddenly it seemed to Socks that the Silver Horse had called up all the help he could get from the birds of the air. He thought he'd seen Thowra transform into a hawk once before, in a similar time of trouble. Had Thowra transferred some of his magic to Socks? Was he, himself, the white hawk?

Because that white hawk seemed to be 'riding off' the Brumby Hunter's horse away from the cliff that was the edge of the Secret Valley, the edge of the drop.

Socks was certain that Thowra had jumped over that cliff and would be — by some marvellous magic — alive, with Boon Boon, down below.

And down below the Silver Brumby, having seen the Brumby Hunter, was filled with dreams of his beloved high mountains, and perhaps of leading the Brumby Hunter a great dance in that high country. To lead him a dance, Thowra must first get out of the valley, and the only way was through Son of Storm's.

Socks watched. There seemed to be no movement below, but there was movement, and quite silently someone crept up beside him! All he knew was that a sudden, cold blast of air carrying snow covered him all over. Someone was there.

Then his withers was nipped! Out of the snowstorm appeared a silver horse and the one who nipped his withers — Son of Storm.

Socks could only think that Thowra had come up through Son of Storm's Hidden Valley.

Now what were they going to do — that silver horse and the big brown son of Thowra's half-brother?

Storm had always run with Thowra, and here was Son of Storm backing him up in some wild escapade in the high mountains.

Son of Storm nipped Socks again on the withers, and bent and tugged at Lightning's ear, so the two friends followed him.

Socks thought he heard a distant sound of galloping hooves coming from the direction in which they were going, but all he really could think of was the cloud of snow that wavered and blew in front of them — Thowra or a ghost!

Then he realised that the sound of a galloping horse was getting closer and closer. Surely it was not the Brumby Hunter returning?

For one instant the snowfall seemed to abate — and Socks saw the Brumby Hunter and his horse quite clearly. Man and galloping horse were heading in a direct line for that willy-willy of snow, and what would happen if they clashed?

With a gasp, Socks stopped to watch the inevitable confrontation, but suddenly the elements themselves took a hand.

Snow came pouring down. Horse and rider, silver cloud, were all invisible, and then out of the snow storm there galloped a great, strong silver stallion, but there was no sign of the Brumby Hunter.

Socks galloped forward to the place where they should have met — what had really happened then? The vanishing Silver Brumby had vanished again.

The Brumby Hunter's horse somehow was gone. What made it invisible?

Socks stared at the shape which he thought was prosanthera bush, but could see nothing. After a while he noticed what looked like the possibility of a depression in the ground behind some bushes.

Socks moved forward, but not as quickly as Lightning did. Lightning's curiosity had been aroused. How could the Brumby Hunter's horse run headlong into the Silver Brumby and then vanish, leaving neither hide nor hair nor even a hoofmark? There must be *something*.

Dog and horse, they looked all around but could see nothing unusual, yet they were sure that there was something strange about this small grassy hollow. Socks moved one foot and the hoof-fall sounded hollow on the ground.

Where had he heard that hollow sound before?

There was a picture coming into his mind of a great grassy flat and a little stream flowing through it; what had this got to do with the two secret valleys?

Quambat Flat? Quambat Flat? It was quite a distance away? But there was a sunken hollow there — where the ground sounded hollow under a horse's galloping hooves.

Socks knew it quite well — remembered the hollow sound. Now he and Lightning stood tense and still — listening. Then, they heard a muffled neigh and — less muffled and quite recognisable — curses in the Brumby Hunter's voice, and a queerly echoing whip-crack. And the whimper of the Hunter's injured dog.

Both horse and dog stopped entirely still — there was something eerie about the sounds — not ordinary. They were close by — there, and yet not there — so close and yet more distant.

Even Lightning was baffled.

He could usually tell exactly where a sound was coming from. This time, somehow, it came from all around them.

Then the neigh came again, and for one flashing second they seemed to see through a cave wall, see a silver horse rearing up, threatening the Brumby Hunter with its forelegs. A scream rang out and everything blacked out.

Both Socks and Lightning sprang forwards and found themselves in a terrifyingly narrow dark space — and galloping hooves rang hollowly far ahead.

Lightning began to sniff a way out of their enclosure in the darkness, Socks following him closely — and both of them listening keenly to the hoof-beats ahead.

It was a narrow passage, but had to have held Thowra *and* the Brumby Hunter's horse and rider.

Then the sound of hooves began to change; fewer echoes, as if they were galloping in a more open space.

The darkness began to go faintly grey — Lightning quickened his pace ... a little faster, a little faster, until suddenly they burst out into glittering, silver light — and were on a platform behind a waterfall!

They stopped! Where was the Brumby Hunter? Where was the glorious silver stallion?

Chapter Four

There had been a legend of Thowra's son Wirramirra escaping from a bushfire by becoming part of the spray of a waterfall; was Thowra vanishing now, by becoming the spray from a wonderful waterfall as it emerged from a hillside?

Cold, cold water, from the depths of the earth; icy water filled with mountain magic.

Socks crept closer, extending his nose, and there he saw the Silver Brumby, standing in the centre of the falling water, a perfect and lovely horse — every line of him expressing love of life, expressing love.

Lightning pressed against Socks's foreleg. Thowra's expression was the same as when he and Boon Boon had stood looking in the friends' sandy cave one night promising safety, and as far as Lightning was concerned, all was right with the world. He and Socks were safe.

The Silver Brumby would be safe and he would guide Socks and Lightning back to his Secret Valley; sometime they would get back to the hollow tree on the Ingegoodbee and Lightning's dear Miss Dingo.

Lightning and Socks stood watching the Silver Brumby, sometimes half-hidden in the silver spray.

Sometimes the spray itself seemed to fly into the shape of a rearing horse.

Then suddenly Lightning's hackles rose. There, above the waterfall, where the stream gushed out of the mountainside, stood the Brumby Hunter's horse, the Brumby Hunter sitting firmly in the saddle.

Perhaps Thowra had seen him and did not care?

What would happen next?

Thowra seemed almost to be teasing, never coming out of the lace of falling water. Lightning got tired of waiting. He knew he could safely walk along the ledge of rock that became quite a wide shelf below the falling water.

He began to tiptoe carefully across. Socks followed as far as he could before the rock grew very slippery. From there he watched Lightning going under the silver spray — shaking the water out of his ears.

Socks took a few tentative steps forward — glistening black as the spray soaked him — then Thowra saw both Lightning and Socks and came towards them, not realising that the Brumby Hunter was following.

Lightning saw what was going to happen and dodged past Thowra, his claws clinging to the wet, slippery band of limestone.

The Brumby Hunter cursed! Lightning hurled himself at the horse and there was a slithering and scrabbling of hooves, a great barking from Lightning, a furious curse from the Brumby Hunter, two neighs from Thowra and Socks.

Quite a commotion!

Thowra seemed to pivot on his neat, hard hooves and almost dive down the waterfall. To Socks it looked like suicide, but he heard a little whinny from Thowra which undoubtedly said, 'Follow me,' and he charged dow through the water — aware, as he went, that Lightning was following.

Thowra leapt from wet, slippery rock to wet, slippery rock — Socks tried desperately to put his feet on the same rocks, and to call to Lightning. From one fairly stable, stone platform he looked back to see if his friend was safe behind, and saw that the Brumby Hunter's horse had slipped off the limestone track and Lightning was forcing it to slide.

He paused for a moment and called, saw Lightning throw up his head and then turn through all the glistening spray and come after him.

Thowra had managed to get a little further ahead. Socks tried to go faster — and found his feet slipping.

He was trying hard to save himself and realised, gratefully, that Lightning was quite close and getting closer. Then he saw that Thowra seemed to be waiting, standing on a flat rock on which the spray kept constantly breaking.

Socks tried to steer his slide towards that rock. Lightning was beside him now, his claws stopping him sliding so fast, but unable to help. Thowra stood waiting.

Socks made a huge effort and slid closer towards the flat rock. Lightning was there already.

Socks's slide slowed and Thowra and Lightning both grabbed him.

Silver horse, black-and-blue dog, black horse with the four white socks — there they all were, covered in glittering spray from the waterfall, tight together on the flat rock.

Thowra gave Socks a little nip to follow him, and tugged at Lightning's ear. Then he jumped into the falling water.

There was nothing for Socks and Lightning to do but follow.

Chapter Five

Water crashed and sparkled all around them.

There was the shape of the Silver Horse ahead —
there shining silver, and then just a shape made of
diamond spray, like Wirramirra had been when the fire
was on 'the tops'.

Socks felt Lightning against his legs, but he knew that
they must both walk forward — however slippery the
rocks were — to join Thowra and go with him.

In fact Thowra was just moving slightly and Socks
could see some sort of a corridor beyond him, and the
creek rushing down the floor of it.

The corridor looked quite dim, and as Thowra moved
out of the waterfall, he walked into darkness.

Socks did not like the look of it, but Thowra gave that
faint, whinnying neigh that quite clearly said, 'Follow
me.'

Socks and Lightning followed. More suddenly than
they expected, they were in the darkness, so thick that
one could feel it. Ahead were the faint sounds of neat
hooves on limestone.

The morning light came quickly. Thowra went
through a horizontal grevillea that Lightning realised hid

this opening from the corridor, and saw that the grevillea grew on the banks of the creek.

They were in the Secret Valley, but both Socks and Lightning were puzzled about the way they had got there. Memory seemed filled with a shining waterfall that clothed a silver horse, or even a silver horse that became a shining waterfall, but Thowra was starting to trot along the valley floor.

That evening Socks and Lightning were curled up on the sandy floor of their usual cave — but Lightning was restless, and when the sky above the valley began to get darker and dingo howls started to echo in the hills around, he got up and began to pace around. The howls were making his longing for Miss Dingo even stronger.

He knew the sound of Miss Dingo's howl among many others, and her howl was not there, but the dingo voices were making him more and more disturbed.

He walked to the mouth of the cave and back again. Socks watched him anxiously.

Then a bark — exactly like Lightning's bark — sounded far away and high above.

The Brumby Hunter's dog!

The Brumby Hunter must have worked his way back to the cliff above the Secret Valley. Perhaps he may never have seen Thowra vanishing in the silver spray of a waterfall.

Socks got to his feet, too, and found himself looking straight at Thowra, who had come to the mouth of the cave.

Thowra gave a very soft whinny to call them to follow, and led them back up the valley, and soon Socks saw that they were going to make their way out of the Secret Valley, the way they had come.

Though the snow had stopped and the sky had cleared, that was not exactly Socks's idea of fun! And how did they jump *up* a waterfall, anyway?

It was best to follow the Silver Brumby without hesitating.

There was that dog barking again. His bark did not sound friendly like Lightning's bark did. Socks felt the hair rising on his back, even as he followed Thowra, and he was shivering as he crept round the horizontal grevillea into the black, dark tunnel.

He followed on, trying to imagine Thowra shining silver in the darkness.

It would not be long till they reached the place where they had jumped down the waterfall. *Was the Silver Brumby going to try and jump up it?*

Lightning was nervous, too, in that dark tunnel, but Thowra kept striding on.

They would soon be out of the tunnel — and what then! Socks was almost holding his breath; Lightning's heart was beating uncomfortably. *His* feet, with their claws, did not slip on the wet limestone. Socks's feet did keep slipping.

He could hear the tapping of Thowra's hooves ahead; it was an encouraging sound in that black, dark tunnel, but he felt his heart beating harder and harder against his ribs.

There had been faint moonlight before they went into the tunnel, but Socks was not expecting a full moon to have risen above the waterfall, and was surprised when suddenly Thowra, in front of him, stepped out of the tunnel into the glittering silver spray, so that he was standing there, cast in silver.

Socks stopped and Lightning bumped into his hind legs, but then looked up in amazement. There was

Thowra, still standing, as though made of molten silver, looking keenly to the right of the waterfall. Something seemed to have cast a spell over him, but both Lightning and Socks realised that he was gazing at the rocks beside the waterfall, working out footholds where they could climb up.

Then the dingo howls started again — a song to the risen moon.

Thowra moved forward a few steps — to the right of the waterfall. Socks, so relieved that they were perhaps not going to jump *up* the waterfall, took a couple of steps after him into the moonlight. Looking down he saw that his own white socks were shining silver. Suddenly he felt as though he were touched by magic, and that his silver fetlocks should be able to carry him anywhere that the Silver Brumby went.

Carefully Socks watched where Thowra put each foot, and he, too, started to climb the great tumble of rocks beside the waterfall.

Thowra might be magic, but Socks felt that his legs had magic in them, too, and looking down beside him, he saw Lightning silvered over by moonlit spray and felt assured that Lightning was fired with magic, too.

Obviously Lightning, with his sharp claws, could climb the tumble of rocks, all wet with spray, more easily than Socks could, but however difficult it was, they would both be lent some magic by the moon.

On and on the enchanted three went, led by the glittering magic of the Silver Horse.

Chapter Six

It was a difficult climb but never impossible, not with the Silver Horse moving on ahead. Socks found it easier if he managed to keep close behind Thowra, putting his feet exactly where Thowra's neat hooves had been.

Lightning was right beside him, climbing easily.

Sometimes they heard the Brumby Hunter's dog bark, but it was some distance away. Lightning knew well not to answer it. *He* knew that they were, all three, really in hiding — or seeking a hiding place that was not in the Secret Valley.

In fact the Silver Brumby was intending to lead the Brumby Hunter right away from his Secret Valley. He knew that there was very little chance of hiding from that man and his dog except in the Secret Valley, and now the Brumby Hunter had an idea where that was, perhaps even had an idea that Thowra had jumped into it, but he certainly would not know just how; not even that clever Brumby Hunter would imagine him jumping over the edge of the cliff, landing on one ledge, and jumping off it onto another, till he reached the valley floor. The way into the Secret Valley would always be his secret; he had never yet shown anyone else. One day he might show

Socks, but Socks would never leave Lightning, and to get down the cliff Lightning would have to fly.

All the time he was thinking, Thowra was moving upwards; clouds had come across and snow was falling quietly; not much snow lay on the ground till they got higher. Flakes were falling into the head of the Crackenback River when they crossed it.

Socks knew where they were going. Thowra was making for the Ramsheads — his country forever and ever.

Socks was glad because he knew the Ramshead country, and the Leatherbarrel Valley, and he followed the Silver Brumby as though he had springs in his legs, feeling wonderfully inspired by the strength of the silver horse. Maybe some of the magic that flowed from Thowra had really gone to him and to Lightning.

Socks glanced at Lightning and saw that he looked pleased and happy, but, he thought, as soon as the dingoes started howling if the moon reappeared, Lightning would worry about Miss Dingo.

Up the three climbed, passing the rocky tor where the last of the snowgrass grew.

Snow was still falling quietly, and except for the wild calls of a flock of currawongs, high above, there was no sound.

They climbed up to the South Ramshead, and the higher they reached, the thicker the snow on the ground became. Thowra trotted almost printlessly over the fresh snow. Socks also knew it was important to leave as few hoofmarks as possible.

With a break in the clouds, the moon appeared, silvering the whole of the main range, and the dingo howls began in the forest below them. Lightning cocked his ears, listening. Socks looked around, just to make sure Miss Dingo and her pups were not following, though he knew that her call was not blended in with the others.

Suddenly he became transfixed with something he saw on the opposite slopes — above the Leatherbarrel Valley — two shadow horses and perhaps a shadow dog; moon shadows. Socks stared at those shadows as he trotted along behind Thowra. He did not realise that they were his shadow, Thowra's and Lightning's — shadows thrown by the now-strong moon. Then, as he looked, he saw the shadow of a third horse — and rider — coming up behind.

He heard Lightning give a low growl and looked quite sharply behind. There, just near enough to throw a moon shadow behind their own, the Brumby Hunter must have worked out that Thowra would make for his own country.

Socks began to feel terrible. Thowra must be quite certain that he was not followed. Lightning should do more than growl. Socks turned round, but Lightning was already running towards the Brumby Hunter, and Thowra had looked around and seen his danger.

Socks saw the Brumby Hunter swing his arm and knew he was getting ready to use his whip — *use it on Lightning* — and in blinding fury he turned and galloped back through the moonlit rock tors. Behind him he heard a stallion's scream of rage and thundering hooves. Thowra was coming, too.

The Brumby Hunter stopped in uttermost surprise; the Silver Horse whom he was hunting was now charging him, and the black horse with white socks was leading him on. Lightning began to bark as he went, flat out, towards the horse and rider, and the dog with the same bark gave a very menacing growl.

That growl was too much for Lightning. Instead of going for the Hunter's horse, he headed straight for the dog, like a hurricane.

The dog dodged to one side but Lightning guessed which way he would go, and hurled himself at him with such force that he knocked the Hunter's dog endways.

Socks heard the whip crack and saw the Hunter sitting on his horse, raising his whip arm. That was too much for Socks. He charged the Brumby Hunter, throwing up his head at the last moment, and hitting him chest-on. The horse winded, it rocked on its feet, and fell, throwing the Brumby Hunter off.

Just then Thowra came galloping back. The Brumby Hunter pulled his horse on to its feet and went to spring into the saddle, but he was still off when Thowra leapt at him and his horse.

The dogs were fighting and got muddled up in the scrum, Socks rushed in to protect Thowra and Lightning. He grabbed the other dog by the scruff and threw him to one side, then he picked up the whip with his teeth and dragged it away from the Hunter's hand.

Thowra simply stood, with heaving flanks, staring at the Hunter who was without a whip or a dog, then, strangely, he bowed his head and backed away, calling Socks in his quiet little whinny.

Socks gave Lightning's ear a tug, so Lightning left the fight. Socks picked up the whip again, and gladly followed Thowra up through the thickened snow.

Looking back, Socks saw the dog get up and go for a pat from his master. He thought to himself that the Brumby Hunter would not give up too easily, and had not the Silver Brumby a gleam in his eye when he bowed to the Hunter? In fact, Thowra was almost dancing along into the Ramsheads.

Snow began to fall more steadily; tracks would be covered.

Socks and Lightning both suddenly felt light-hearted and happy, as though they would follow the Silver Brumby forever.

Chapter Seven

Thowra looked back through the falling flakes and the intermittently moonlit night. There was no sign of the great Brumby Hunter, but the Silver Brumby knew better than to think that the Hunter would give up so easily. There was a round snow dome ahead of them, just asking to be climbed. He trotted on, Socks and Lightning trotting happily with him, but both aware that the Brumby Hunter was somewhere behind them, invisible in the curtain of falling snow.

As they got higher up the North Ramshead, wind began to swirl the snow in spiralling gusts around them.

Socks noticed that Lightning looked behind them very often. The dog was somehow carrying the Hunter's stockwhip, but he was having difficulty in climbing steeply. Suddenly he opened his mouth and barked. His open mouth dropped the whip. He had seen the Brumby Hunter not far away.

Socks and Thowra both heard the Brumby Hunter's horse galloping, and came down a little way to meet him. Lightning ran too, but then he remembered the dropped stockwhip and turned back.

Out of the flailing snow storm came the Brumby Hunter. Lightning knew better than to bark this time.

With his teeth clamped on the whip handle, he rushed at the horse.

Socks came galloping down the lower slopes of the North Ramshead. He was afraid that his beloved Lightning might get hurt and was going to punish the Brumby Hunter, and make sure nothing happened to Lightning.

Socks knew that brumby stallions had gone for bush-walkers before this, and he was well aware that he could frighten off the Brumby Hunter.

Then he heard Lightning bark. 'If he has opened his mouth to bark, he must have dropped the whip,' thought Socks.

Socks went faster, but the Brumby Hunter was going faster still. Lightning grabbed the whip, but knew he was powerless to crack it. He went hurtling on towards the horse and rider, and really felt he should turn on a terrifying, screaming bark — which would mean opening his mouth.

He heard a scream behind him, Socks's stallion scream, and saw the Brumby Hunter check his pace.

Lightning felt comforted — knowing that Socks was coming in support. He was getting very close to the Hunter's horse. He opened his mouth and barked — and the whip fell!

Lightning picked up the whip by the handle and made a great rush at the horse. The Brumby Hunter sprang off his horse and made a run at Lightning's mouthful of whip handle. Lightning dodged and bit the Hunter's hand.

'You bugger,' the Hunter yelled, and pulled out his handkerchief to mop up the bleeding hand. Then he seized on the whip again, and pulled hard.

Lightning dug in his toes and hung on. Socks was coming, so he *hung on*.

A wild, stallion call rang out from further up the North Ramshead. Thowra had seen what was happening and he was going to join in, too.

Socks was a heavy horse, and anything that got the full force of his charge would find it difficult to keep on its feet.

The Brumby Hunter was knocked flat in the snow, but he still wanted his whip, and hung onto it for grim death.

Lightning hung on, too.

Socks circled around to line up for another charge, and saw out of one corner of his eye that Thowra was quite close. He was glad. Support was coming.

'Drop it, you mongrel!' the Brumby Hunter shouted at Lightning, and gave a tremendous tug at the whip, twisting the handle so that it hurt the dog's mouth.

Then Socks charged again, and this time sent the Brumby Hunter flying. When he could clear the snow out of his eyes, the Hunter saw Thowra rearing up over the top of him.

Then the rearing image of a silver horse became a whirlwind willy-willy of snow — something that could not be caught with a lasso, or hit with a whip.

The willy-willy died down, and there was the Silver Horse again.

'Good God,' the Brumby Hunter swore, 'am I chasing a horse or a ghost?' and just then Socks knocked him flat again. But Socks and Lightning and the Silver Brumby thought it was now time to go, taking the whip with them.

This time Thowra led them round the North Ramshead and over the rock tors of the Ramshead Range. They chased the Brumby Hunter's horse off, and could hear him calling it! Socks was amused. He looked back once and saw the Brumby Hunter on his feet, running after Lightning, calling him to come, because he badly wanted his whip. Thowra looked back, too — with a gleam in his eye. The Brumby Hunter was not accustomed to walking, but his horse was standing fairly close, waiting to be caught.

Thowra headed into the granite tor country that he knew so well, and that Socks knew, too, so Socks was happy. Only Lightning was missing Miss Dingo. She had been with them on their last visit, and he kept thinking he should see her, kept thinking he should hear her.

Somehow he was sure she was close. The wind swirled the snow around and a dingo howl came, carried and twisted by a willy-willy, and echoing in the rocks.

Suddenly Lightning barked. He felt he had to let Miss Dingo know where he was and he barked again.

The wind dropped for a moment, and in the eerie silence moonlight came through the falling snow, making the lunar landscape of the Ramshead tors more ghostly still. A dingo howl sounded from fairly close, yet it was as if it rolled round a rocky cavern. Lightning barked again. He was certain that Miss Dingo had come to find him. He even hurried ahead of Thowra, going straight for the opening of the cave where he and Socks had hidden before.

There, in the opening, he saw Miss Dingo who was making excited greeting noises. She had left the older pups with the job of looking after the younger ones while she was away, and asked one of her friends to look in on them now and again. She had learnt from the death of her male pup that it was no longer safe to leave her youngest puppies alone.

Lightning bounded forward, Socks close behind, Thowra, too, and as they all squeezed into the cave in the rocks, Lightning licked all around Miss Dingo's face.

After a while, Thowra went out to see if there were any signs of the Brumby Hunter, though he knew that his tracks and Socks's would be snowed over or blown away in the wind.

Socks went out with him and they both stood there staring through the falling snow. Suddenly they saw the shadowy horseman coming slowly along, his horse's shoes balling up and then the balls of snow breaking down on one hoof so that it trod unevenly.

Thowra crept round the back of the rocks that hid their cave, and then through a rock passage that led out in front of the Brumby Hunter — there he reared up and danced around on his hind legs, half-hidden by falling snow.

The Brumby Hunter's dog barked. The Brumby Hunter reined in and sat staring at the Silver Horse dancing in the snowflakes.

Ghost or horse? Ghost or horse? The apparition vanished. Even the watchers from the cave could no longer see it, but presently Thowra crept into the cave from a back way.

Chapter Eight

Thowra knew it was the start of what was going to be a very heavy winter, and he thought that they should all get going for lower country immediately — not wait for daylight as a big dump of snow might come in the night — so he nudged Socks and nipped Lightning on the ear and led them off into the blizzard.

Thowra found ways through the bush that neither Socks nor Lightning had ever known, and they, with Miss Dingo, followed with implicit trust in that great silver horse.

Both Socks and Lightning still felt that somehow they had been given some of Thowra's strength and power — some of his magic — when they followed him up the waterfall from the tunnel that led from the Secret Valley. It was as if they, too, possessed magic that would take them safely through the mountains — safely through blizzard and tornado, through flood and fire, and over a frozen land.

Sheet-ice might be beneath their hooves and feet, and there would always be the sound of slithering and sliding, but the magic touch of Thowra would give them strength and balance and speed to cope with all dangers. Feeling this strength, like a gift of magic, Socks and Lightning went on with the Silver Brumby through the half-moonlit, snowy night, and Miss Dingo trotted happily along beside Lightning, asking no more than to be with him again and heading back towards the hollow tree on the Ingegoodbee River and the pups that were waiting for her.

They crossed three creeks before those creeks come together, above the waterfall, to make the big body of water which they could hear crashing below. Were they going to jump into the waterfall and go down that way? If so, how would Miss Dingo manage? Then they were there beside the spray that flew up and all around them.

This was the place where Thowra had hurled himself down, becoming part of the water, part of the spray — a shining silver horse. Lightning and Socks had hurled themselves down, too — somehow filled with the courage and magic of the Silver Brumby.

Would this magic still work?

What about Miss Dingo?

But Thowra was thinking of her, too. He took her by the scruff of her neck, walked a few steps into the spray, then sprang into the centre of the fall.

Lightning watched, horrified for a moment and then became completely trusting as he saw Thowra's head above the falling water and the little dingo held above the turbulent stream.

They bobbed up and down a few times, but mostly Thowra held Miss Dingo above water. Lightning and Socks kept up with them because they were anxious for Miss Dingo, but, even though anxious, there was certainty of her safety with Thowra. Soon they were all standing together below the waterfall. Thowra was helping Lightning to lick Miss Dingo dry.

There was still the long, dark tunnel to get through, but Miss Dingo would see better in the dark than Lightning or Socks, Socks thought, and realised he did not much like the limestone passage himself.

As Thowra started to move towards the tunnel, Lightning got closer to Miss Dingo.

'It's time,' Socks thought, and found himself wishing that he and Miss Dingo could soon be at the hollow tree on the Ingegoodbee, all warm and snug with the pups.

Thowra looked around once and then began to walk towards the tunnel. He tugged Miss Dingo's ear to tell her to follow.

The last Socks saw of Thowra, Miss Dingo and Lightning, they were going into the dark tunnel through a curtain of half-lit snowflakes, Miss Dingo right beside the Silver Brumby, and his beloved Lightning beside her.

Then Socks went into the dark himself, and when his eyes got used to the gloom, all he could see was the faint shape of a silver horse and the blur of Miss Dingo. His blue-black Lightning was invisible.

He knew the Secret Valley was ahead, beyond the end of the tunnel that was masked by the grevillea bush. As he followed Thowra, Miss Dingo and Lightning round the grevillea bush, Socks could see that snow was barely falling, just a few big rose-petal flakes, and through those flakes, he could see Boon Boon waiting for them, and dear Son of Storm.

Chapter Nine

Snow was falling thickly the next morning. Thowra had felt quite rightly that it was the start of a heavy winter. Now Socks thought he and Lightning and Miss Dingo should make for home. The hollow tree on the Ingegoodbee was perhaps low enough not to get too much snow. Anyway, Lightning and the pups would catch rabbits even if there were snow — they had done it before.

So that morning Thowra, knowing they should go, came to see them off round the cliff into Son of Storm's valley.

A robin redbreast flew along ahead of them, round the cliff, scarlet breast against the snow, it flitted from rock to rock, bush to bush. Once it sang for them — the robin's song of winter which said, 'Happiness, Happiness'. They edged around a swamp. A few dried flower heads of candle heath stood up out of the snow, and the robin balanced on one. Socks crept along the track, watching the robin, occasionally giving a little whinny of encouragement to Miss Dingo.

Miss Dingo did not really need any encouragement at all. She knew they were headed for home and it made her think about how much she missed that dog pup, who had been mauled by the Brumby Hunter's dog. She knew how empty the hollow tree was without him. She had not wanted to stay in the nice warm cave in Thowra's Valley, but had longed to get home, particularly as the snow falling more heavily made travelling difficult. Somehow, subconsciously, she still expected to find her dog pup.

They found the valley of the Cascades full of snow, and that made Socks hurry even more. The three travellers kept close together, even closer when they saw a strange dingo, and when they heard the swiftly repeated staccato bark of a giant glider possum.

Socks knew all the bush birds and animals very well, knew their voices and habits, but even he was disconcerted when he saw an owl sitting beside the Ingegoodbee Pools.

It did not seem to have seen the three travellers, and all of a sudden it gave a call — 'Mopoke! Mopoke!' — and another owl answered from some distance off, 'Beware winter! Beware winter!'

Socks stood quite still, thinking. It is true what the owl says. 'Beware winter!'

The snow started to fall more heavily. Thowra knew it was going to be a heavy winter. Son of Storm knew it, too. Poor Miss Dingo was going to miss her dog pup even more in the long, dark days ahead.

Socks watched the mopoke take off towards Rawson's Flat. He would not hear that call again till spring and mating time, but before that he might hear the bronze cuckoo's mournful whistle, just like Lightning's master's whistle. He started on towards the hollow tree, thinking of the mopoke and the old dead stockman and Lightning.

Darkness came in and no promise of moonlight shining through falling flakes. The hollow tree stood out above the river and Socks walked towards it, watching Lightning and Miss Dingo walking together. The other pups came out to greet them. Miss Dingo was pleased to see them, but she obviously felt that the one who was missing should have been there.

When they went into the hollow, there was the round nest that the dog pup had made himself, and in which he had always slept — but no dog pup came, however much Miss Dingo expected him to appear. She went over to the nest and howled once, then came back to the other pups and Lightning.

There was no food, no rabbits, so Lightning had to go hunting and bring some rabbit back. Presently they all settled down for the night. Miss Dingo looked over at the dog pup's nest, and finally curled up in it herself, whimpering. After a while Lightning curled up beside her and licked away her tears, and they slept there together.

But Lightning had a score to settle. The Brumby Hunter's dog had killed the male pup.

Socks was wondering about Thowra. He knew he would have to go back because the Brumby Hunter was still somewhere near the Secret Valley — and so was his dog — but he suspected that Lightning wouldn't go back with him, even if he did have a score to settle with the dog.

So it was that Socks set off on his own for Thowra's Secret Valley, leaving the hollow tree one night as the full moon was waning.

Lightning licked his nose in farewell as Socks put his head down to the old dog. Then Socks went on his rather lonely way — wondering what he would find — Thowra in his Secret Valley, or Son of Storm with news of a big struggle and perhaps news of the death of the Brumby

Hunter, trying to get down the cliff. Or would Thowra have gone off on his own to the Ramshead country — *his* country?

As he passed the Ingegoodbee Pools, Socks was beginning to feel more and more certain that Thowra would lead the Brumby Hunter a dance in the high country. There he would be absolutely in his own well-known country. He would know every hiding place.

Socks quickened his pace. He reached the Cascades in much better time than usual, in spite of quite heavy snow on the ground. Then he took an easterly line towards Thowra's Secret Valley, ploughing through heavy snow as he got higher up.

At last he crept into Son of Storm's Hidden Valley, thinking it might be best to go from there to Thowra's Secret Valley and check whether Thowra was there before looking elsewhere for the Brumby Hunter.

Son of Storm seemed to know he was coming and greeted him with pleasure and friendship, then, as the dawn had not yet come, he escorted Socks to the nice dry cave in which Lightning and Socks had slept. There Socks lay down to rest, because he had covered a long distance very quickly and was tired.

He slept and was surprised to see Son of Storm asleep, too, when he woke; and wonderful, too, was it to see Lightning, who had travelled through the whole night to join him.

At the first grey sign of dawn, the three of them started round the cliffs to Thowra's Secret Valley. Then through the grey dawn they could just see Thowra's shape, and yes, Benni the kangaroo. They appeared to be almost tiptoeing, if a kangaroo could tiptoe! Thowra was making no sound at all, and looking all around as he climbed.

Socks had heard tales of Benni the kangaroo, and he guessed that Benni had come with a message for Thowra — perhaps something about the Brumby Hunter. Then he heard the whispering snowflakes, and their whisper as they fell through the sky told of the Brumby Hunter looking for the Silver Brumby's tracks along the edge of the cliff, where surely he must have jumped — tracks that would tell if he had jumped to his death, or not.

There was Thowra, marvellously alive! What did the Brumby Hunter believe about him, anyway? Was it, as some said, just a ghost that the Hunter was hunting?

Chapter Ten

The 'ghost' climbed silently up the cliff track, Benni beside him. When he reached Socks and Son of Storm he signalled them to follow him back. Except for going into Son of Storm's Valley there was nowhere to get to from the top of the track, and from the whispering snowflakes, they were safer hidden in the valley than getting out into the bush above.

Socks was wondering where Lightning was? He would like to have a go at punishing the Hunter's dog himself. That dog deserved a hiding for killing Miss Dingo's pup.

Thowra led them down onto the valley floor, and they got there just as the snowfall slackened. Thowra looked up and for one instant saw the Brumby Hunter. By the way he stared down, as though transfixed, Thowra was sure he had been seen. It was almost as if there had been eye contact between the Hunter and the hunted — the man and the Silver Horse — but the cliff top was too distant.

It was not too distant, however, for the man to make out the misty form of a silver horse standing on the valley floor in the falling flakes. 'Like a cat with nine lives', he cursed. 'How the hell did you get there?' Then the snow began to fall more steadily and blocked the man's vision, making Thowra less clear.

Socks's eyelids were matted with flakes, but he could still see the man and his dog and he heard the swearing; at the same time he wondered, 'What now? Here are we, and here is that man. How can I get at the dog and pay him back for killing that dear pup? How can I stop the man hurting Thowra?'

Thowra knew what to do. He climbed back into Son of Storm's Valley, leading Socks and Son of Storm, and then got up onto higher ground so that he could go round to mock the man on the cliff top. Socks wondered what way Thowra would take. Of course, if he were going to go jumping over the cliff, Socks would not know the way, but perhaps he would just lead the Hunter up into the Ramshead Range.

Socks followed with perfect trust, finding again that he seemed to have gained something from Thowra, more spring, more ability to climb slippery rocks. But something wasn't right — he couldn't hear Son of Storm behind him. He turned around to look for his friend, but he was nowhere to be seen. 'He must have gone home,' thought Socks. 'Maybe there is more than one entry to the valley.'

They hurried, hoping to find the Brumby Hunter still there — and there he was, determined to find a way down into the valley, but the snow had covered the indented front hoofmarks where Thowra had jumped.

Thowra skirted round, far enough behind the Hunter and his dog to be neither seen nor heard, and went on further up through the bush, apparently looking for something. He found his way through the prosanthera bushes which suddenly opened out and revealed a promontory of rocky slate. Thowra stepped up onto it without making any sound and looked down on the Brumby Hunter. He was too far away to make eye contact now. Instead he threw up his head and neighed, one of his most come-hither neighs. Up from down in the bushes there floated a furious curse, 'You bugger! I'll get you!'

Thowra melted backward through the bush, and then led Socks on upwards. Presently they both heard the Brumby Hunter's horse crashing through the scrub, following.

Thowra quickened his pace a little. He had his mind set on those rock tors of the Ramshead area. Already he could imagine the snow flying from his galloping hooves as he dodged around the rocks, and hear his neighs echoing off those rocks as he hid from the Brumby Hunter. Perhaps he might even stop to roll in the snow. Such fun, such fun!

But there was quite a long way to go before he and Socks reached the Ramshead tors, and once they got above the tree line they would not hear the Brumby Hunter's horse following.

The Brumby Hunter could still hear Thowra's mocking neighs, and they made him more careless than he might have been.

Once Thowra stopped and watched till his hunter got quite close, then from behind huge rocks he snorted snow at him — and then vanished!

It was easier for Thowra to disappear in a snow storm than for the black horse, Socks, but Socks was learning a few tricks from Thowra. All the same it was Socks, himself, who thought of standing under a snow-bowed young tree and shaking it so that its snow fell in great blobs on his black hide.

They had travelled very fast but, in spite of their speed, it was already getting dark and the wind was rising. They could sometimes hear the wind's howl round the rocks. A willy-willy of snow swirled and rose up from the Leatherbarrel, buffeting them, filling up their hoofmarks.

A little further to go, and they would be among the rocky tors. The snow was wind-hardened now that they were getting higher up. Once they heard the Brumby Hunter's horse neigh. It was then that Socks saw the crevice in the rocks where he and Lightning, Miss Dingo, and the pups had once sheltered, and wishing that they were still with him, he went towards the narrow opening.

Just then the Brumby Hunter's horse neighed and Socks neighed a wild call to the sky. Startled, Socks pushed his way into the narrow opening, away from the hundred and one echoes — some of them going far and wide, some of them muffled by the falling snow.

Thowra was looking startled, too, and he surprised Socks by quickly squeezing through the opening and, once inside, throwing a wild neigh.

Socks and Thowra were almost deafened by the enormous cacophony of calls.

They realised that the wild echoes would cause the Brumby Hunter to wonder where they were.

Both Socks and Thowra made out the Hunter's shape go past two or three or four times ... searching ... searching ... searching ... Thowra threw another echoing neigh, to confuse the Hunter even more.

A dingo howled in the distance. Socks was certain it was Miss Dingo so he stuck his head out of the crevice, where there would be no echoes, and called, but Thowra pulled him by the ear. They were going to return to the Secret Valley.

Chapter Eleven

Thowra ducked back through the fissure just once more. Socks felt him go but even so he was not expecting the wild, rolling, echoing neigh. Then the echoes were taken up by the rocky hills around and above and rolled about.

The echoes were still rolling around as Thowra and Socks started for the Secret Valley, but as they turned down off the Ramshead Range, the lingering howl of a dingo was carried on the wind, and the howl was followed by a bark. Socks knew that Lightning and Miss Dingo were looking for him, and he began to go a little faster, urging Thowra on.

Another bark, just slightly different, stopped them in their tracks. It was not Lightning's and was above and behind them. Suddenly Socks turned back — he would try to confuse the Brumby Hunter again. He hurried, cantering through the snow. It was not far to go to that fissure in the rocks. In his impatience to set those wild echoes ringing in every direction, he put his head through the narrow opening and called. Then he stepped back to listen. The sound came booming and rising to a high note. He pushed his head back in again, and this time gave a stallion scream. It almost pierced his eardrum; it was *wild*. As the echoes rolled, dying round the Ramshead tors — eerie in the falling snow — he heard the faintest of whinnies from close by, and knew Thowra had come back for him, so he stepped down from the fissure that led to the echo cave.

As Socks joined Thowra, he heard the distant dingo howl again, and was even more certain that it was Miss Dingo. Then came the bark that he absolutely knew was Lightning's, and could hardly stop himself from neighing in answer. Dear Lightning, he missed him so, missed his company. Even though they had only been apart for a short while, it seemed like a lifetime because so much had happened and there had been so much uncertainty. Socks was glad his dear friend was safe. He remembered the old stockman's whistle that was so like a bronze cuckoo's in springtime. Poor Lightning, how the cuckoos' calls had upset him when he heard them, and he knew his old master was dead.

Socks thought he would risk sending his special neigh to Lightning, and hope the Brumby Hunter did not hear it.

He and Thowra kept trotting along, listening and looking, looking into the bush on either side. They only heard the dingo howl that simply had to be Miss Dingo saying 'Here we are', but they could not see anything.

Lightning, however, must have seen them — the ghostly Silver Brumby and, perhaps, Socks's four white legs in the darkness. Lightning's low growl alerted Socks, and he trotted towards the dog and Miss Dingo, rubbing his head on the dear old dog's coat.

They all stood together, Miss Dingo, Lightning, Thowra and Socks — Socks so delighted to be with Lightning again, and Lightning rubbing against him.

Then Lightning seemed to hear a distant sound.

Socks and Thowra put their heads up to listen too. Far away they could all hear a heavy horse breaking through the bushes. It seemed to go more quietly for a few moments. There was just the whispering sound of many animals creeping.

They all listened for a while, and then Thowra led off again, moving more quickly now, because he knew that the Brumby Hunter was on their trail, and that now there would be Lightning and Miss Dingo to add to their tracks.

They went through patches of thick scrub, knowing that the snow shaken off the leaves would cover their tracks.

Socks and Lightning were so pleased to be together that they almost danced along — and Miss Dingo, knowing that Lightning was happy, danced along, too, and occasionally rubbed against Lightning.

The wind was coming now, in stronger gusts, and the taller trees were creaking. Strong limbs rubbed against each other, and a giant flying phalanger barked its repetitive bark. Everything was normal in the bush — for a night of rising wind — except for the whispered sound of animals creeping.

When they stopped to listen once, Socks saw that Lightning's hair was standing up along his backbone, and he thought, 'They're getting closer!' Thowra thought the same but also thought, 'I've done it before, I can do it again, even if it is snowing hard. At least my tracks will be covered. He won't see my exact take-off place!' He trotted on a little faster, then faster.

Socks had an idea what was going to happen, but he was anxious. The snow was falling too thickly. He could hear the Brumby Hunter getting close. It was time to tug at Lightning's ear and get further into thick scrub then head to safety, while the Brumby Hunter peered uselessly through the snow storm, listening for sounds he would never hear.

He urged Lightning and Miss Dingo into a thick wall of scrub, where he knew they could stay, and got a spot from which he could see out himself. By the sound of cantering hooves there would not be long to wait.

He saw Thowra hiding in another band of scrub, some distance from the cliff above. Then he saw him, all crusted with blowing snow, standing in a clearing, then rising up in a half-rear and suddenly throwing up his head and neighing, 'Come and get me. Come and get me!'

The Brumby Hunter appeared, with his dog just at his horse's heels. Lightning gave a faint growl and was ready to bound out at the dog, but Socks took hold of his ear.

Then Thowra took off at a gallop straight for the two candlebarks through which Socks knew he was going to jump. The Brumby Hunter leapt forward with a shout, but all he would have seen was the ghost of a horse leaping through the falling snow, as his horse slid to a stop on the snow-covered edge of the cliff.

Chapter Twelve

Two days later, Socks stood between Thowra and Son of Storm, staring up at the cliff top where the Brumby Hunter was walking about looking at tracks, or trying to find tracks that had vanished under the snow.

Benni the kangaroo had arrived at the Ingegoodbee, saying that Thowra might need help, and Socks and Lightning had gone back to the Secret Valley.

Socks touched Lightning with his nose. Lightning's sixth sense should tell him what the Brumby Hunter was doing. Suddenly he felt Lightning's hackles rising. Something must be happening up there!

Lightning stepped a few steps forward. He growled a deep growl.

Socks strained his eyes into the distance, through the faint pre-dawn light. He realised that the dark bulk which he could see, hovering on the edge of the cliff, was the Brumby Hunter's dog.

Lightning gave another throaty growl.

Then it seemed as if the dog on the cliff top took two tentative steps forward, hung there for a moment, then a half-step.

Even in the grey dawn, Socks could tell that the dog was trembling.

Socks knew that cliff top well. There was barely a foot hold for a cat, far less a heavy dog — but he watched.

Lightning watched, too, faintly growling way down in his throat.

Just then a great cloud of white rose-petal snow drops began to fall from the grey dawn, whispering snowflakes.

The dog on the cliff tried to bark. Socks and Lightning both saw that his feet were slipping. They could imagine the dog's breath taken in sharply, and Lightning barked in sympathy, as though it were his feet slipping on the horrifyingly, steep cliff. Then there was the Brumby Hunter's voice, calling his dog — but it was too late ...

The dog had slipped and hurtled through the air. He gave one cry, and Lightning leapt forward as he landed on the first of Thowra's landing places. He was apparently unhurt, though shaken. He had not folded his legs underneath like Thowra did when he jumped.

Lightning raced forward, heard the cry that the dog gave, but could see no way of reaching him, no way of him getting further down — or back up.

Suddenly feeling that the dog *must* be saved — even if he had killed Miss Dingo's beloved pup — Lightning turned to Thowra to save him, but he found that Thowra was standing close behind him already.

They heard the Brumby Hunter calling his dog, and a faint whimper from the dog.

Lightning whimpered, too, suddenly feeling desperately anxious that the dog should be saved — even though he had a score to settle with him. Little did Lightning know that the instinct that was driving him was a family bond — the Brumby Hunter's dog was in fact his half-brother.

250

Lightning looked anxiously at Thowra — his eyes pleading. Then he pressed against Thowra's leg, asking him to help.

Thowra looked down at the old dog as he moved closer to the cliff, bent his head to him for one touch of friendship, and then looked up at the cliff again. By going round through Son of Storm's Secret Valley and jumping over the cliff, he could land beside the dog on the little ledge. But that would give his escape route away to the Brumby Hunter. Better to keep his secret if possible, and find some other way.

He stood for a while, staring at the cliff — at the various little landing places for leaping down after the first wild jump through air.

Lightning looked from Thowra back to the cliff again. To him it looked impossible, but then so had the waterfall that Thowra had jumped into with Miss Dingo!

Then he saw Thowra begin to move forward, his eyes fixed on the cliff.

Lightning watched. Even if, by some miracle, Thowra got up to the dog, how could he get him down?

But Thowra was magic.

Thowra, too, was wondering how he could get a heavy dog down the cliff — even if he risked going round to the top and jumping, how would he get him down?

In the end, that was what he did. Thowra went round the track to Son of Storm's Valley and went silently along the top of the cliff, hoping not to meet the Brumby Hunter.

Lightning saw him, like a shadow between the two candlebarks, all masked by falling snow — and knew what he intended to do.

Still the question remained — how would he get the dog down — and somehow that big dog had to be helped down!

Lightning and Socks watched, both realising that it was a perilously anxious moment — Socks anxious for Thowra, Lightning knowing that he desperately wanted Thowra to save the dog.

Thowra knew that his escape route to the Secret Valley would probably be no secret any longer — not if the Brumby Hunter saw him.

There was no sign of the Brumby Hunter. Between the candlebark trees for one moment it seemed as though the horse was backing into the scrub, perhaps to enable him to get a run-up for a jump.

Just then the snowflakes thickened. Lightning's eyes involuntarily closed against them, so the next thing he saw, through the falling snow, was the Silver Stallion airborne, floating and dropping through the flake-filled air. And it seemed to him that Thowra was flying with great white wings, his legs folded underneath him.

Lightning closed his eyes, almost praying for that beautiful silver horse and the dog who was stuck on the cliff, but he had to open his eyes again to see what was happening.

He saw Thowra unfold his legs and land on the ledge beside the dog ... but what could he do? Then Thowra was climbing, like a cat, around a faint track to one side of the ledge.

He heard him give a little whinny to the dog, saw the dog get up, limping, and follow him along the faint track, limping as though he had hurt a leg, or even his back, when he fell.

Thowra had stopped on a small, flat rock, and was

252

looking carefully around. Occasionally he looked upwards, as did Lightning, but they could see neither hide nor hair of the Brumby Hunter.

Still watching Thowra, Lightning wondered, 'What now?' — then he saw Thowra gather himself together and jump.

For a moment from below Thowra looked like a great white bird, legs pulled up underneath him. For a moment it seemed to Lightning that he hung or floated in the air directly above him — a huge silver horse with white wings folded along his back and then spread to steady himself. But were they really wings, or was the white hawk there?

At the moment the Silver Brumby had jumped the dog had given a cry — Lightning had nearly echoed it because he felt — just for a moment — that the poor dog had been deserted on the cliff side. However, Lightning knew immediately that Thowra would not desert the dog, and he gasped as the dog jumped and flew through the air — yelping with fear and pain.

Lightning felt his muscles become ready and taut as he saw Thowra extending his legs and landing on the soft valley floor, and he gave another sigh as he realised that the dog was going to land in nearly the same place.

Lightning began to run to the spot where both Thowra and the dog had dropped into the valley. He got there just as the dog gave a sharp cry of pain as it landed. Lightning ran over to it, putting his head down to where it lay whimpering slightly. Then he began to lick away the tears that trickled from its eyes. 'Poor dog, poor dog,' Lightning thought, then Socks and Thowra came close by too.

Lightning looked at the dog's face. Somewhere he had seen that dog's face before — reflected in the calm, sunset-coloured water — the Ingegoodbee Pools ... not far from home ... dear Miss Dingo should have been beside him in that reflection. It was his own face Lightning saw ... the poor dog. All animosity forgotten, even if this dog had killed his pup.

Then Lightning lay down beside his old enemy and licked his sore leg, feeling a sudden tenderness go through him. After a while Thowra nudged both dogs to get up, and he led them to the cave that Socks and Lightning now seemed almost to own.

He turned back and gave the dog a little tug on the ear to lead him, limping, to the nice dry cave. As soon as the dog saw the cave, he lay down on the sand.

Lightning lay down beside him and continued licking round his eyes. The dog stopped whimpering and licked lightly in return.

Snow was still falling as whirling circles but the cave was sheltered and dry, and Miss Dingo, having followed them, was there and had killed two rabbits and laid them on the sandy floor for the dogs.

Outside, a weak dawn light fell through the snow shower, and Lightning could hear the comforting call of the bronze cuckoo.

The Silver Brumby was obviously restless; so was Socks. Socks knew that Thowra might be thinking that his secret place might be secret no longer, because the Brumby Hunter would know that he had led the dog down into it.

Socks heard the bronze cuckoo, too, and got a little closer to Lightning. Somehow he was sure that the Brumby Hunter would not leave them alone.

The only answer was to get the dog back to his master. The dog seemed to be perfectly happy with

Lightning, but he would be better off with his master, *and* less danger to the Secret Valley.

Thowra knew he would have to find another way out of his Secret Valley — and a way that the lame dog could manage.

That night, when the snowflakes began to fall through the moonbeams, the Silver Brumby went like a ghost along the valley floor, below the track that led to Son of Storm's Valley, and he found a way where he thought he could lead the dog back to his master without leaving any tracks. Thowra left the Brumby Hunter's dog just away from the edge of the cliff, where he knew the Brumby Hunter was bound to find him. He waited in the trees until the Hunter arrived to collect the wounded animal.

Thus it was that the Brumby Hunter found his dog was back with him, and he did not know if a ghost horse had brought him there.

He never knew whether or not he had dreamt that his dog was brought to him in the snowy night, by the ghost of the Silver Brumby.

Lightning found that the dog had gone, saw Thowra's hoofmarks leading down the valley floor, and knew that the dog was all right.

Chapter Thirteen

Socks, Lightning, and Miss Dingo decided to head for home before the Hunter gathered himself together again from his slide right to the very brink of the cliff, which had indeed been a brush with death.

There would be another legend to add to the legends already told about the Silver Brumby, and still no one, not even the Brumby Hunter, would know if he were a ghost or a living horse.

The Brumby Hunter might yet claim that he had chased a ghost, and that it had nearly led him over a cliff — or would he feel stupid?

It would not do to appear to be stupid — after all, he was known to be the greatest of all brumby hunters in the mountains.

Though Miss Dingo was in a hurry to get home, they did not go very fast. Lightning was pleased to get into the deepest of the Ingegoodbee Pools. Socks drank long and deeply. Miss Dingo just lay at the edge of the pool in which Lightning swam.

After a while she got up, barked at Lightning, and headed for home. Socks gave her a friendly rub of the ears, and Lightning leapt out of the pool and pounced on a young rabbit which was hidden in a nearby tussock. He brought the kitten rabbit to Miss Dingo, who seemed very hungry because she sat down and ate it.

Then they all hurried on to the hollow tree. Lightning caught another rabbit on the way and carried it for Miss Dingo, giving it to her when she curled up in what had been the dog pup's nest. She whimpered as she got the whiff of the pup's scent again, but Socks noticed that she accepted the rabbit gratefully and was happier when Lightning lay down close to her.

Socks found himself thinking she would get snappy soon, and suddenly realised that he knew she was going to have a pup or pups.

Lightning knew what was about to happen when she cleared everyone out of the hollow tree. The time had come for Miss Dingo to give birth.

A day or so passed — in which she ate ravenously and drank the Ingegoodbee nearly dry; and dear old, patient Lightning waited to be invited in to see the pups. He almost tiptoed in.

There in the dead male pup's nest was just one pup — and both Lightning and Miss Dingo were overjoyed because it was a male pup, to be loved and cherished like the one that was killed by the Brumby Hunter's dog.

Socks found himself invited back into the hollow tree, too, and was delighted to find Miss Dingo friendly and loving again, and it seemed as if they would all live happily together in the hollow tree above the Ingegoodbee River.

Night closed in, and presently the bright stars of a clear winter's night shone above. Far south of the Ingegoodbee, the Southern Cross shone brilliantly. No snow was falling.

Lightning did not curl up and sleep all at once. He could sense that lots of little animals were on the move through the bush, as if something were driving them from the north. After a while, he got a faint whiff on the breeze, he found his hackles rising before he even knew what the scent was — or that it was dangerous.

The image of that dead pup rose in his mind before he realised that the scent was of the dog that had killed the pup, and also of the Brumby Hunter's horse.

An echidna scuttled past the hollow tree, and then three wallabies; up in a candlebark, a giant flying phalanger barked. Lightning was too disturbed by the general movement of small animals to even catch a young hare for Miss Dingo. He was also wondering what to do, where to go — if anywhere?

It was too late to go anywhere.

There was the Brumby Hunter's dog at the hollow tree's opening, and there he was with his hackles up, leaping at the dog in a wild fury. They rolled each other over in the mud outside the hollow tree, growling and biting and struggling.

Then suddenly the Brumby Hunter had his whip in his hand and was cracking it over both dogs.

Socks saw Lightning get one crack from the whip, and it was time for him to intervene. He caught a vision of the brilliant stars in the dark sky, and he sprang out of the hollow tree and charged at the Brumby Hunter, knocking him off balance, as he raised his whip again. The horse stumbled on a tree root, the man cursed. Socks charged again and again and got a stallion's bite in on the Brumby Hunter's horse's neck. For a moment there was chaos when Miss Dingo sprang at the strange dog too. Then the man collected himself and called his dog off, and peace reigned.

Socks lay down across the entrance to the hollow tree to guard his 'family', but he felt fairly sure that there would be no more fighting visitors.

Just once, in that shining night, he woke and saw, against the stars, the silver shape of Thowra. The Silver Brumby simply stood there looking into the hollow, and then he bowed his head down to Socks's nose and blew him a soft farewell and vanished, back to his Secret Valley. No snow fell that night, and Socks and Lightning remembered forever seeing the noble head of the Silver Brumby against the stars, and remembered having jumped with him down the waterfall, and climbed with him up the ice-coated rocks, ice chips flying from their hooves and feet off the rocks — up into the country that was the Silver Brumby's forever and forever.

OTHER BOOKS BY ELYNE MITCHELL

SILVER BRUMBY SERIES

The Silver Brumby (1958)

Silver Brumby's Daughter (1960)

Silver Brumbies of the South (1965)

Silver Brumby Kingdom (1966)

Moon Filly (1968)

Silver Brumby Whirlwind (1973)

Son of the Whirlwind (1979)

Silver Brumby, Silver Dingo (1993)

Dancing Brumby (1995)

Brumbies of the Night (1996)

Dancing Brumby's Rainbow (1998)

The Thousandth Brumby (1999)

Wild Echoes Ringing (2003), published for the first
time in this edition of *The Silver Brumby*

OTHER CHILDREN'S FICTION

Kingfisher Feather (1962)

Winged Skis (1964)

Jinki Dingo of the Snows (1970)

Light Horse to Damascus (1971)

The Colt at Taparoo (1975)

The Colt from Snowy River (1979)

Snowy River Brumby (1980)

Brumby Racer (1981)

The Man from Snowy River (1982)

AFTERWORD

Let me tell you about my favourite books of all time — Elyne Mitchell's *Brumby* books — and how I came to be a devoted fan of these tales.

In the early 1970s I was given the first four *Silver Brumby* books for Christmas by my mother, who knew I liked horses. In these stories the horses talk to each other and to other bush creatures, a unique feature of the series. Initially this concept of dialogue between the horses put me off the books as I didn't really appreciate fantasy, so I only read a few pages of *The Silver Brumby* before setting all four of the books aside. This was a time in my life when I thought electronic dictionaries were good reading!

It wasn't until I found myself in bed with the flu and nothing to do that I looked at the books again, and found, to my surprise, that they were fantastic. I have read the stories of the *Silver Brumby* series many times, often starting again as soon as I have finished reading them. I have even created lists and family trees for most of the horses that appear in these stories just for the fun of it, which you can find on my website: *www.blaze.net.au/~sasami/brumby/*

In each story Elyne Mitchell describes in detail the beauty of the Australian high country in a way that only someone who has lived there could. Even though these books were written for children, if you love horses I recommend you read these stories, no matter what your age.

I can only say thank you to Elyne Mitchell for sharing with us these beautiful creatures of her imagination, and the bush through which they run.

Ken Stone, 2002

FAMILY TREES

**THE FIRST GENERATION —
HOW IT ALL BEGAN**

BEL BEL / MIRRI **YARRAMAN** BROWNIE

THOWRA STORM ARROW ARROW'S SISTER

**THE MERGING OF THE SUN
AND THE MOON**

WINGANNA YARRAN

WURRING ILINGA

KAREE YURI

THOWRA'S CLAN

? THE BROLGA ? ?

STEEL KALARI CLOUD

YURI KOORA BOON BOON GOLDEN **THOWRA** CIRRUS

WIRRAMIRRA DILKARA WINGILLA LIGHTNING KUNAMA

STORM — THE BROLGA'S DAUGHTER   ARROW'S SISTER — ?

WINGILLA — SON OF STORM — DANDALOO — ?   SPEAR

BRI BRI   CHOOPA*   YAROLALA
Adopted by Son of Storm,
if not fathered by him

CHESTNUT RACEHORSE — LUBRA — ? — CLOUD — ?

? — WIRRAMIRRA   GOONDA — LIGHTNING — KUNAMA — TAMBO

TIARRI   BARINGA — DAWN   MOON

KALINA